PENGUIN

Nothing Stays Buried

Praise for P. J. Tracy

'Fast, fresh, funny, and outrageously suspenseful'
Harlan Coben

'A fast-paced, gripping read with thrills and
devilish twists' *Guardian*

'A thrilling page-turner with a nail-biting finish'
Sunday Telegraph

'A powerful thriller and an ingenious plot' *Observer*

'Some of the best new blood work in the genre . . .
Scary funny, witty, and genuinely perplexing
right to the end' *Glasgow Herald*

'P. J. Tracy is about to become a household name'
Daily Mirror

'Vivid scenes, realistic characters and humorous
dialogue' *Time Out*

'[A] smart thriller' *The New York Times*

'A killer read in every way' *People*

'An engaging puzzle with a vigilante twist . . . Gripping
and original' *Kirkus*

ABOUT THE AUTHORS

P. J. Tracy was the pseudonym for the mother-and-daughter writing team of P. J. and Traci Lambrecht. Together P. J. and Traci were authors of bestselling thrillers *Want to Play?* (a Richard and Judy Book Club pick), *Live Bait, Dead Run, Snow Blind, Play to Kill, Two Evils* and *Cold Kill*. P. J. passed away in December 2016.

Find out more at www.pjtracy.com or at facebook.com/PJTracyAuthor.

Nothing Stays Buried

P. J. TRACY

PENGUIN BOOKS

PENGUIN BOOKS

UK | USA | Canada | Ireland | Australia
India | New Zealand | South Africa

Penguin Books is part of the Penguin Random House group of companies
whose addresses can be found at global.penguinrandomhouse.com.

First published in the United States of America by G. P. Putnam's Sons 2017
First published in Great Britain by Michael Joseph 2017
Published in Penguin Books 2017

001

Set in 12.5/14.75 pt Garamond MT Std
Typeset by Jouve (UK), Milton Keynes
Printed in Great Britain by Clays Ltd, St Ives plc

A CIP catalogue record for this book is available from the British Library

ISBN: 978–0–718–18583–1

www.greenpenguin.co.uk

Penguin Random House is committed to a
sustainable future for our business, our readers
and our planet. This book is made from Forest
Stewardship Council® certified paper.

In loving memory of P. J. – mother, partner, best friend, soul mate. You made magic happen for me from the moment I was born, and being your daughter was a magnificent gift. I will miss you every second of every day.

I love you more than all the stars in the universe.
That's how we always signed our cards to each other, and we really meant it.

Prologue

Something horrible was going to happen to Marla. Somewhere down the road there had to be payback for her perfect childhood, her perfect career at the veterinary clinic, her perfect apartment in Minneapolis, her consistently perfect life. Friends who adored her envied her in equal measure, and secretly waited for the tragedy to come, because they believed in the law of averages and the irrefutable balance of good and bad in every life. And also because in the darkest moments of their own less than perfect lives, they just had to believe that someday Marla would get hers.

'Good things come to good people,' her father was fond of telling her on those rare occasions when the shower of her good fortune made her feel just a little bit guilty. But if that were really true, why did the rest of the world believe the opposite? The notion that goodness was punished was so pervasive that even the language was permeated with warnings. Only the good die young. Nice guys finish last. No good deed goes unpunished. Phrases like that had often given Marla pause; made her think she should try harder to do something bad occasionally, like forget to return a library book, just to even out the scales.

And then she'd run over the bunny.

'Stop crying, Marla. And stop calling it a bunny. It was

just a goddamn rabbit.' Her father had tried to comfort her with semantics. 'Probably the same one that ate every lick of my spinach plants last week. Every last lick.'

But he hadn't known the worst of it, because she could never bring herself to say it aloud. The bunny hadn't died right away. She'd seen it in her rearview mirror, trying to drag itself off the road with its front legs, because the hind legs wouldn't work. She'd had to go back and run over it again.

It had been the right thing to do; but oh my God, that image in her rearview mirror would be with her to the end of her life, and although her father had felt great sympathy for her distress, he hadn't felt a bit for the rabbit. How could that be? How could you feel sorry for someone for being sad and not feel sorry for something being dead?

She spent the next week imagining that the bunny had been a nursing mother, and that somewhere baby bunnies were cold and mewling in a hidey-hole, slowly dying of starvation. She never admitted that to anyone, because people tended to think you were a bit unbalanced when you empathized with animals to the point of torment. But empathy was the disease Marla had inherited from her mother, and there were no boundaries to it. She couldn't help connecting to everyone and everything she encountered; she couldn't stop speculating about their lives, their families, their pain – even that of silly rabbits that ate her father's entire spinach crop and then ran out in front of a speeding car.

Normally Marla didn't mind the night drive out to the farm, especially on a Thursday, when the freeway was empty. Tomorrow night the frenetic weekend race to lake cabins would fill the two lanes heading out of Minneapolis with a jam of lights, white and red, crawling bumper-to-bumper for sixty miles before it started to thin out. But tonight, and every other summer weeknight, the road shot straight and true into deeper and deeper blackness where the exits were few and far between. Her exit, just three miles up, was what worried her. That particular two-lane road was one bunny shy this week, thanks to her, and she greatly feared a repeat of last week's carnage.

She took the ramp more slowly than usual, stopped at the top and spent a long time looking both ways before easing right onto the two-lane road. There was no moon tonight, and the darkness seemed to swallow the beams of her headlights, as if she were shining them down the throat of a monster. She slowed even further as she approached the S curve through the woods where the bunny had once lived, and that was the only reason she didn't run right over the large black shape in the middle of the road.

As soon as her headlights hit the thing, she recognized it as one of those large plastic bags the volunteer crews used to pick up the occasional litter on road cleanup days. Still, it had startled her, and she could hear her heart pounding in her ears as she pulled over onto the shoulder and stopped. She sat there for a minute trying to catch her breath, her fingers still curled tight around the wheel, eyes wide and fixed on the bag.

Relax, Marla. Blink, for God's sake. It's not an animal, not a person; it's just a bag of trash. Normally these bags were carefully placed on the shoulder for the township truck to collect, but this one was smack-dab in the middle of the two-lane road, and a genuine hazard to any vehicle coming around the blind S curve at a normal rate of speed. It never occurred to her to simply drive around it and go on.

Her mind was already busy imagining a speeding car zipping around the first bend in the curve, slamming on the brakes, veering off the road, and plowing head-on into a tree.

It was only after she got out of the car that she also imagined that same speeding car running into her while she was trying to drag the bag off the road, which made her move a lot faster.

It was surprisingly heavy, and it made a terrible scraping sound on the pebbly asphalt as she tugged and pulled it by inches toward the shoulder, and that was when she began to suspect what was really in the bag. She released it with a little squeal and a shiver, and backed away.

Motorists killed more deer on this particular curve than all the hunters in the county managed to bring down during hunting season. You didn't think much about what happened after the accidents unless you happened to see the roadkill crews making their rounds, loading grisly remains into the open-backed truck that hauled them away. Sometimes the job got messy, and then they had to use a shovel and a bag. Apparently this particular bag had fallen unnoticed off the back of the truck when it accelerated on the curve.

Marla looked down at the bag with a mixture of sadness and distaste, understanding the heaviness now, seeing the telltale swells and lumps that clearly marked a large object and not a collection of discarded cans and paper. At least she hadn't killed this one; hadn't witnessed its violent end, which made the job ahead a little easier. She wondered absently why it didn't smell, murmured a brief prayer that the bag didn't rip when she tried moving it again, then bent to her work.

This time she put her back to the side of the road and tried pulling the bag toward her. The large animal inside shifted and rolled with the first tug. Marla winced, but kept at it, right up until the moment the bag snagged on a sharp piece of broken asphalt, tore open, and a bloody human arm fell out.

Marla snapped upright and stifled a choked gasp. For a minute her mind didn't work at all, and then when it started up again it manufactured terrible pictures. Not that there was a dead person in that bag, because that was a reality she just couldn't accept at the moment. What occurred to her instead was that in the movies, just when the heroine thought she was safe, the supposedly dead person's hand jerked out and grabbed her ankle.

'Oh God, oh God, oh God.' She began to back very, very carefully away, toward her car, keeping her eyes focused on the inky blackness of the road ahead, because she didn't dare look down at the bag again.

And then suddenly, twin white lights pierced the darkness and began rolling toward her, faster and faster. Too small for headlights. They're reverse lights. Dear Jesus, there was a truck up there, so close, and she'd never even seen it. And now it was coming for her.

Marla was totally paralyzed for a few moments, trying

to regain her composure, rationalizing for the sake of her sanity, because none of this made sense in her perfect world.

The truck is not coming for *you, it's coming to* help *you. This is the country – people stop to offer assistance when they see a car on the side of the road, because in Buttonwillow, Minnesota, everybody is your neighbor, even if you live twenty miles apart. It's probably somebody you know, maybe even somebody you went to grade school with. And there's a perfectly reasonable explanation for that body in the trash bag . . .*

Marla snapped back to reality. No, no, no, there wasn't. There was no perfectly reasonable explanation on God's green earth for a dead body in a trash bag in the middle of a deserted country road. No perfectly reasonable explanation for this truck, suddenly appearing out of nowhere. And now, because she'd been thinking too much again, it was too late to duck into the safety of her car and screech away. Too late to call 911 or Jacob, because the truck had rolled to a stop a few feet in front of her car and now the driver's door was slowly creaking open. At that point, she abandoned all thought, succumbed to panic and instinct, and bolted into the woods.

Every inch of her felt like it was on fire as she leapt through the brush and bramble, dodging trees in the darkness, clambering over fallen logs, tripping over exposed roots and scrambling back to her feet. She knew these woods – Cutter Creek was to her right, and a few hundred yards up ahead there was a clearing and then Hank Schifsky's cornfield. Another quarter of a mile up was his long dirt driveway and his old farmhouse. She could make it.

And then she felt herself falling, felt her ankle give way as she tumbled down a steep, washed-out gully that hadn't existed when she'd run wild in these woods as a kid.

She choked back whimpers of fear and pain and dragged herself to the base of a large oak tree, trying to make herself as small as possible. And as stupid as it was, she hadn't lost hope; she was still waiting to hear the call of a friendly voice behind her. 'Ma'am? Ma'am! Don't run, I'm here to help you!'

But all she heard was relentless, crashing footsteps in the woods behind her. The raspy pant of her pursuer.

Something switched off inside her. She divorced herself from her immediate reality, from her physical being, and retreated deep into the core of her soul. There it was peaceful, a place where she could think of her past and her future. She should have married Jacob. And if he'd still have her, she'd do just that. They'd have babies and live in Buttonwillow until the end of their days. They should have done it a long time ago, back when they were both eighteen and Jacob had given her the promise ring she still wore on her right ring finger, even though she was a grown woman.

The footsteps were getting closer now, crunching through the dead branches and old, dried leaves that littered the forest floor. Things couldn't end here. She had to leave something so Jacob and her father would know she'd been here, had made it this far, and could maybe piece together what had happened if she didn't make it out of these woods alive.

She pulled the ring off her finger and placed it by the base of the tree where she was hiding, and as she heard the labored breathing getting louder, she got up and started running on her swollen, ruined ankle, screaming at the top of her lungs.

The lights were what Walt would always remember. They didn't belong in this dark night in the countryside. They lit up the thick woods on the north side of the narrow road, throwing spooky shadows through the tightly packed tree trunks and brush.

They shed unwelcome light on the north side, where there was a turnaround with space enough for one car to park, for the daring anglers who skidded down the treacherous slope to drop their lines in the creek below. You fished at night during the few weeks when the suckers were running, but for the rest of the summer, only kids parked there at night to kiss and hold hands, and sometimes more than that, before the clock ticked to curfew.

The turnaround had been there as long as Walt had been alive. He'd parked there with Mary, his high school sweetheart, before sneaking back home, and he'd proposed to her there, too. Right there, where the path down to the creek carved a hole in a stand of cottonwoods far older than he was now.

All these things belonged here, had always been here, but not the lights, and yet tonight they were everywhere, startling the early spring frogs into silence, as if the whole place had been swept clean of night creatures.

Marla's car, the white Ford Explorer he'd bought for her when she graduated from college, was sitting in the turnaround, visiting the very spot where she might have been conceived all those years ago. It was spotting from the gentle April rain that had just started to fall, and Walt's eyes brushed over it as if it wasn't there, because it shouldn't be.

He had been standing here so long while the Highway Patrol set up the lights and county deputies paced the grounds. He was glad the Highway Patrol was here. The more departments, the better. It gave the scene, the tragedy, a level of import that promised careful attention.

The crime-scene techs, who looked like astronauts in their white suits and booties, hurried to cover that dreadful, bloody place in the middle of the road that was surrounded by blinking red lights and peppered with iridescent yellow crime-scene markers. One of the techs, who had known Walt since he'd worked for him baling hay as a high schooler, looked over his shoulder at the old man.

'Probably isn't human blood at all,' he said with a fake, forced shrug. 'Raccoon, squirrel, deer more than likely.'

Walt didn't move. He kept looking at the plastic now covering the blood, protecting it from the rain. 'Marla hit a rabbit last week on this very road,' he said.

'Could have been a rabbit,' the tech said, but it was too damn much blood for anything that small and he knew it.

Marla had been missing for only a few hours, but out here, there were no time limits on reporting a missing person. This was Marla. They all knew her, like they knew every person in their district, and they knew she would have called her dad if she was going to be late for dinner.

A deputy approached Walt and tipped his brown plastic-covered hat. 'Mr Gustafson, is that Marla's vehicle?'

Walt hesitated because no one ever called him Mr Gustafson. 'It is.'

The deputy sighed and looked down. 'We'll find her, sir. Don't you worry.'

'Appreciate it.'

Jacob was here, too, coming out of the woods now, his face a frozen, unreadable mask. He'd been the first to arrive, getting here so soon after Walt had phoned him that he worried about how fast the boy had been driving, and how carelessly. He'd been sweet on Marla damn near forever, and was the one person in this world who was as panicked as Walt, trying hard not to show it. He was sheriff now, like his daddy before him, but he was more than that.

'How are you doing, Walt?'

'Not so good. Just like you.'

Jacob scuffed his boot through the agate stones scattered in the turnaround near Marla's car. Harry Michaelson's bluetick hounds started baying in the far distance, the first dogs on-site long before the patrol brought in their own hounds.

Jacob looked in the general direction of the sound as if he could see through the black of the woods beyond the lights, and looked back at Walt's face. It was partly in shadow, and he looked younger than his seventy-odd years, with his teeth clenched and his jaw muscles bulging as he looked toward the baying sound, too. His pupils were dilated so wide, they ate nearly all of the blue of his eyes, and Jacob knew the man had to be dying inside at this moment. What had the dogs found? The seconds ticked by with interminable slowness before his shoulder unit squelched.

'Coons,' a voice came from the other end. 'A whole mess of 'em.'

Walt took his first breath in a while and released a shaky exhale.

He's in hell, Jacob thought, just like he'd been ever since he had gotten the call. 'Sorry, Walt. Damn blueticks. The Highway Patrol dogs should be here any minute, and they don't sound at a goddamned coon.'

Walt nodded, took another breath. He bobbed his head toward the Explorer without looking at it. 'Maybe she broke down.'

Jacob shook his head. 'Keys are still in it. It started right up. Tires are all okay.'

'Still, maybe it broke down earlier and just fixed itself sitting there. Maybe Marla . . . I don't know, started walking, got tired, fell asleep somewhere, she works so hard, you know . . .' His voice faded as he pressed a hand hard over his gut, because the agony was eating at him from the inside out.

Jacob looked away, pretended he didn't hear the absolute desperation in Walt's speculation, pretended he didn't see anything but a lot of people, a lot of lights, and an empty car.

Nightmare. Jesus God, I'll do anything, just let her be safe . . .

'What's on your mind, Jacob?'

'Walt, the hounds picked up a clear trail in the woods. It ended in a washed-out gully near the creek.'

'What does that mean?'

Jacob reached into his pocket and pulled out an evidence bag. 'I found this at the base of a tree in the gully.'

Walt took a sharp breath. 'That's Marla's ring. The ring you gave her in high school.'

'I think she left it for us, Walt.'

One

Life was weird in unquantifiable ways: One day you were an urban depressive, living in the emotionally burned-out shell of a house you had once shared with your philandering ex-wife, watching unremarkable years slowly ooze by like cooling lava. The next, you were living on a tranquil lake an hour outside the city with a baby on the way, carried by the mercurial woman who had owned your heart since the first, combative encounter. Of course, back then she'd been a person of interest in a string of serial murders he'd been working, and who wouldn't get a little prickly over something like that?

But Minneapolis homicide detective Leo Magozzi was pragmatic and cynical above all, and certainly no idiot – as over-the-moon as he was with the prospect of first-time fatherhood, he harbored no illusions about a traditional coupling with a complicated soul like Grace MacBride. There might never be a sentimental march down the aisle, maybe not even a happily ever after, although it was his fervent wish. Sometimes he thought such things of permanence were as antithetical to her nature as vegetarianism to a tiger.

But babies were about as permanent as you could get, and Grace seemed to be flourishing as a pregnant woman; a happy side effect of that was she seemed to be opening the door for him just a little. Not more than a crack, but it was marked progress by previous standards and something he could work with.

For instance, she occasionally touched his arm in public – a shocking development if there ever was one. Even more shocking was the fact that lately, they were spending a couple of nights a week together. And those little things allowed him to be guardedly optimistic about the trajectory of things in the future. His situation still wasn't free of uncertainties, but he was finally okay with that – he and Grace were now forever tethered by a miraculous little human that they had created together.

He suddenly thought of his grandfather, years dead now – a curmudgeonly man fond of dispensing coarse nuggets of realism whether you wanted to hear them or not. Magozzi had spent a lot of time with him during his formative years and he was truly the one who had prepared him for a perfectly imperfect life, had taught him that nothing was simple or preordained.

Everybody's got problems, Leo, doesn't matter how old you are, who you are, where you come from, or where you're going. They get better, they get worse, but they stay with you until the day you die, so get used to it. And the minute you think you've got the world by the balls, think again. If you want a sure ticket, join the priesthood like your great-uncle Dom. Life will never surprise you if you're wearing the cloth.

I don't think I'm cut out for the priesthood, Grandpa.

Most of us aren't. So ride the storm. Just because you got benched from the big Homecoming game and now Miss Jenny Perky Tits won't give you the time of day doesn't mean life is over . . .

Grandpa! God . . .

Don't take the Lord's name in vain, son.

Sorry.

Don't tell me you're sorry, tell your Lord. Ten Hail Marys and ten Our Fathers should cover it.

Her name is Shelly.

Shelly, Jenny, whatever. You're only sixteen years old and you're gonna go through a lot of Shellys and Jennys before you settle on one, so like I just said, ride the storm. Women will make a mess of you, but if you find the right one, she'll put you back together again.

Magozzi cringed and smiled at the same time, remembering his deep distress over his grandfather's scrutiny of his high school sweetheart's anatomy, wondering why taking God's name in vain was worse than using vulgar language to describe a woman's breasts. It was only later that he'd learned his grandfather was beginning to suffer dementia. Apparently one of the symptoms was losing your filter for polite conversation.

He was thinking of these things as he lay sweating on the floor beneath a partially assembled crib, wondering why in the hell he hadn't ponied up the extra thirty bucks to have the store put it together for him.

He rolled his head to the side, trying to release the crick in his neck, and got a good look at his partner Gino Rolseth's white calves and Sperry Top-Siders, the only things visible of him from this position on the floor. He'd seen worse things in his life, but not by much. 'Okay, Gino, I'm waiting for my logistical support. It's eighty-eight degrees and I don't have central air. It's getting hot down here.'

'Count your blessings, you're on the floor and heat rises. It's fifteen degrees hotter up here and I'm only five-seven. I wouldn't stand up if I were you.'

'Come on, let's get this show on the road. What do I do next?'

'I'm working on it, but this damn instruction manual is written in Mongolian or something. This is purely interpretive work on my part.'

Magozzi sighed. 'Then give me the drill, I'll figure it out.'

'You don't need a drill, says so right here in Figure 8. You need one of these nut-thingies.'

'What's a nut-thingie?'

'This cheap tin piece of crap that's supposed to tighten the nuts on the legs.' He tossed it under the crib. 'Jesus, Leo, why didn't you buy this thing already put together?'

'I was just thinking about that.'

'Yeah? So what did you come up with?'

'Real men don't buy things preassembled.'

He heard Gino snuffle. 'Yeah, I went down this very same road seventeen years ago when Angela was pregnant with Helen. "Let's buy it assembled, Gino," she begged. "No, honey, it'll be a piece of cake, I've got this covered," I reassured her. Well, guess what? We spent two days trying to put the damn crib together and we almost got divorced over it. Lesson number one – don't ever argue with a pregnant woman, or she'll take a pound of flesh, and it's not the flesh a man wants to lose.'

Magozzi crawled out from under the crib. 'That's kind of a generous weight estimate, isn't it?'

Gino smirked. 'Speak for yourself. So, are you giving up already?'

'No, I'm going to get us some beer and we're going to figure this out before I crawl back under there.'

'Let's do it down on the dock and throw some lines in while we're at it. Fishing is good for the thought process. Plus, it's cooler down by the lake.'

'That's what I was thinking.'

Gino looked around the spare bedroom that was slowly metamorphosing into what Magozzi apparently thought was a nursery, which meant there was an almost-crib in a bunch of empty space. 'You're going to need a changing table, a rocking chair, a dresser, stuff on the walls . . .'

'Why? Babies are born blind, right?'

'That's kittens.' Gino narrowed his eyes. 'You're kidding, right?'

Magozzi gave him a noncommittal shrug.

'Please tell me you're kidding . . . Never mind. So what does Grace think of the green walls?'

'Desert Sage. And she hasn't seen them yet.'

Gino frowned. 'I thought she was pretty much living here.'

'Part-time. She stays here a couple nights a week, but she's still got her house in the city, and the Monkeewrench office is only half a mile away.'

'Yeah, yeah, it's convenient for work, but how's that going to fly once you two have the baby? I mean, that's like shared custody, except between two houses instead of two people.'

And that was the problem with Gino. He saw everything in black and white. But with Grace MacBride, nothing was black and white. And Gino had a point, except the shared custody thing also entailed a third party – Monkeewrench. Harley, Annie, and Roadrunner, Grace's business partners and the only family she had ever known. Their baby was going to have a whole lot of parents, which probably wasn't such a bad thing. 'We'll figure it out, Gino. Come on, let's get those beers and go fishing.'

'Yeah. Hey, just for the record, I like the green walls. Nice and neutral.'

'Desert Sage.'

'Whatever.' A goofy grin suddenly gobbled up Gino's face. 'This is so awesome, Leo. A few months and your life is going to take on a whole new meaning.'

'It's beyond awesome. I'm the first man in the history of the planet to father a child.'

'It feels that way, doesn't it?'

'You mean I'm not?'

'There were a few trillion before you, but who's counting?'

In the kitchen, Magozzi splashed his face with cold water, then grabbed two frosty bottles of beer from the fridge while Gino wandered into the living room. There was a wall of floor-to-ceiling windows that overlooked woods and the lake beyond.

'You really scored with this place, Leo, you know that? It was the real estate deal of the century.'

'Tell me about it. If there hadn't been a double murder here in December, I never could have afforded it.'

'Yeah, I can see how that might make some potential buyers a little skittish.'

'One of the perks of being a homicide cop, I guess.'

'Any bites on your place in town?'

'The realtor had a couple open houses, but no offers yet. He gave me a list of staging suggestions he thinks will help it show better. Pictures on the wall, new hardware on the kitchen cabinets, plants, stuff like that.'

'What's wrong with the hardware on your kitchen cabinets?'

'Hell if I know.'

'Well, it couldn't hurt.'

'Yeah, but some of it's ridiculous. There's a limit to how much time I'm willing to piss away arranging flowers and folding the throw on my sofa just right. I've got enough to do with this place.'

'You're heading into town tonight, right?'

'To have dinner with Grace, not to stage my house.'

'So leave a half hour early, stop somewhere on the way, and pick up a couple of ferns or something. Hopefully you'll sell the house before you can kill them.' Gino wiped his brow with the back of his hand. 'You really need to look into central air. It's barely June, what do you think it's going to be like in July?'

'This is an anomaly. It'll probably be snowing next week. It might even be snowing in July.'

Two

Aside from an occasional workout routine in the basement of her Minneapolis home, Grace MacBride never
exercised – she'd always thought it to be a deplorable waste
of time. But she'd been genetically blessed – for all her
thirty-odd years, she had been thin, toned, and unreason-
ably healthy for a woman who spent most of her time
sitting in front of a computer.

She was still toned and healthy, according to her doctor
visit two weeks ago, but the thin part had gone out the
window a while ago. She still did double takes whenever
she passed a mirror and saw her burgeoning belly awkwardly fused onto an otherwise svelte body. Grace thought
it looked hysterically funny and absolutely fantastic.

She'd chosen a doctor on a whim, through an online
referral service. He was only the second she'd been to in
her adult life. He turned out to be a kind, elderly gentleman who had probably surpassed retirement age by
several years. He smelled of antiseptic soap and cigarette
smoke and had been befuddled by her lack of history.
And later, probably a little terrified by it.

I can't find your records in the database, Ms MacBride.

I don't have any records.

You've never been to a doctor?

Once. I had to have a physical to get into college.

And yet I find no record of that visit.

I was using a different name then.

Perhaps I could try that . . . um . . . alternative name.

That person doesn't exist anymore.

Oh . . . I see. Then perhaps you could tell me a little about your family history.

I don't have a family history, either. I never knew my parents.

Well, then. Right. So let's deal with the present, shall we? What I can tell you right now is that you seem to be in excellent physical condition and so does your baby, at least as far as I can determine without an ultrasound, which I recommend you schedule soon. Do you exercise?

I still go to the shooting range every week, does that count?

She smiled, remembering the expression on the doctor's face. The poor man. In retrospect, she probably could have been more tactful, but that was another thing she considered a deplorable waste of time.

Magozzi stirred next to her and sighed in his sleep. Bars of early sun were beginning to seep through the partially open blinds, laying strips of warm light across his dark, wavy hair. For some reason, she wanted to reach out and touch it, but she didn't.

Grace didn't particularly like to share her bed. Sex, yes, cuddling in sleep, not really. She and Magozzi slept together occasionally – obviously, she thought, drawing a hand over her belly – but the truth was that her history sometimes made the sudden touch of another human being during sleep terrifying.

Magozzi wasn't terribly happy about her aversion to closeness. All his life he'd dreamed of a fairy-tale marriage complete with a white picket fence and a baby carriage. And as it turned out, he was getting the baby carriage without the rest of it. But he never pried too hard, never pushed too hard, this man whose stock-in-trade was getting people to tell the truth. He was endlessly patient and respected her boundaries, which was probably a big part of why she loved him, although he wasn't in short supply of other admirable characteristics.

But things had started changing gradually, and now, six months into this pregnancy, she found herself wanting to feel him next to her at night. She had spent a lot of time ruminating over this disturbing shift in her persona and finally rationalized that some biological dominion mandated she have a protector in her vulnerable condition. Some animals did it, and humans were nothing if not animals, albeit in some cases, a much poorer version.

'I can hear you thinking,' she heard Magozzi's sleep-thick voice talking into his pillow.

'You're still sleeping. It's just a dream.'

'I'm pretty sure I'm awake.'

'Okay, so what am I thinking?'

'That you want me to make you French toast for breakfast.' He rolled over and gave her a sleepy, lopsided smile.

'I don't like French toast.'

'You'd like mine. I dip the bread in melted vanilla ice cream before I fry it.'

Grace smiled a little. 'That's actually pretty clever.'

'Of course it's clever.' He reached out and brushed a few strands of black hair from her face. 'Good morning.'

'Good morning.'

And then Magozzi's cell phone started ringing. He looked at the screen and sighed.

'It's Gino. Rain check on the French toast, okay?'

'I'll go make coffee.'

After Magozzi had rushed out with a mug of coffee and a banana, Grace fed her dog, Charlie, his morning kibble, then went back upstairs to get dressed, which was getting more and more difficult to do these days. In another month, she'd be wearing a tent.

She finally tossed her favorite belt holster into the purgatory bin of things that didn't fit her anymore and retrieved her old shoulder holster from the top shelf of the bedroom closet. It didn't fit much better, but her boobs were still smaller than her stomach, and there was no way she was going to go out into the world unarmed just because she was six months pregnant. In fact, being pregnant was double the reason to carry – she wasn't just protecting her own life anymore.

Charlie snuffled his approval from his perch on the bed. 'You like?'

The dog's stump tail wagged back and forth, but he didn't bother to lift his head. He'd been moody like this for a while, falling into a deep melancholy whenever they came back to the city. And who could blame him? At Magozzi's lake house, he could run to his heart's content, chase squirrels and butterflies, explore the woods, and on one regrettable occasion, he'd found a dead fish on shore to roll in. There, he could do the things a dog was born to do; here, he was confined to a tiny fenced-in yard which probably felt like a prison to him now.

And in truth, Grace was beginning to feel the same way. Not long ago, her small house had been her inviolate sanctuary; a physical and emotional fortress jealously guarded by fear and paranoia and every security precaution imaginable that kept everything and everyone out. But recently, her very carefully planned and constructed security blanket was starting to feel suffocating. Whether Charlie's discontent was mirroring her own or the other way around, she would never know. And in the end, it didn't matter. As she had learned these past few years, things changed – life, people, animals – all without your permission, no matter how zealously you fought to maintain supreme control.

She sat down on the bed and stroked Charlie's head. 'I know, buddy, I'm sorry. We won't be here long. Just a couple days.'

Charlie blinked at her and whined.

'Somebody in this relationship has to work, you know. Your kibble doesn't grow on trees.'

The dog snorted, as if he knew all about the multiple zeroes at the end of her bank account balance. Grace sighed, stood up, and patted her thigh. 'Come on, let's go to Harley's.'

At the sound of Harley's name, the dog's malaise vanished and he scrambled off the bed, anticipating the banquet of people food that was always waiting for him at the Monkeewrench office. Charlie loved Harley, of course, and Annie and Roadrunner, but Grace had always suspected that food was the main attraction. There was such a striking resemblance between dogs and men.

Grace followed Charlie into the kitchen and out the door, then felt a kick in her belly as she was locking up the house. Baby was already anxious to get out.

'Stay inside as long as you can,' she murmured. 'It's not safe out here.'

Three

When Harley Davidson was a kid, not one person had ever asked him what he wanted to be when he grew up. It was such a little thing, but it left a lonely hole in his heart when every other kid was asked the question a million times by a million people. Maybe nobody had ever inquired about his hopes and his dreams for the future because they didn't think he had any – the odds were dismal in the foster-home system for a bitter, aggressive boy with a bad mouth and a worse attitude. Or maybe they just didn't care.

Put your hand there, Harley. Feel the kick. You're the only one who hasn't done that.

I didn't want to be . . .

Harley. This is the newest member of our family. You need to introduce yourself.

Harley's hand moved to the swell in Grace's belly and jerked back, startled, when he felt movement against his palm.

Oh my God. There's a person in there.

Yes, there is.

And then Grace did the strangest thing. She put her hands on his cheeks and pulled his head against her belly.

I read a book that said babies in the womb respond to voices, remember them subliminally after birth. What do you want to say to the baby, Harley?

He released the breath he'd been holding against Grace's stomach and whispered, Baby, what do you want to be when you grow up?

Whoever is in there will want to grow up to be just like you.

This was what Harley was remembering as he perched on a ladder in one of the spare bedrooms in his Summit Avenue mansion, putting the final screws into the frame of an ornate, ceiling-mounted bed canopy. He could see Annie and Roadrunner in his peripheral vision, supervising from across the room. He thought Annie's fulsome figure looked particularly fetching today in a lacy dress that had some kind of shiny beadwork on the neckline. 'Your cleavage is damn near covered, Annie, what the hell is the matter with you?'

She lifted her chin haughtily. 'Sometimes the magic is in what you don't see.'

'What's wrong with seeing stuff?'

'Nobody's ever accused you of being refined or a gentleman,' Annie sniffed.

Harley smirked down at her. 'Show me a woman who wants a gentleman, and I'll show you a woman who is a liar.' Before Annie could retort, he made a broad, sweeping gesture toward the canopy. 'What do you guys think?'

'It looks centered,' Roadrunner commented blithely as he assessed the layout and dimensions of the room.

'Jesus, of course it's centered, you think I'd drill into a plaster ceiling without taking measurements? And I wasn't asking what you thought about my carpentry skills, I was asking what you thought about the canopy. This sucker is hand-carved, gold-leafed mahogany, painstakingly crafted in Bavaria over three hundred years ago.'

Annie clucked her tongue. 'It's beautiful, Harley, but you are one crazy fool. The child is not going to care about gold leaf or anything else.'

'Maybe not right away, but in time, little Leo or little Grace will grow to appreciate all the finer things in life, including my wine cellar.'

'Uh-huh. In a couple decades. Where are you going to hang the mobile?'

'Mobile?'

'The things you hang above a crib that have dangling animals and rainbows and whatnot. Babies love mobiles, it keeps them calm and puts them to sleep. Babies also have horrible eyesight, and this ceiling is eighteen feet high – no infant is going to be able to see a mobile hanging way up there.'

Harley clomped down the ladder, his jackboots a couple of sizes too large to negotiate the rungs with any grace. 'Not a problem. I'll put in a chandelier lift for the mobile, job done.'

Roadrunner politely cleared his throat, then his shoulders started shaking in suppressed laughter.

Harley scowled at him. 'What?'

'No offense, but for a couple of geniuses, you're really overcomplicating things. You don't hang mobiles from the ceiling, you hang them from a doodad that attaches to the side of the crib, problem solved.'

Annie tapped her lower lip thoughtfully. 'Is that so?'

Harley wagged his head adamantly. 'Oh, hell no. Nothing's getting attached to the side of this crib. You haven't seen it yet, but it's the pièce de résistance, and it just got delivered this morning . . .'

They all looked toward the open bedroom window when they heard a happy bark and a car door slam.

Harley started brushing the plaster dust from his hair

and beard and off his shoulders. 'Damn, Gracie's here already. Annie, you and Roadrunner go downstairs and distract them while I clean up. I don't want her to see the nursery until it's finished. And feed Charlie – there's poached chicken for him on the kitchen counter.'

'What about the frittata?' Roadrunner asked.

'Oh, shit, I forgot about it. Pull it, Roadrunner. I don't want to burn another one.'

Four

Harley usually cooked one of two things when he made breakfast for the Monkeewrench crew: donuts and sausage, or canned chili and beer. That was surely why the rest of them couldn't identify the aromas emanating from the kitchen while they waited at the round table in the breakfast room.

Annie was drumming her manicured fingernails on the rosewood impatiently. 'What on earth is he doing out there, and what's that smell? Bacon? Ham?'

Grace shrugged. 'Maybe both. But there's something else I don't recognize. It almost smells like food.'

Next to Grace, Roadrunner took a deep breath and flared his nostrils, sorting through the scents, expanding his chest until every rib was outlined against his white Lycra biking suit. 'It's a frittata. And it smells a lot better than it did when I rode over here at eight. This is the third time he's tried to make it.'

Harley's movements were always accompanied by an orchestration of sounds composed by Hells Angels. There was the pounding of his heavy motorcycle boots as he approached, then the jangle of chains and grommets and the squeak of leathers, and then suddenly his muscular, tattooed bulk filled the room as if someone had just pushed a boulder into it.

His left hand swung a champagne bucket by the

handle, spilling ice on the parquet floor. In his right, he clutched a bouquet of crystal flutes. 'Open this, Gracie, would you? Last time I put a cork through a window.' He plunked the bottle next to her, leaving a pool of water on the table.

Annie gave him a stark look of disapproval. 'You're serving alcohol to a pregnant woman?'

'Do you think I'm an idiot? This is sparkling grape juice. Come on, Roadrunner, give me a hand in the kitchen.'

Once Harley and Roadrunner had left the room, Annie arched an eyebrow at Grace. 'You do realize that Harley is going to be the most doting, meddling uncle on the planet, and he'll spoil that sweet little bun of yours rotten unless you're careful.'

'This from a woman who's already filled up an entire closet with baby clothes?'

Annie averted her gaze demurely. 'Well, you know how I love to shop, and baby clothes are just so precious.'

'We don't even know the sex.'

'Of course we do. It's a girl, mark my words.'

Grace smiled. 'I think so, too.'

'You're not tempted to find out for sure?'

'I like surprises.'

'Since when?'

'Since about six months ago.'

Annie let out a tinkling laugh. 'So how is the daddy-to-be?'

'He's acting strange. He already childproofed all the cupboard doors at the lake house, and he's turning the entire lower level into a playground.'

Harley appeared with a monstrous frittata and proudly plunked it down on the sideboard. 'Behold, my famous frittata.'

Annie craned her neck to get a closer look, and Grace covered a smile with her hand. It was obvious Annie was very interested in the frittata, but she would rather fall on a sword than let Harley know it. 'Since when did you have a famous anything?'

Harley gave her a smug smile. 'Oh yeah? You want to get busy with my phone book and start making some calls to a few of my lady friends?'

'You're disgusting.'

'And you, my dear lady, have a lascivious mind, because I was talking about my secret culinary gifts.'

'Yeah, right. Pig.'

Oil and water, Grace thought, uncorking the grape juice. Annie and Harley had always seemed like a perfect match of opposites, and yet the fates had never seen fit to throw in an emulsifier to bring the two together, and she wondered why. Maybe destiny had a team of actuaries working full-time, doing risk assessment on relationships, and for whatever reasons, her two friends didn't pass muster as a couple.

It took Harley and Roadrunner three trips to haul the rest of the food to the breakfast room's sideboard. Breakfast here was a little like going to eat at Paul Bunyan's logging camp, even when the fare was canned chili. The amount of food he prepared was almost obscene, and this morning was no exception. Grace eyed the frittata, the bacon, the ham, the four kinds of sausage, the fried potatoes, and asked, 'Do you have any fruit?'

'You're drinking it. Besides, you need something more substantial, being in the family way, and you're looking a little pale lately. How the hell do you do that when it's ninety degrees and sunny every day? I go out to get the mail and come back in looking like George Hamilton.'

'Well, the frittata looks fabulous.' Grace took a very small slice, greatly fearing the crooked orange decorative border came from canned cheese food.

'Harley,' Annie said, 'this is an unexpected act of gentility, serving real food.'

'Oh my God, was that an actual compliment?'

'Of course not.'

'Just wanted to double-check. Now eat up, all of you. I've got a proposition to make.'

Annie talked around a mouthful of bacon. 'Is this anything like when you wanted us all to buy that ostrich farm together?'

'I wasn't really serious about that. Well, I was, until I found out the damn things kick like mules. But this is different. An old sheriff buddy who works a county in southwestern Minnesota called me the other day for a favor.'

Annie arched a brow at him. 'Since when do you have an old sheriff buddy?'

'Since he arrested me for doing ninety in a thirty a while back. He thought I looked like a troublemaker, so he threw me in the pokey. But of course I charmed him with my stunning intellect and charismatic personality, and we ended up drinking whiskey and playing Texas Hold'em all night.'

'So what's your proposition?' Roadrunner asked as he

arranged his fried potatoes in a perfect ring around the rim of his plate, then began eating them one by one.

'Jesus, Roadrunner, do you have to do your OCD thing . . .'

'Spill it, Harley,' Annie said sharply.

'Well, I was thinking – we totally killed all the corporate security jobs last year, made a ton of money, pinned down some bad guys for the cops, but never spent a second on what we used to love doing more than anything else – helping people. Sheriff's got a friend – an old farmer named Walt. He lost his daughter a couple months ago. She just disappeared without a trace, and he wants to hire us to find her.'

Grace shifted uncomfortably in her chair. 'We have too many urgent requests from law enforcement all over the country, and we can't divert our attention away from that right now. You're talking about a missing persons case that's two months old, and as much as I hate to say it, it's probably a recovery mission. But the majority of the cops asking for our assistance are talking about murderers operating in their jurisdictions right now. We need to set priorities.'

'I think this should be one of our priorities. There are four of us, no reason we can't take this on as a side project and still get the other stuff done at the same time.'

Grace folded her arms across her chest. 'That's not what's going on here, is it? The real priority is to wrap me in cellophane for the next three months and keep me safe on a shelf.'

Harley shrugged. 'Now that you mention it, it wouldn't hurt you to take it easy for a little while instead of chasing bad guys, but that's not why I'm laying this out. I want to do something closer to home, something a little more personal. Walt lost his wife a few years ago, and his son before that, and I'd like to help find out what happened to his daughter, give an old man some peace in his final years.'

Grace leaned back in her chair. The upholstery was cushy and soft, and the chair seats were large enough to curl up your legs. She loved this room, and she loved each person in it, geeks and freaks every one of them. But that's all they were. They weren't cops, they weren't detectives, they were just a motley collection of computer geniuses who'd developed crime-solving software that connected all the faded dots and made it easier for the cops to catch bad guys. 'Where does this man live, Harley?'

'Buttonwillow. Southwest of us, about a two-hour drive.'

'So we'll send our software to the cops down there.'

Harley shook his big head. 'Won't help. It's a one-horse department with an old computer that can barely spit out a mailing label. No chance they could load the software, let alone run it.'

She raised her brows. 'You've been there?'

'Yeah, well, I took the Hog down to the guy's farm yesterday, talked to him for a while, stopped at the sheriff's office on my way home. Look, I'm not asking for a commitment from any of you, I'm just asking a straight-out favor that you all take a drive in the country with me and meet him before you make a decision, that's all.'

Roadrunner had finished eating his potato necklace. 'I'll take a ride with you, Harley.'

Annie passed a sour face on to Grace. 'The last time you took me on a country drive is not exactly my favorite memory.'

'Hey.' Grace grinned at her. 'You swam with dead cows, you connected with Mother Earth, you saved the world. And you were magnificent.'

Annie grunted and looked off to the side. 'Yes, I was.'

Five

Magozzi stepped out of his house in the city and into a steamy June morning that smelled like the lilac perfume his grandmother used to wear. It was just past dawn, but the air was already sodden, like somebody had thrown an invisible wet blanket over the city. Just as the radio weatherman had prognosticated on his way here from Grace's, it was going to be a hot one – a classic Minnesota colloquialism that meant you would sweat your balls off before noon if you had to be outside in a suit for more than ten minutes, a reality that loomed in his immediate future. And that future was not going to smell like Grandma's perfume, because it involved a homicide.

He watched an unremarkable MPD Ford sedan roll through a stop sign at the corner and heard the engine make a feeble attempt at a roar as Gino goosed it. He was driving too fast down Magozzi's residential street, dodging arboreal wildlife foolish enough to be cavorting on a city thoroughfare.

It was still weird to see Gino behind the wheel of anything but the drug-confiscated, supercharged Cadillac loaner they'd finally had to relinquish to the MPD auction block last November, something Gino was still bitter about, especially since it had in all likelihood been sold back to another drug dealer. The economy sucked, but the drug trade was doing a booming business in the city this year, all thanks to the Mexican cartels setting up shop along the I-35 corridor from Texas all the way to Minnesota.

The heroin overdoses had doubled in the past few months, pills, meth, and cocaine were flooding in at an alarming rate, and Vice and the DEA were going nuts. Law enforcement could deal with the local gangs that were distributing, but as long as product kept pouring in, there was always somebody to sell it, no matter how many people you put in prison.

Gino pulled up to the curb in front of the realtor's FOR SALE sign staked in the front lawn.

'You almost killed two squirrels in one block,' Magozzi said as he hopped in and buckled up.

Gino slurped from his travel mug, dribbling a brown line of coffee droplets onto his pant leg. He didn't seem to notice. 'Yeah, they were the two emaciated squirrels that run this piece of crap. I was aiming for them. Dammit, I miss the Caddie.' He draped his hands over the steering wheel and scrutinized Magozzi's house through the windshield. 'You ever heard of curb appeal?'

'My realtor may have mentioned it. What are you saying?'

'I'm saying that no matter how many houseplants you buy or what hardware you put on your kitchen cabinets, you are never going to sell this thing unless you do something about your scorched-earth yard. Potential buyers don't want a house that looks like it was built on a toxic waste dump.'

Magozzi shrugged. The truth was, his scruffy, barren yard had never really bothered him, not until he'd bought the lake house. It was nestled in the woods and there was nothing but lush, unrelieved greenery as far as the eye could see. It was like living in a tree house. 'There's a perfect buyer out there somewhere.'

'Well, I hope your realtor is sending out flyers in Braille.'

Magozzi scoffed. 'Hey, there are a lot of people who hate to mow as much as I do, and this is perfect for them. Bring in a couple loads of pea gravel, throw in a cactus or two for the summer, and you've got yourself a maintenance-free lawn. No mowing, no watering, no fertilizing. You take the cactus in for the winter and start all over again in the spring.'

Gino let out a defeated sigh and pulled away from the curb, driving much more reasonably now that he had a passenger on board. 'Nothing wrong with having two houses, either. Half the state owns a city house and a lake cabin somewhere else.'

'It's a pain in the ass. The first reasonable offer that comes in, I'm dumping this place. In the meantime, it comes in handy as a crash pad when we work late.'

'You ever think about keeping it as a rental property?'

'That would be an even bigger pain in the ass . . .'

Gino suddenly slammed on the brakes hard and leaned on his horn as a mindless text zombie walked out into the street against the light, oblivious to everything but his phone. He jerked his head up at the sound of the horn, mouthed 'Fuck you,' returned his attention to his phone, and kept ambling illegally against the light.

'Can I kill him, Leo?'

'Vehicular manslaughter?'

'I really want to shoot him.'

'Your choice. Although you could just arrest him.'

Gino honked again and held his shield out his open window. 'It's your lucky day that I'm on my way to clean up a dead body, otherwise you'd be in cuffs right now.'

The text zombie's eyes grew wide, then he bolted across the street and disappeared down an alley.

'Dumbass. What the hell is wrong with people?'

'I hope that's a rhetorical question.'

'It is.'

'So where's this dead body?'

'You know that off-leash dog park by the VA hospital?'

'No. I don't have a dog.'

'Well, if you're a dog, it's a great place, filled with hills and bluffs and woods. Apparently, it's also a great place for killers.'

The silence that followed was typical of every ride to every homicide scene. They'd make small talk, joke a little, Gino would rant about something, but as they got closer to their destination, they ran out of distractions and the heaviness of what waited for them started to sink in.

Six

You could almost predict what kind of crime had gone down by the way the emergency vehicles were parked. At active crime scenes they were strewn all over any existing space in a haphazard scatter that always reminded Gino of his son's Lincoln Logs after he'd demolished something he'd just built. God, boys were destructive little people.

In the lot of Minnehaha off-leash dog park, every vehicle with a bubble on it was parked in careful, painful order, each one a door length away from its neighbor, front tires perfectly aligned. There were no urgent fishtail stops at a homicide scene to gain extra seconds, because everyone knew they were too late to help the victim.

Gino parked behind a row of squads and a set of barricades, and they stepped out into the stifling heat that seemed to be getting worse by the minute. But even Gino didn't complain about it – they were alive and a woman somewhere in this park wasn't.

The Bureau of Criminal Apprehension's crime-scene unit was already on-site, and Magozzi saw techs walking across a green expanse of lawn toward a tree line. Uniforms were interviewing a few people beneath the shade of a stately old maple tree, and Sergeant Baker out of Third Precinct was crouched in front of a weeping young woman who was on her knees, hugging her panting husky and worrying the dog's fur like it was a stuffed animal.

Baker caught sight of them and waved, then found another cop to stay with the crying woman before he walked over.

'Hey, Sergeant.'

'Detectives. Haven't seen you two in a while.'

'And I'll bet you didn't miss us,' Gino said.

Baker shook his head sadly. 'No.'

Magozzi gestured toward the woman the sergeant had just been talking to. 'I'm guessing she found the body?'

'Yeah.' He grimaced and looked down at the ground. 'Actually, I think the dog found it first. And listen, it's pretty bad. Well, they're all pretty bad, but this one is worse than most, just so you know. I've got the scene laced up tight, but let's get you two in there before things get crazy on the fringes and the media starts showing up.'

'Where's the victim?' Gino asked.

Baker pointed to a thick cluster of trees in the near distance that was swallowing up the techs Magozzi had seen earlier. Urban Minnesotans loved their beautiful city parks, with all the lakes and trees and tidy, sheltered paths that carved through all kinds of terrain. They were the city's greatest resource in Magozzi's opinion, and gave people a chance to pretend they were out in the woods or on a lake someplace else, where there weren't a million other people breathing down your neck, vying for space, and possibly plotting your demise.

But as Gino had intimated earlier, a park was also a good place for the less well-intended to either hunt their prey or stash their dirty deeds. And maybe that would be the next brilliant government plan to crack down on crime – defoliate all the parks. No place to hide a body, problem solved. They would of course totally ignore the fact that woods weren't the real problem, human nature was. That would be prejudicial, implying that there were actually homicidal maniacs out there in spite of the tree cover. It might hurt the homicidal maniacs' feelings.

'Take us on a walk, Sergeant,' Magozzi said, tiring of his own cynical thoughts. 'You have a way cleared?'

Baker grunted. 'Basically, we have a way trampled. This park is loaded in the morning. Last walk for Fido before his owners split for work and lock him in the house so he can chew the windowsills off. When the husky started howling, a lot of other dogs followed, and then their owners. The place looks like the tail end of a cattle drive.'

'Super,' Gino grumbled. 'So, who's running the show?'

'This is your lucky day. Jimmy Grimm is in the building.'

Magozzi felt at least a couple of the six hundred muscles in his body relax a little, hearing the name. Jimmy Grimm was the head tech of the BCA's crime-scene unit and the gold standard, and it was indeed a lucky day if he caught your scene. Not that there weren't a dozen talented, seasoned techs in line for his throne when he finally decided to throw in the towel, something he'd been threatening for a while; but Jimmy was special, more like a third partner.

Magozzi, Gino, and Baker crossed a dew-spangled lawn that was dotted with picnic areas, then mounted a rough jogging trail that led through shady woods that didn't do much to mitigate the swelling heat that was building as the sun lifted higher in the hazy sky. Gino was huffing and puffing after a few minutes, wiping his brow repeatedly with a handkerchief. 'Hot,' he muttered, loosening his tie.

After a few minutes, they hit a phalanx of police officers standing behind a far-reaching cordon of crime-scene tape that disappeared into the trees where techs were placing markers. Baker lifted it for them before veering into the brush and heading north down a slight incline. 'A little tough going, guys,' he warned. 'Watch your step.'

Twigs crunched beneath their feet as they negotiated more rugged terrain, and Magozzi felt the sting of sandburs grabbing hold of his pants and sinking their little needles into his flesh. 'She was dragged in here,' he said, pointing out a trail of broken plants just to their right. 'Dead or alive?'

Gino paused to crouch near a crushed thornbush. 'Get a tech over here with a bag and a marker, Baker. This bush took a bite out of someone.'

'Probably a dog. Or maybe the victim.'

'Or maybe whoever was dragging the victim,' Gino replied, and Baker closed his eyes. He was never going to make Homicide.

Magozzi lifted his head toward the tree canopy when a bird issued a sweet, tuneful call; it was far too cheery a soundtrack for the movie they were all in, already spoiled because they knew the ending. But the pretty birdcall wasn't loud enough to obscure the hissing buzz of flies.

'Jesus,' Gino whispered, pausing at the perimeter of some sick asshole's idea of a good time.

Magozzi moved up to stand next to him and stared down at the pretty face of a young woman. He always started with the face. Person first, murder victim second.

Late twenties, maybe early thirties, brown hair, brown eyes he wished he could close.

She was splayed on her back, arms outstretched above her head as if she were about to do a backward dive into the shallow, limestone ravine just a few steps beyond. There was a dark necklace of bruising around her neck, and when his eyes moved down her torso, he felt his stomach coil tight and his throat close: her Nike-emblazoned sports tank was crisscrossed with deep slashes where flies were feasting. They'd seen this before. 'We've got a cutter, Gino.'

Gino's breathing was fast and shallow, and the collar of his blue shirt was already dark with sweat. 'More like a butcher. Sick bastard spent some time on her. And she's fresh, and not that far off the path. Had to be a night job, or early morning before sunup. Even if he'd disabled her before he dragged her here, you can't do this kind of carving in broad daylight with people walking on a trail a couple hundred yards away.'

'And what does that remind you of?'

'Christ, yeah, I know. Megan Lynn, McLaren's unsolved from last May.'

'That's what I was thinking,' Jimmy Grimm said solemnly as his head suddenly popped into view just below them.

'Hey, Jimmy. See anything down there, like a bloody knife?'

'At first glance, no, nothing but a lot of dog crap. I'll have the team comb through it when they finish with the primary scene.' He lost his footing and slid down the slope a few feet. 'Dammit, I can't get back up. Give me a hand.'

Gino made a daring and treacherous move, balanced on the incline, and offered his hand to pull him up.

Jimmy dusted himself off, put on a new pair of gloves, and regarded them with steady eyes once he was back on solid ground.

'Different park, same scene as Megan Lynn's last year. Strangulation. Cutting on the torso. No outward signs of sexual assault.'

Magozzi nodded. 'Did you check her for a card?'

'Not yet.'

Gino was the first to see what they'd all been fearing – the outline of a small rectangle beneath the fabric of the girl's tank. 'Oh, shit,' he murmured.

Jimmy crouched down, delicately reached beneath the fabric, and pulled out a bloody playing card. 'Four of spades,' he said quietly.

Gino looked down at his dusty shoes, trying to ignore the unsettling sensation of stepping into a patch of quicksand. 'Megan Lynn had the ace of spades.'

'Yep.'

'So where's the two and three?'

Seven

Timothy Wells had just finished feeding and burping Abbie and Allie, and was now rocking them to sleep in his arms, spellbound by their curling little fingers as they flexed and gripped. Most people referred to them as 'the Twins,' maybe out of convenience, or maybe because it sounded cute, like a title. That was fine, but he'd never understood the generic designation, as if they were a single entity and not two totally different, miraculous little people who deserved to be called by their names.

Allie was a little fussier – inherited from his side of the family, no doubt; but Abbie, a calm and gentle mama's girl through and through, was already sound asleep, her soft eyelashes fluttering every once in a while. It looked like she was dreaming, and he wondered what babies dreamed of after only six months on this earth. Probably food. Mom. Dad. The animal mobile hanging above the crib.

His cell was set on vibrate, and it suddenly started skittering on the sofa table behind him. He smiled and didn't bother looking at the caller ID, because Charlotte always called to check in after she'd gotten settled in at work. She couldn't help it. 'Hey, honey,' he whispered into the phone.

'Tim? This is Jenny.'

Tim frowned. Jenny was Charlotte's office manager. 'Oh, hi, Jenny. What can I do for you?'

'I'm trying to reach Char. Is she on her way?'

Tim rolled his eyes up to the grandfather clock by the front door. It was half past nine. Charlotte was half an hour late to work. Not like her. She was usually half an hour early. 'She's probably stuck in traffic. She didn't call?'

'She hasn't checked in and she's not answering her phone. I just wanted to make sure everything was okay, because that's not like her, especially since she has a presentation at eleven.'

Nothing's okay now. Tim's hands started shaking, imagining a car accident, or a bad fall in that dog park she liked to run in, with all the hills she thought would help her lose her baby fat faster. 'She left early this morning to go jogging. She was planning to shower and clean up at the gym before work. Are you sure she's not there?'

'Positive.'

Just keep Jenny on the phone a little bit longer. Charlotte will walk in any minute. 'Oh, there you are, Char!' And then Jenny would thank him and apologize for bothering him, and the world would settle back into its proper place.

'Tim?'

Allie started squirming in his arms. Even Abbie was starting to fuss.

'Let me try her, Jenny. I'll call you right back.'

He listened to the entire outgoing voice message on Charlotte's cell phone that she always, always answered when he called, because what if one of the babies was sick? She even took the damn thing into meetings and the restroom so she wouldn't miss a call – the new mother's certainty that the one time she didn't pick up, it would be something serious.

Tim had thought that was an overabundance of caution, because he was a terrific stay-at-home dad, and nothing was ever serious. But he wasn't thinking that way today.

He looked down at the two little people he loved second and third best in all the world, then squeezed his eyes shut. *Oh my God, oh my God, what do I do now? Who do I call? Who can help?*

And then the doorbell rang.

There were twin babies in Charlotte Wells's house, crying in a back bedroom, wailing actually, and the sound was killing Magozzi. It was as if those babies knew he and Gino were out there, and somehow knew why.

Timothy Wells sat on an IKEA couch opposite them. There was a bargain-basement coffee table in between the seating areas that held a baby monitor, a television remote, and a framed photograph of the happy family. He was utterly expressionless, but his hands clutched each other, trying to hang on to a life that had just vanished in the few seconds it had taken Gino to say, 'I'm sorry, Mr Wells . . .'

After he'd asked the first, painful questions every survivor did as they worked through denial and tried to process shock, and after he'd heard the answers, he'd stood up woodenly, like a Punch and Judy puppet, excused himself, then walked out of the room. They could hear him throwing up through the bathroom door.

'Jesus Christ,' Gino muttered, looking around the neat but cheaply furnished living room. New parents on a shoestring budget, putting all their spare dimes into their babies. Every flat surface was cluttered with the kind of photos new parents collected. Charlotte Wells in a hospital bed, one new baby cradled in each arm, tired dewy face oddly serene with the soothing enormity of what she had just accomplished; Dad with the babies, awkward and baffled, then all four of them on a bed a few months later, when fat toes kicked at the world and proud parents mugged for the camera.

'I know what that feels like, and pretty soon you will, too,' Gino said. 'Tired as hell, but you can't wipe that goofy grin off your face. He's not our guy, Leo.'

Magozzi nodded. You got a feel for these things after a while. Not a certain knowledge, of course, but a sense of what people were made of and what reactions were real. But they still had to pick him apart like a crab and pry every last bit of information out of him they could. He wished he was still in Grace's bed, before the day had shattered from sunlight to shadows.

Timothy Wells came out of the bathroom a few minutes later, his face gray, his gait unsteady. The tears hadn't come yet. Grief visited everyone differently. 'I have to get the girls,' he mumbled.

Gino stood up and followed him to the back of the house.

Once the twins were safely in their father's arms, they calmed down. They were blond, perfectly chubby, and cherry-cheeked from crying. Tim stroked their foreheads as they both yawned in concert. When he looked up again, Magozzi saw raw fury in his eyes, but he kept his voice soft and soothing for the benefit of his babies. 'I'll tell you anything you need to know. Just find the monster who murdered my wife.'

Eight

Notifications always left human wreckage in their wake, and Gino and Magozzi always took a little of that away with them. They'd waited with Timothy Wells until his parents and in-laws arrived, then made a quiet exit so the forlorn could grieve in peace. It wasn't always like that – sometimes the mourner was a prime suspect who had to be observed, but it wasn't the case with Timothy Wells. He was a wrecked man with a wrecked life who deserved some privacy with his loved ones, and more than anything, he deserved justice as fast as they could deliver it. But speed wasn't trending for them at the moment, and this wasn't an average, cut-and-dried case with an obvious solution.

'Goddamnit,' a mostly silent Gino finally blurted out as they approached City Hall.

'Is that a general "goddamnit," or a specific one?'

'General. Specific. I don't know, both. We just spent the past three hours frying our retinas watching surveillance footage, and interviewing every single person who ever had regular contact with Charlotte Wells. And what did we get? Nothing except enough tears to fill twenty swimming pools. No stalker lurking around the water cooler at work, no creep at the gym who hung around while she worked out, no guy with an I AM A SERIAL KILLER T-shirt hanging in front of the security cam across from the dog park.'

'So we're going with a serial for sure?'

'I don't know how we can't, with the MO and the playing cards. But how the hell is he selecting his victims? He had to have some kind of contact with them, even if it was indirect.'

'The parks have to be the point of contact. Megan Lynn was a jogger, Charlotte Wells was a jogger. Joggers have routines, and routines make for good targets. And maybe there's some connection between the two victims, like they used the same handyman or whatever.'

'A psycho handyman. That would be helpful.' Gino parked on the street, turned off the ignition, and flopped his wrists over the steering wheel. 'So this guy has a year lag between murders here, and we're missing the two and three of spades. Maybe he was operating somewhere else.'

'Just what I was thinking. We have a lot of specific crime-scene details to plug into ViCAP. If this guy was operating somewhere else, chances are good we'll get some kind of a match.'

'If the cases ever got entered into the system.'

'Ritualistic stuff like this gets entered into the system, even if you're running a one-man department in the Alaskan wilderness.'

Gino scratched his jaw pensively. 'Then again, there might not be a two and three of spades. What if this guy has some weird, OCD numerological fixation and he does every fourth card? Or maybe he hates prime numbers.'

Magozzi rolled his head to look at Gino. 'A psycho handyman who hates prime numbers. Now we're getting somewhere.'

'I might be overthinking this. Oh, shit. That's a Channel Ten news van over there. Get ready to no-comment your way to the office.'

Amanda White was waiting to ambush them at the front door of City Hall. She was Channel Ten's new replacement for the obnoxious Kristin Keller, a journalist who had never let the facts interfere with her reporting or derail her career trajectory. She'd finally gone national last year, and was now spreading her misinformation to a larger audience, but this White character was even worse. She was young, starvation-hungry for any scoop, and so borderline unethical, she made Kristin Keller look like Gandhi.

She pushed her mini recorder in their faces, her hungry eyes burning brightly. 'Detectives, can you tell me anything about the murder you're currently investigating?'

Magozzi looked at her wearily. 'You know the answer to that, Ms White. We have no comment at this point.'

'Will there be a press conference?'

'Media will be notified.' Magozzi opened the door to City Hall and felt a wonderful wave of chilled air hit him as he left the heat and Amanda White behind.

Or not.

'Off the record?' she persisted, following him and Gino into the lobby. She made a great show of clicking off her recorder.

Gino turned around and stared her down. Most reporters knew enough to never, ever mess with Gino after a crime scene, a notification, or an autopsy, particularly when any two of that unholy trinity happened in one day; Amanda White had yet to learn that. 'Off the record, give it up, leave us alone, and let us do our job.'

Magozzi watched the stare-down continue, admiring Gino's restraint. Amanda White wasn't backing down either, but she changed her tack and put on a new mask in a split second, giving Gino wide doe eyes and a sympathetic moue. It was actually kind of creepy.

'I know it's early in the investigation, Detective Rolseth, I know you and Detective Magozzi are not going to talk to me at this juncture, but the reason I asked about a press conference is that I'm concerned for the welfare of the women of this city. If it's not safe to jog alone in our parks right now, then it's my job to give them a warning, even if you won't.'

'Your point is?'

'I'm putting two and two together.'

'So you're good at math?'

'Megan Lynn.'

Magozzi decided to step in before things escalated. 'Megan Lynn?' He frowned a little, as if trying to recall the name.

'Nice puzzled look, Detective Magozzi, it's just not very convincing.' She rolled her eyes, something she would never have done on camera, and Magozzi was surprised at how snotty and ugly it made her look. 'Megan Lynn,' she continued. 'The girl found in Powderhorn Park last year. Same MO as this one, right down to the knife cuts.'

The scary thing was, she didn't even wait for a response, she just gave him a predatory smile with oversized, over-whitened teeth, turned on her heel, and walked away.

'God, I hate that woman,' Gino seethed after she'd left. 'And those teeth – she looks like a shark without a face. This is what we get for not locking up all the witnesses that went running up to that nightmare scene to find their stupid, howling dogs, then spilled their guts about what they saw. You know what I hate about her more than her teeth?'

'Her hair?'

'No, I hate that she's actually got a point about warning the public. And if she does it before we do, then MPD is going to look bad.'

Magozzi tried to rub away the headache that was creeping in at his temples. 'So you want to let the press dictate when we hold press conferences and what we say? Cart driving the horse. Besides, it's not our call.'

'Thank God.'

Nine

Gino had always thought that walking into Chief Malcherson's office was like walking into a model home somewhere, dusted and buffed and ready for company. Very rarely had he seen anything out of place, or some foolish piece of dust daring to linger on his mahogany desk.

It was a weird feeling, walking into a place so put together when he lived in a virtual booby trap of a house that cherished the evidence of family rather than the essence of tidiness.

Having a second child twelve years after the first had brought him happily back to the warm clutter of growing little people. He was forever moving a tricycle off the front walk or spilled crayons off his recliner, and minded not a bit. In his opinion, there was something sad about perfectly dressed people in a perfectly decorated environment, as if someone had taken a Mixmaster to their priorities.

Malcherson was pretty much a reflection of his office, or maybe it was the other way around. Buttoned down, pulled together, and basically impeccable. In stature and bearing, he looked like an Armani Viking. In manner and speech throughout his seven-year tenure as chief, he had always been the political voice of reason; a stellar representative for the MPD. Gino had always admired the wavering line he walked between the cop he had once been and the politician he became.

He looked up when they walked in, his full jowls hanging a little lower than usual. 'Detectives, come in, sit down.'

'Thanks, Chief.' Gino and Magozzi settled into cushy upholstered chairs.

'Tell me how things are progressing.'

'We've been beating the bushes, sir,' Gino said in his best, Sunday-company voice. 'No persons of interest yet.'

Malcherson's face darkened. 'Have you found anything to dispel our fear of a serial?'

Magozzi shook his head. 'If anything, we're more sure than we were before.'

The chief cleared his throat. 'That's unfortunate.'

'Yes, sir. But that's not the worst news,' Gino said, always a ray of sunshine. 'We ran into Amanda White on the way in. She's fishing the serial killer angle, pulling together Charlotte Wells and Megan Lynn, and she basically told us if we didn't warn the public, she would.'

Malcherson looked truly alarmed. 'She doesn't know about the playing cards, does she?'

'No way. She's just looking for a scoop, never squander an opportunity for hysteria, right? If she knew about the cards, she would have already been yakking about it on TV.'

Magozzi watched the chief fold his hands and stare down at some of his paperwork for a moment, inevitably running multiple scenarios and risk assessments.

'I'm not certain an official statement intimating that the two murders may be connected would be productive at this point.'

Gino leaned forward and gave the chief a square-jawed look, which was kind of a miracle, because his extra chin had swallowed his square jaw a long time ago. 'You know, Chief, I've been thinking.'

Malcherson sighed heavily. 'Of course you have, Detective Rolseth.'

'Yeah, well, we pretty much knew that this was a serial the minute we saw the four of spades on Charlotte Wells, and we all decided to keep a cover on it until we could confirm one way or the other. But like I was telling Leo, the first call I made when I left the crime scene was to Angela, telling her and the kids to stay out of the parks. It doesn't seem fair that I'm making sure my own family doesn't get hurt while I leave the rest of the city to fend for themselves.'

Malcherson's lips were pressed together in a thin line. 'We're still not a hundred percent certain we have a serial. And we don't have all the evidence processed. Far from it, according to your most recent reports. Not only would it be irresponsible to prematurely start a citywide panic a few hours into an investigation, we also risk the possibility of sending our perpetrator underground.'

'Think of it as a tornado, Chief,' Gino persisted. 'It's a watch, not a warning. We don't know if the tornado is on the ground yet, but there's a possibility one may be forming. No cause for panic when it's only a watch, just be prepared. So get the cows in the barn and the flashlight in the basement and don't take any chances until the system passes.'

Malcherson rubbed his forehead. 'I'll make a statement.'

'Great,' Gino said after they'd left the chief's office. 'I

can hear the script now. "Detectives Magozzi and Rolseth have yet to come up with a person of interest, so, ladies, be careful in the parks, because we've got a serial killer who likes to carve up his victims with a KA-BAR after he strangles them."'

'I think he'll be a little more subtle than that.'

Ten

Detective Johnny McLaren sat at his desk with his chin in his hand, grinning like an idiot across the aisle to where Gloria had commandeered Magozzi's desk as if she owned it. Actually, she owned any space she occupied, always had, and everybody in Homicide was glad to have her back, manning the check-in desk and running the day-to-day show with military precision.

They were the only two in the office at the moment, and as far as McLaren was concerned, that constituted a date. 'Don't get me wrong, Gloria. I believe in marriage with all my heart, but if that doesn't work for your mis-guided feminist views, I'm perfectly okay with just having sex and a few children.'

Gloria gave him a haughty look and wadded up the waxed paper that contained not a single remaining crumb of the massive sandwich she'd just put away. 'You know, honey, they have medications that help with psychotic breaks with reality. You ought to look into it.'

McLaren's grin got bigger. 'I get it. You're in denial. That's probably why you took a year off to go to law school. I was becoming irresistible, and you were afraid you couldn't trust yourself around me anymore. My the-ory is you quit school because you realized you couldn't live without me. The ebony-and-ivory thing can work out, you know.'

Gloria stood up and stomped a few feet to tower over McLaren's desk, her five-foot-seven frame augmented by three-inch heels the same blaze orange as her silk caftan. Her beaded cornrows danced as she bent over and got in his face. 'Some theory. I quit because lawyers are all boring scumbags. And what would I do with a pasty little white pencil of a man like you, anyhow?'

'Anything you want.'

'Trust me, you wouldn't survive the night, munchkin. And what the hell happened to your face? It's redder than your hair.'

McLaren touched a flaming cheek and winced. 'I went golfing with Willy Staples. The sunscreen didn't work.'

Gloria cocked her head and narrowed her kohl-lined Cleopatra eyes. 'The rich guy who owns all the shopping malls?'

'Yeah. He picked me up in his Bentley.'

Gloria put a hand on an impressively proportioned hip. 'Well, my oh my, aren't you all that, rubbing elbows with the swells. What business you got with him?'

'He's working on a franchise deal in Russia, and I'm the only translator he trusts because I'm not Russian. Plus, I work cheap on the weekends, as long as there's some poker or golf involved.'

Gloria regarded the little twerp with grudging admiration. Everybody in the department knew McLaren had one of those spooky photographic memories and a special aptitude for language, as unlikely as it seemed in such a wimpy, innocuous little vessel. 'You speak Russian now?'

McLaren clucked his tongue. 'See what you miss out on when you take a leave of absence? I aced it last year while you were figuring out that lawyers are all boring scumbags.'

She rolled her eyes to the ceiling. 'What on God's green earth possessed you to learn Russian?'

'Hey, we're essentially still in a Cold War with them, figured it might come in handy someday. Plus, I was thinking Russian oligarch might be a great second career for me.'

They both looked up when Magozzi and Gino came plodding in with suit coats slung over their shoulders. Their button-downs were limp, and there wasn't a tie in sight.

Gloria folded her arms across her bosom, clear disapproval in her face. 'There is a dress code here, you know.'

Gino made a failed attempt at a smile. 'It's good to have you back, Gloria. I didn't catch shit the whole time you were gone, and it made me feel empty inside.'

'Well, I guess I'll give you a pass this time, with the heat and humidity and all.'

'Bad scene?' McLaren asked.

'Bad scene, worse notification,' Gino muttered.

McLaren's rusty brows peaked on his sunburned forehead, blending in as he looked from Magozzi to Gino. 'Oh yeah? What's up?'

Magozzi sank into his desk chair. 'We think we have another Megan Lynn.'

McLaren's face froze and his thin shoulders collapsed, like somebody had just pulled a plug on him. 'Jesus Christ, no.'

'Yeah.' He looked at Gloria, who could keep her mouth shut tighter than a bear trap when it was required. She wasn't a cop, but she engendered more trust in Homicide than almost anybody else in the department and probably held a lot more secrets than all of them put together. She also knew when to make a graceful exit. Not that she wouldn't nose around later and read every single piece of paper that came in, which was fine by Magozzi.

Gloria gave a stern look of determination in the general direction of her front-desk domain. 'Well, I hate to leave this party early, but I've got a few slackers I need to beat up and set straight.' She sashayed away, throwing back an admonition to Gino and Magozzi to drink some water.

Magozzi let out a weary breath, then reached into his briefcase and placed an eight-by-ten photo on McLaren's desk. Charlotte Wells in a sundress, smiling on a white sand beach somewhere, proudly pointing at her baby bump while turquoise-blue surf foamed in the background. Surf and life frozen in time. Timothy Wells had printed it out for them before he and Gino had left him to deal with his two motherless baby girls and his ruined life, and every time Magozzi looked at it, he was physically sickened because he couldn't stop his darkest fears from transposing Grace's face onto that pregnant body.

'Charlotte Wells. Pretty young brunette, just like Megan Lynn. Devoted wife and mother of two six-month-old twin girls, working her way up the corporate ladder at General Mills. Went jogging early this morning before work in the Minnehaha dog park, like she does a few days a week to get rid of her baby fat, according to her husband, Tim.'

Magozzi paused to let that sink in; he wanted McLaren

to know a little of who she'd been when she'd still been breathing, because he got it. He would remember her, and not just as a nameless victim represented by random numbers on a case file that would hopefully get solved one day.

He pulled out another photo of Charlotte Wells in situ at the crime scene and placed it next to the beach shot. 'Exact same MO as Megan Lynn,' he continued. 'Strangulation, postmortem cutting on the torso with some kind of serrated knife, according to the ME. No sexual assault. Personal effects all intact. But the big kicker is she had a four of spades in her shirt.'

McLaren dragged his hands through his clown-colored hair. 'It's the same son of a bitch, it's gotta be. The playing-card angle never saw the light of day, so it can't be a copycat. Jesus. He's marking his victims. He's keeping track.'

'We're thinking this is definitely a serial.'

'Fuck. Yes,' McLaren muttered. 'And if he's going in order, then there are two victims out there somewhere with the two and three of spades on them – we just haven't found them yet.'

'Been there, we already plugged it into ViCAP. No matches on the national database for our MO or the playing cards. If he was operating anywhere else in the country during the year he took off between murders here, it's not in the system.'

McLaren frowned. 'So maybe he's not going in order and there aren't two additional victims.'

Magozzi reanimated after draining a half-liter bottle of water, per Gloria's advice. 'That crossed our minds, and it makes sense. Megan Lynn and Charlotte Wells were left in public parks near trails where they were sure to be found. He's showing off his handiwork, and putting a cherry on top by marking his victims with cards. The sick bastard is signing his work, showboating. This kind of killer isn't going to deviate and hide some bodies and not others. But we don't know that for sure. We can't get into the mind of a crazy, who knows what his twisted fantasy is.'

McLaren leaned back in his chair and started drumming a paradiddle on his desk with his fingers. 'I'm thinking about the year time lag. Not out of the norm for a serial, but still, there's a chance our perp could have taken an involuntary vacation that interrupted his killing jag. It's a long shot, but worth a look.'

Magozzi nodded. 'We'll have Tommy Espinoza work his computers for prison records, see if there's a violent offender who got put on ice after Megan Lynn's murder and released before Charlotte Wells's murder.'

'Did you get anything from the husband?'

'An absolute nightmare of a notification, and that's about it,' Gino said, unwrapping a flattened turkey sandwich he'd pulled out of his briefcase and assessing it for food safety after it had spent a few hours in a boiling hot car. Hunger eventually won out over good judgment.

'How about associates?' McLaren asked.

Magozzi shook his head. 'According to everybody we interviewed, including the husband, Charlotte Wells was social, gregarious, loved by all. She had no grievances with any coworkers, no sketchy characters in her past or present, no enemies. We've got a couple more friends to talk to and we'll go through her cell phone records, but that's probably going to be a dead end.' He cringed. There were too many goddamned idioms in the English language with the word 'dead' in them. Dead end. Dead ringer. Dead reckoning. Dead to the world. Dead on your feet. Dead to rights . . .

McLaren jiggled his mouse and woke up his sleeping computer. 'I'll pull all the files I've got on Megan Lynn and forward them to you. Maybe there's some kind of dovetail between her and Charlotte Wells, like they went to the same coffee shop or the same gym or whatever. What about surveillance footage?'

Gino tossed the crusts of his sandwich into the garbage can by his desk. 'No cameras in the dog park, just a traffic cam that semi-covers the main entrance. Nothing jumped out at us. But there are a million ways to sneak in without using the main entrance, according to the park police, which is what I would have done if I wanted to stake out a sweet hiding spot.'

'Let me take a look at it. I've got all the Powderhorn Park surveillance from last year, plus the traffic cams from the immediate area. I've looked at the films about a thousand times, so something from the dog park might hit a nerve with me.'

'Thanks, Johnny.'

'No thanks necessary, let's just string this bastard up by his nuts and send him down the river for life times two.'

'Amen.'

McLaren refocused on his computer, but that never stopped his mind or his mouth. 'Hey, Leo, what's the news on Junior?'

Magozzi suddenly felt an astonishing, cleansing emptiness as serial killer butchers and dead women completely evacuated his mind, replaced by joyful visions of what his near future might be like. 'He's kicking like a maniac.'

'It's a boy?'

'We don't know. But I think so.'

'Fantastic. Did you sell your place in town yet?'

'Hell, no,' Gino interjected. 'His yard looks like White Sands after a bomb test – it's never going to sell, I keep telling him but he doesn't listen.'

'Why, are you interested, Johnny?' Magozzi asked.

'Maybe. A man needs a house if he's going to start a family.'

'What?'

'Gloria and I. We're going to start a family, she just doesn't know it yet.'

Eleven

Buttonwillow, Minnesota, was indeed a one-horse town, minus the horse and minus the town. Aside from a feed mill, a gas station, and a Dairy Queen at the freeway turnoff, it was just an empty, unrelieved landscape of rolling hills, farm fields, and woods, speckled with electric fences, cows, and an occasional farmhouse.

Five miles off the freeway, Harley turned his Hummer onto a washboard dirt road and rattled their teeth for ten minutes before easing into a driveway with potholes slightly smaller than the Grand Canyon. Even Charlie, seated in the backseat between Grace and Annie, grunted at the impacts, then went rigid with attention, ears pricked forward, when the Hummer braked to a stop.

'I think Charlie's scared,' Annie said.

Harley looked at the dog through the rearview mirror as he slid the gear into park and turned off the motor. 'Bullshit. He's eyeballing all those trees in the yard. It's been a long ride.'

But when Grace opened her door, Charlie followed her out with doggie restraint, not running for the trees, not tearing up the grass as dogs sometimes do. He just stepped out of the car slowly, almost respectfully, then sat down promptly, his eyes and ears focused on the house.

The house was a big two-story box, probably built at the turn of the last century in classic rural Midwestern style, which meant a roof, four walls, and enough space for a brood of sons who would start working the land the minute they could walk. It sagged a bit on one side, as if it were about to tip over from sheer exhaustion, but Annie saw a Southern touch in a big wraparound porch with rocking chairs and a railing that had once been white. Whoever built this house had been wealthy by the day's standards, because wraparound porches were not common in the history of the Midwest. Settlers had had neither the energy nor the wherewithal to waste good lumber and labor on a porch made for sitting – in those days, houses were for sleeping and little else. Daylight took you out to the fields, dark took you to a bed, and that was life.

There were overgrown flowerbeds and a scraggly lawn; and behind it all, a fading red barn surrounded by rusting, discarded pieces of unidentifiable equipment.

The front door of the house opened and a man emerged. Somewhere in the back of her mind Grace had imagined that all old farmers would look the same: stooped from a life of hard labor, seamed faces ravaged by the sun, raw-boned wrists hanging from too-short sleeves. But this man put a lie to the image. Tall, erect, with a full head of snow-white hair and wiry arm muscles showing themselves beneath the short sleeves of a denim shirt, defying the seventy-plus years that Harley had estimated. She saw Malcherson – chief of Minneapolis Police and Swedish to the core – in the man's stature and coloring, but there was a subtle difference in his bearing as he drew closer. There was wicked stress in his shoulders, pulling them forward as if he were carrying the weight of an incomprehensible world pushing him down, threatening to drill him into the earth.

'Everybody, this is Walt,' Harley said.

'Morning,' the old man said to Annie and Roadrunner when Harley introduced them, but there was no smile, and now, Grace saw, no joy in that face.

'And this is Grace,' Harley finished, and Walt looked right into her eyes for a long time before giving her a nod that seemed meaningful in some way she didn't understand. Grace thought the most extraordinary part of the exchange was that Walt's gaze never wavered down to her conspicuous stomach, which was almost unavoidable at this stage in pregnancy.

He held his left hand away from his side, palm down, and Charlie walked right into it. 'Nice-looking dog.'

Grace raised a brow to see Charlie's sudden and immediate acceptance of a total stranger.

Walt finally took a step backward, signaling the end of niceties, and gave the Hummer a baleful glance. 'What the hell is that contraption?'

Harley looked like he was about to beat his chest. 'That, my friend, is a Hummer, upscale off-shoot of a military vehicle, and it can handle any terrain you've got.'

Walt grunted. 'So will my old pickup. Paid fifteen hundred dollars for it used ten years ago. What did that thing cost?'

Harley blinked at that one. 'Uh, well, around seventy, eighty grand.'

Walt looked at him, and for the first time, he smiled a little. 'You got robbed, son. Well, pile back on in there, I got something you need to see.'

'Like what?'

'When we get there, you'll see it, and then I won't have to waste my breath telling you.'

Annie folded her arms across her breasts, a sure sign to anyone who knew her that what she was about to say was the way it was going to be. 'I do believe I'll wait for you all here, if you don't mind.'

Walt looked straight at her without a trace of expression on his face. 'But I do.'

'You do what?'

'I do mind.' He walked right up next to her and offered his arm, and there was absolutely nothing Annie could do. It had been a long time and a long road, but there was enough South left in her that made it impossible to refuse a man's arm when it was offered. Especially when it was offered by an irascible old Minnesota farmer. She'd seen a lot of them on television news shows and documentaries, but never expected to see this kind of civility north of the Mason-Dixon Line.

It took them fifteen minutes to negotiate the hillocks and deep holes tractor tires had dug into the farm road during the early spring snowmelt. Every few minutes along the way Walt said something incomprehensible to Harley in the front, while Annie suffered greatly in the back, jostled by Grace on one side and Roadrunner on the other. 'Only got eighty bushels an acre off this forty last year.'

Annie rolled her eyes. Eighty bushels of what? And who cared?

'One-ten off this parcel, and that's after that nincompoop from the co-op double-sprayed the ammonia. Goddamn idiot.'

70

She didn't ask what he was talking about, for fea[r] he would tell her; besides, she was too busy trying to ke[ep] her breasts in her bra and her butt on the seat during this god-awful carnival ride.

She just didn't get it. Cornstalks rose in perfectly measured rows on either side, each plant exactly the same distance from its neighbors, the earth beneath them as flat and smooth as an ironed sheet. Seemed to her that if they could make the field that level they could have done the same with this stupid road that kept throwing her around like a hot kernel in a popper.

Worse than that, this place was ugly. Corn, sky, road – that's all there was, and she wouldn't have given a plug nickel for one inch of the space.

The road improved a bit as it turned away from the cornfields and plunged into a wood, but here there were only trees crowding the Hummer, barely a scrap of sky visible above them, and that only reminded her of the time she'd been hunted like an animal in a place in Wisconsin called Four Corners. 'Honey, I want you to know I do dearly hate this place,' she whispered to Grace, softly enough so the sound wouldn't reach the hearing of the old man in the front seat.

'Nothin' wrong with my ears,' Walt said without turning around. 'So why do you hate this place? You haven't even met it yet.'

Embarrassment and Annie had always been strangers, so it didn't really bother her that he'd overheard. Besides, she didn't know the man, and always kept ninety percent of any truth under wraps when she was talking to people she'd never see again. 'It's in the country, that's why.'

'Well, now. That sort of sets me back on my heels. Figured you for a lady who fits just right on one of those porches with the big white columns, just sitting there sipping on a tall drink with ice in it, looking out over a big lawn.'

He'd recognized her as a lady, which she liked, but he'd also pulled the most distant piece of Annie's past, or at least what Annie's past should have been, right out of his head as if he knew all about her, and she didn't like that one bit. 'Well, sir, it would seem you figured wrong.'

'Maybe.' Walt shrugged just as the Hummer poked its front end through a hole in the woods and pulled into the open. 'But I'd face that porch right here, was I to build one for that kind of lady. Isn't much of a lawn the way it is, but I can see the way it ought to be.'

And so could Harley. He stopped the car, draped his big wrists over the wheel and sighed while the rest of them followed his gaze out the windshield.

The trees thinned as the land rolled down to a lake, but there were a few giants shading the trip down. The grass was long and seed-heavy at the top, waving in the breeze with a synchronicity that looked choreographed. Beyond that, the earth hollowed out and cupped the lake that showed them all the sky.

Surrounded by the strangeness of farmland, the sight still evoked that same Zen quality of peace Roadrunner felt and appreciated at Magozzi's new lake house. 'Pretty,' Roadrunner murmured. He wasn't much fonder of the countryside than Annie, unless there was a paved bicycle path cutting through it, but there were some slices of this world that just took your breath away whether you wanted to be in them or not.

'So that's the farm,' Walt said. 'Two hundred acres, more or less, including the lake and all the land around it. Plus the three cabins on the other side of the lake, right by the apple orchard, or where the orchard was before the drought of '97. Used to be a migrant camp, but the cabins are all plumbed and wired, so no reason you couldn't rent them out to fishermen if you had a mind to. There's a muskie in that water that goes thirty, forty pounds.'

'Migrant camp?' Harley asked.

'Seasonal workers, they call them nowadays. They'd come up from south of the border to help us out during the harvests. Hard workers, they were. So there it is. Had three banks appraise the property last week, got the papers at the house. Bottom is over a million, top is over two. Is that enough to pay for your time? Enough to find out if my daughter is dead?'

Twelve

Sheriff Jacob Emmet, six years into his service for one of the largest, emptiest counties in Minnesota and four years from his fortieth birthday, was beginning to think that every good reason he'd run for this office was fading fast.

The first two years had been dandy. He'd found any number of lost kids who'd wandered off into the countryside and lost their way, reuniting a lot of happy families; he'd shut down the first flush of urban transfers who thought rural areas were God's gift to meth labs; he'd cleaned up after a lot of traffic accidents and put away his share of drunk drivers. That's what a rural sheriff was supposed to do – get rid of the chaff and protect his meager populace, mediate silly arguments between neighbors, smooth feathers, and help make his slab of Minnesota farmland a place where kids felt safe and people always lent a hand to neighbors. He liked the state, he liked the jittery, fickle weather, but mostly he liked the people linked to the land through generations.

And then everything started to change. Small family farms sold out to agricultural conglomerates when times got rough, and now strangers with no tether to the community worked the fields for anonymous corporate overseers. Cottonwood County's farms had always employed seasonal laborers – mostly Mexicans – to help during the abundant harvests, but before the sell-off to big ag, the farmers and the hired help lived and worked side by side, and the same workers came back year after year to the same farm. Their families knew one another, their children played together, and there had never been a lick of trouble. But things were different now.

The change had been slow at first – it had started out with a few drunk and disorderlies, then property crimes like theft and vandalism. Then there had been a stabbing, and the first two murders in the county's hundred-year history, and for the first time, people started locking their doors at night.

And now, with the cartels spreading north like poisonous vines, things were dicier than they had ever been. And dangerous, because some of these so-called seasonal workers had no interest in honest labor. They were the cartel's shadow operatives who hid among the innocents, traveling unchecked, unnoticed, and unabated on Interstate 35 from the Rio Grande all the way up to the Canadian border, carrying heroin and cocaine and heartache in their trunks. And it was damn near impossible to tell the sheep from the wolves.

It tormented Jacob. As a child, he'd fished and swum in Walt's lake with the children of the workers. They'd giggled, shared lunches, played games, and the language barrier didn't matter one whit. He taught them some English and they taught him some Spanish. Not once had it occurred to him that his foreign friends were anything but kids, just like him. They were just like him.

Now he saw grown-up versions of those faces and automatically wondered if they were in the stranglehold of the cartels; if they had drugs in their trunks and murder on their minds and decapitated bodies in their pasts. And when he thought such things, a black rage consumed him, because the blood they'd found on the road near Marla's abandoned car traced back to a felon with multiple drug convictions in the U.S., four deportations, and a well-documented association with the vicious Sinaloa cartel.

When the blood work from the scene had finally come back, Jacob had done plenty of mental acrobatics, trying to convince himself that the blood and Marla's disappearance were entirely separate; a coincidence. But as a cop, he knew the most obvious solution was probably the right one. Marla, with her gentle, kind heart, would stop to help anyone in trouble, anyone she even suspected was in trouble, without thinking twice.

Jacob jumped up out of his chair and started pacing the floor until he felt sweat trickling down the hollow of his spine. He'd never shot a man before, had certainly never killed one, but if Monkeewrench and their technology could help him find the monster who took Marla, that would change.

Thirteen

'For God's sake, Harley, turn up the air. I seriously think I might actually perspire,' Annie complained from the backseat of the Hummer.

Harley grunted, deeply insulted. 'What do you think you're riding in, a frigging Prius? You've got individual temp controls right in front of you. Seat included, if you want to chill that magnificent backside, so crank your own air down and quit busting my balls.'

'How much farther?' she asked as she fiddled with the temperature controls. She should have known better than to ask that. It gave Harley an excuse to talk to the sexpot who lived in his custom GPS, which told them several minutes later that 'your destination is point-zero-five miles, you big handsome lug.'

'Harley, you are the dumbest man alive, and the most pathetic. Why didn't you just say we were almost there?'

'Hey, I programmed that thing myself. Pretty cool, eh?'

'Thus proving my point. You're one step away from a blow-up doll.' Annie glanced out the window as they turned into a short gravel drive that led up to a small, square concrete block building. 'This cannot be the sheriff's office.'

'Can, and is. Well, actually he called it a satellite office. His real one is thirty miles west in the county seat.'

Annie closed her eyes. 'I am in the third world.'

Harley parked next to the single patrol car and shut off the Hummer. 'Be nice. This guy wanted to meet up here to save us the drive. Besides, you're going to like him.'

'I am not. The man works in a concrete bunker in the middle of nowhere.'

Grace was first out of the car, eyes scanning the lush fields of corn and blooming alfalfa that surrounded them. It was absolutely silent except for the occasional trilling of blackbirds and the faint rumble of some kind of machinery in the distance. It felt lonely, and to a lifelong city dweller, it also felt a little sinister, like all that empty space was just waiting to swallow you up.

Roadrunner walked up to stand beside her, casting a long shadow on the gravel. 'It's pretty out here. What are all those purple flowers?'

'Alfalfa,' Annie said, joining them just as she caught a glimpse of movement through a narrow, horizontal window carved out of the concrete block. 'What's he looking at?'

'Us.' Harley moved up after locking down the Hummer as if he were parked in the Bronx. 'We're probably the prettiest people he's ever seen.'

'Then why does he look so suspicious?'

'He's a cop. It's his job to be suspicious.'

Jacob wasn't totally surprised by the group that piled out of the Hummer outside. When Harley Davidson was the first player you met, you kind of assumed his three business partners might look a bit out of the ordinary, too. Besides, Harley had given him a vague heads-up about all of them riding the road less traveled, whatever the hell that meant. So he barely raised an eyebrow at the skinny guy in a shiny one-piece suit that made him look like a trapeze artist, but the women made him uneasy.

He'd never been all that good with the fairer sex, but these two sure as hell didn't look like the kind he was used to, and made him even more uncomfortable than usual. The window he'd been peering through like some spooky Peeping Tom was pretty much caked with rain-streaked dust, so Fat Annie, as Harley had called her, was basically just a shape, and a large one at that. Jacob had actually flinched at that 'Fat Annie' label, and sure as hell hoped Harley didn't introduce her to the locals by that name. 'Fat' was a word you never used to describe anyone anymore, and especially not a woman.

The other woman was pregnant – five or six months along, he figured – but otherwise as long and lean as Annie was short and wide. She was dressed all in black as if the color of her hair had leaked down to her clothes; she looked like a semicolon on a green page with the hayfield behind her. But there was an air about her that reminded him of meeting Clarence Krueger and his near-feral rottweiler on the road. You never knew if that damn dog was just going to sit there and pant, or try to rip your arm off. Come to think of it, Clarence made him feel pretty much the same way.

The minute the front door opened and the sheriff stepped outside, Annie crossed him off the potential list. He wore one of those brownish uniforms all Minnesota sheriffs wore, which was a fashion cruelty since the color didn't complement any complexion on the gene tree. And they always pressed creases in those silly pants that looked polyester even if they weren't. Sure, he was a few inches over six feet and looked like he threw cows over fences every hour of the day, but what good was that when you ran around with a grass stem stuck between your teeth? A hayseed was a hayseed, and the moniker was well placed. The only thing he had going for him was that he'd come out of that crummy building to greet them instead of sitting inside with his feet on his desk reading the latest issue of *Tractor and Field*.

But then he'd come a little closer, hand held out to Harley like they were best friends, and she saw the steady sky eyes and the blond hair stuck at weird angles out of his silly hat. The hat sucked. The eyes were better. They lay in the shade cast by the brim, and you only caught a glimpse of the color when he pushed his hat back on his forehead and looked down at you like you were something he'd never seen before. Trouble was, she couldn't tell if that was a compliment or an insult.

'Nice of you all to give Walt a listen. We're grateful for your time, and we could surely use the help. Come on, let's get you out of the sun and the heat.'

The building's interior was as spartan as the exterior, but surprisingly cool considering it didn't have air-conditioning, just a slowly rotating ceiling fan that probably did more to distribute dust particles than provide any real relief. There was a desk, some empty shelves, and a stack of metal folding chairs propped against the unpainted cinderblock wall. The only decor, if you could call it that, was a bulletin board that had old, yellowed WANTED posters tacked to it. Annie thought it had all the personality of a prison cell. In fact, the single cell near the back of the room looked more inviting.

The sheriff gave her a wry smile while he gathered four folding chairs and arranged them around the desk. Apparently he'd seen her expression of disdain as she'd looked around the room. 'This place hasn't been in use for years, but it was the most convenient spot to meet up with you and save you a drive. Please, everybody take a seat.'

When they were all settled around the desk, Harley lifted a slender folder labeled 'Marla Gustafson' and passed it to Grace. 'Don't tell me this is all you have on Marla's disappearance.'

Jacob Emmet switched instantly from the affable rural sheriff to a very serious lawman. 'Hell, no, there's a mountain of official paperwork and physical evidence locked up at headquarters. This file is just my personal thumbnail sketch of the investigation so far. I record a daily summary, pulling out things that might mean something later for quick reference. Thought it might help you get ahead on the case, see if it's something you can work with. If you're willing to take it on, then I'll establish a chain of custody for digitized versions of all the reports. Wish I could give it all to you right now, but legally, I have to clear it and be in possession and present during any transfer of evidence.'

Grace thumbed through the pages of Marla's file, scanning and recording as much as she could to memory. 'Walt told us some things about the case, but probably not everything. We'd like to hear it from you.' She saw a pained expression on Jacob Emmet's face that he was trying hard to hide. There was something more here, beyond a sheriff worrying about a missing constituent.

'Unfortunately, there isn't much to show after two

months. We found her car abandoned on the two-lane over by Cutter Creek, less than a mile from Walt's. She was on her way there for dinner. Marla made the drive down from the Cities at least twice a week to check in on her dad and bring him a meal. We tore that scene and the car apart, bolt by bolt, and recovered not a scrap of evidence that anything had happened to Marla. The car was fully functional when we found it, so she stopped for some other reason. If you knew Marla, you'd know she'd stop for anything or anybody in trouble. That's where the blood in the road comes in. We found a puddle of it right by her car.'

Grace lifted her eyes. 'Not her blood?'

'No, ma'am. The blood was in the CODIS registry, which stands for Combined DNA Index System –'

'We know about CODIS.'

The sheriff nodded. 'The blood belonged to a violent multiple felon named Diego Sanchez – a Mexican national, illegal, with known ties to the Sinaloa cartel and four deportations on record in the States. We haven't been able to track him down, but God knows I've tried. I hit up every domestic federal agency, the Federales in Mexico, and Interpol. He hasn't been on anybody's radar for three years.'

Harley smoothed his beard, more in the interest of contemplation than fastidiousness. 'This Diego Sanchez, he has cartel affiliation? Is there a big drug problem in Cottonwood County?'

'Drugs are a problem everywhere, and we've seen our fair share lately. Mostly small-time stuff, but that's how the cartels do business. They get the product in and disperse it in controlled quantities to low-level operatives or local dealers. That way, a drug bust in a place like this won't ever get the time of day from the DEA.'

Grace felt a pall of sadness settle over her, and she saw the same emotion in the faces of her partners as they listened quietly. They all knew this was the beginning of a story that probably had a very bad ending, but she was anxious to get back to the reason they were here. 'Did you find any trace of Marla other than at the immediate scene?'

'The hounds caught Marla's scent trail through the woods, but it ended at Cutter Creek. We found her ring at the base of a tree there. I think she left it there for us to find. Like she was leaving a message, that she'd gotten that far.' He covered his mouth and cleared his throat.

'She was chased into the woods,' Grace said quietly.

'I believe so. And she didn't get out of those woods on her own, and God forgive me for saying this, but probably not alive. Walt doesn't think so either, just so you know. But there's one thing I still haven't been able to wrap my mind around – there was no blood trail in the woods to the creek, just Marla's scent. The logical assumption is that Diego Sanchez is our perp, with his criminal record and all, but we didn't find his blood in the woods. In fact, we didn't find any blood in the woods.'

'You said there was a puddle of his blood on the road. How much?'

'Enough that Diego Sanchez should have left some if he'd chased her.'

'So you think there might be a third party involved?'

The sheriff gazed up at the ceiling fan as it spun lazily, stirring the thick air. 'Can't rule it out. Also can't rule out the possibility that his blood on the road and Marla's disappearance are totally unrelated. But the four of you probably don't believe in coincidences any more than I do, at least when there's a crime involved.'

Grace nodded her agreement and added the new information to her growing, mental list of notes. 'Were her personal items still in the car?'

'Yes, ma'am. Purse, cell phone, the spaghetti and meatballs she and Walt were supposed to eat together that night – but nothing came out of any of it. The last text on her phone was from her boss, reminding her that it was her turn to bring donuts for Friday morning's meeting. She worked at a veterinary clinic in Minneapolis.'

'Did she have a computer?'

'Yes. I've got it in my car. I figured you'd want to take a look for yourselves, although there's not much to see. I'm at a dead end, which is why I called you. I will move heaven and earth to find Marla one way or the other and bring her home. As it stands, it's like she never existed at all, and there isn't a person in this county who wouldn't give anything they had to spare Walt the kind of hell he's going through.'

Grace looked around at each of her partners – Harley and Roadrunner were looking at her expectantly; it was obvious from the beginning that they both wanted to help Walt and this sheriff. Annie's tell was slightly more subtle; she simply lifted a round shoulder, which Grace interpreted as 'Why not? Let's do what we can.'

'Sheriff, tell us why you think we have a chance of finding out what happened to Walt's daughter when you couldn't.'

'I'm hoping that software of yours might turn up something I missed.'

'I hope so, too. We have a mobile computing lab we could bring down for a day or two. That will make things easier for the transfer of evidence, and if we need access to additional physical evidence, we'll be right here.'

'That's about the best thing I've heard in a while.'

'Good. Can we take a look at Marla's computer while we're all here?'

Sheriff Emmet was out of his chair before Grace had finished her sentence. 'I'll be right back.'

Fourteen

Cassie Miller had grown up in very small town America, where all the school grades were in one building and every single year your new teacher asked all the kids what they wanted to be when they grew up. The cool thing was that they kept a running record of your answers every year, and when you graduated, they tucked a copy in your diploma. Cassie had wanted to be a grocery store clerk from kindergarten to fourth grade, and now here she was at age thirty, living her childhood dream at the Minneapolis branch of Global Foods.

When she arrived for her afternoon shift, she placed her purse and sweater in her locker in the employee lounge, fluffed the short Marilyn Monroe haircut that was starting to show a little dark at the roots, reapplied her pink lip gloss, and checked in five minutes early with her employee ID card. The computer would then tell Big Brother management that she was a diligent worker, never late, but never too early, which might imply that she was taking advantage of the shift change for her own benefit. She was the perfect employee, beyond scrutiny.

Well, almost perfect, because the last thing she did before taking her place at register four was to undo the top button of her hideous tangerine uniform to show a nice piece of cleavage. She couldn't do it every day, only once a week or so, so the store's owner, Mr Dalek, didn't think it was intentional. It drove him absolutely batshit, and his reaction never varied. At first his eyes would squint into lascivious crescents and whatever depraved scenarios lay behind them, she couldn't begin to imagine and didn't want to. But then the spastic little troll would snap out of his perv fugue state, remember his position, and race toward her, tapping his neck, hissing, 'Button up, Miller!' Cassie would always pretend to be embarrassed, but truly, those were the moments she lived for.

This is what happened when you weren't allowed to kill people. You had to think up new and creative ways to torture them.

When she got to the floor, things were quiet just as they usually were at this time of day. The noon slam of grab-and-go customers had scurried back to their work cubicles to eat overpriced, organic salad and sustainable aquaculture sushi from the deli section. The floors were being polished and the stockers were busy refilling emptied shelves and bins in preparation for the evening rush. The only customers were a yoga mom who was browsing the gluten-free section and an older, professorial type examining the vast selection of free-trade coffee.

And then there was Sarah, the mousy little fully buttoned girl who ran register three on this shift. What she lacked in self-esteem she made up for in sanctimony. She didn't even bother to greet Cassie when she took her place at her station, just gave her a stern look of disapproval and said, 'You're going to get fired if you keep doing that.'

Cassie ignored her. The Sarahs of the world were yippy little Chihuahuas – a nuisance but not a threat.

'You should really be ashamed of yourself,' she pressed. 'This is a nice store for nice people, and that just looks cheap.'

Cassie broke open a roll of quarters on the edge of the register drawer, pretending it was Sarah's head. She didn't dislike the woman; she was just too stupid to live. Stupid enough to be really dangerous. She decided to try being magnanimous. 'You better start learning to stand up for yourself, Sarah, or you're going to get rolled right under the big machine.'

Sarah pressed her lips together until they disappeared. 'I don't even know what that means.'

'That's what worries me most.'

'You always say stupid stuff like that that doesn't make any sense. But you better button up or I'm going to report you.'

Oh, dammit, now she'd gone too far and she was going to have to do what the stupid cow said. She couldn't afford trouble, not after all the time and effort she'd invested in Global Foods. After an interminably long probationary period, Dalek finally trusted her enough to put her on the roster to close the store tomorrow night and the timing couldn't be more perfect. A 'flour' shipment from Illustrious Bakers – which was the code name for cartel shipments this month – was due to arrive anytime. She just needed a few more pieces of evidence to tie this thing up in a neat little package and get the hell out of this place.

Sarah's prissy whisper scattered her thoughts. 'What's going on in the back?'

Cassie's head snapped up and her eyes narrowed, traveling down the main aisle just in time to see Dalek rushing through the doors that led to the loading docks. She knew exactly what was going on, but she wasn't about to say anything to Sarah. This was her little secret. 'I heard him mumbling about a late shipment,' she lied. 'Truck got hung up on the interstate or something and he was worried they'd try to dump a bunch of spoiled produce on him.'

Sarah looked doubtful, but just shrugged. 'Oh.'

'I have to use the can. Hold down the fort, 'kay?'

Sarah grunted. 'Hurry up.'

Cassie felt her heart thumping hard in her chest as she passed by the bathrooms and cautiously approached Dalek's office. The door was cracked open – a miraculous oversight, because the office was always locked. She pushed the door open a little farther and under the glow of a desk lamp, she saw another miracle – his open laptop. His desktop computer would be here tomorrow night and she could deal with it then, but the laptop never left his possession and she might never get another chance at it.

Cassie looked over her shoulder, then craned her head toward the loading dock doors. She could hear muted conversation, the screech and rattle of a semi's back door being lifted open.

This is it, this is it, in and out in a minute or two.

She felt the sting of adrenaline prickling through her veins and tried to keep her breathing as steady and even as possible as she ducked into the office. She double-checked the room for any security cameras that might have magically appeared overnight, but of course there were none. And what a great irony that was – Dalek didn't dare keep a digital documentation of his activities here, which left it wide open for compromise.

With her eyes fixed on the door, she plugged a very special flash drive into a USB port on Dalek's laptop, punched a few keys, and watched the progress bar flash as the contents of his hard drive uploaded. *Come on, come on*, she screamed in her mind as her sense of time warped and seconds became hours.

And then she heard two things: the loading dock doors opening again, and her heart pounding in her ears. Her hands started to shake almost uncontrollably as she canceled the upload, yanked out the flash drive, and restored Dalek's screen saver. Her hands hadn't shaken like this since her first day on the gun range at Quantico. And son of a bitch, there was no time to scrub her tracks. She'd fucked up big-time, taken too much of a risk, because if Dalek got suspicious and started poking around in his system manager, she was burned. Or worse.

She sprinted out of the office, spun around, and closed the self-locking door behind her just as Dalek appeared in the hallway.

'What are you doing, Miss Miller?'

She turned and gave him a sweet smile, forcing her breathing into an even, normal rhythm. All those Kapalbhati yoga classes were paying off. 'I noticed that your door was open when I came out of the ladies', so I thought I'd close it for you.'

Joe Dalek looked a little befuddled. 'It wasn't closed?'

'No.'

'Oh. Well, thank you, Miss Miller.'

'Anytime, Mr Dalek.'

'Miller?'

'Yes?'

'Button up.'

In the old days, Joe Dalek would have watched Cassie walk the long aisle back to her register for the sheer pleasure of watching her little ass move under her skirt, and eventually, he would have caught her alone in the storage room and shown her things she'd never seen before. But that was before his new side business and the thugs that went along with it. There were too many rules now, too many eyes watching him, making sure he didn't step out of line, get slapped with a sexual harassment suit, and call attention to this squeaky-clean gold mine they shared.

Dalek had never once set foot on the moral high ground, but his innate cowardice had always kept him from going too far to the dark side, and he wouldn't have done it this time if he hadn't been offered the deal at gunpoint, looking down at a bunch of photos of dead people who'd been stupid enough to refuse.

They'd propositioned him at exactly the right time. He'd been about to lose his franchise and everything else he owned, which he probably deserved for investing in a store that catered to rich, pretentious bitches in this borderline neighborhood. Still, it wasn't his fault. He was just another victim of the economy, that was it, and what choice did he have but to find a supplemental income?

He was filthy rich now after only a year, and it had been so easy, so smooth. Not a hint of trouble.

He entered his office and froze in the doorway. Dear God. Not only had he left his door open, he'd left his laptop on the desk. For twelve solid months he'd carried that thing everywhere he went, even the bathroom, and he would have done the same thing today if those stupid assholes unloading the truck hadn't dropped a banana crate full of cocaine in the back lot and watched like idiots as white powder flew everywhere. That alone was enough to get him killed, and now he would have to do damage control and explain the loss of product down to the last gram. There just hadn't been time to grab his breath, let alone his laptop, before racing outside to shut down the loading dock and direct the cleanup.

With an odd sense of trepidation, he approached his desk. Nothing was disturbed; nothing was out of place, and his laptop's screen saver was on, just as it should have been. He watched the big rotating globe that was part of the company logo until GLOBAL FOODS began to orbit around the sphere like a ring around Saturn. When he touched the mouse pad, the locked password screen appeared and he let out a sigh of relief. Not that a dim bulb like Cassie Miller posed any threat, but there were others in the store who did. She'd done him a favor today, and he'd have to think of a very creative way to repay her for her loyalty.

Cassie walked back to her station like she didn't have a care in the world, but her mind and her heart were still racing at breakneck speed as she sorted through the possible scenarios in her immediate future. The best case would be if Dalek had bought her story about closing his office door on the way back from the can. He'd let her close up alone tomorrow as scheduled, she could upload his desktop hard drive, and be on her merry way once and for all. The worst case would be that Dalek, paranoid as hell and with good reason, would take today's discord as a bad omen and tighten things up at the store for a few weeks or even months. He wouldn't let anybody close up shop alone, wouldn't ever leave his office unlocked again, and maybe, just maybe, he'd figure out that somebody had been messing with his computer.

Cassie made a snap decision as she approached the registers, and she didn't have to manufacture a look of distress and panic. When Sarah saw her, her perennial, pinched, world-hating expression went from disdain to empathy, just like that. She suddenly saw a possible ally in Sarah against Dalek if it ever came to that. But it would take careful cultivation and nurturing to turn Sarah to her side, and Cassie didn't know if she had the stomach for it, or if such a distasteful prospect would be necessary at all.

'What's wrong, Cassie?'

Wow. She'd used her name for the first time since she'd started working there six months ago.

'Female troubles,' she easily lied. 'Bad ones. I need to take my break early.'

Sarah, apparently no stranger to bad female troubles, nodded. 'Sure, go ahead.'

'Thanks. I owe you one.'

Cassie jogged out to the parking lot and slipped into the Ford Fiesta the agency had assigned to her for this job. It took her roughly five minutes to log into her work computer and send the partial of Dalek's laptop hard drive to the office, along with a succinct note telling her handler that she would try to get a full copy of his desktop drive tomorrow night. Something was better than nothing. Then she put her computer back in the lockbox on the passenger-side floor, right next to her service weapon.

As she walked back into Global Foods to finish her shift, she never noticed the man watching her from the loading dock bay.

Fifteen

Nothing hopped up a homicide unit like the possibility of a serial killer, primarily because they were so hard to catch. It took a lot of hands on deck to sort through the reams of mostly useless information from all the interviews and reports while they searched for a connection, any connection that might point to a suspect. The trouble was, there was rarely any personal connection between a serial killer's victims and the killer himself – he just liked the way they looked.

Former patrol sergeant Eaton Freedman, a recent addition to Homicide and McLaren's new partner, had established himself at a desk near Gino's and Magozzi's. He was deep into a tall stack of papers, occasionally scribbling notes on a pad.

Chief Malcherson had finally pulled him off precinct control, partly to give the homicide unit a little color, partly because Freedman was carrying a load of muscle that slowed him down on the street, and he refused to stay off the street and let the officers under him do the running. The man was very big, very black, and had a nice combo of people skills and terrifying stature that slid into Homicide as easily as he had aced the detective exam. He could scare a suspect to death by asking his name, and soothe a grieving relative with a genuine empathy he tore out of some squishy soft spot.

Gino shook out a few tropical-fruit-flavored antacids from the bottle he always kept on his desk, then crunched them down with the dregs of neon-green Gatorade. 'You getting anywhere, Eaton?'

'Fuck no . . .'

Gino rapped his knuckles on his desk. 'Goddamnit, Freedman, how long have you been working Homicide?'

'This is my second glorious week.'

'And how many times have we told you that if you use that kind of language in Malcherson's house, he will shit-can your black ass right out of here.'

'You want to give me an English lesson or do you want to know what I found out?'

'You said you didn't find out anything.'

'Yeah, well, now I'm going to tell you how I didn't find out anything. None of the early tips panned out, and I can't find any connections between the victims so far. They revolved around different suns and probably never crossed paths. If this guy has a hunting ground, it's either big, or I'm just not seeing it. I'm starting to wonder if he might not be an opportunist. Creep takes his little murder kit, picks a park, hides out in the brush, and waits for his archetype to jog by. Which is the problem with serial killers. They're usually smarter and better organized than the average dirtbag, and you have to wait until they get sloppy.'

Gino rolled his eyes up to the ceiling. 'Thanks for that inspirational thought. Another great line for Malcherson's press release – we're just going to wait for this guy to get sloppy, and hope he doesn't finish the whole deck before we find him.'

Freedman raised a brow, sending a cascade of wrinkles

up his forehead to the shiny cap of his shaved head. 'Shit. You think that's where our perp is going?'

Gino shrugged. 'It occurred to me. Where's McLaren?'

'He's in Tommy's office, working on the prison records and eating stinky kung pao chicken from The Lucky Panda.'

Gino's face brightened for the first time all day. 'We'd better go check it out.'

Tommy Espinoza, MPD's resident computer geek, had a lot in common with McLaren. They were both single and on the prowl for female companionship, they both consumed more junk food during the course of a day than even Gino did, and their desks continually vied for domination as the world's most trashed desk.

Johnny McLaren smiled and tossed Gino a pair of chopsticks when he walked into the room. 'I figured you'd sniff us out eventually.'

'Freedman outed you.'

'Knew he would. Come on, help yourself, I got extra.'

'Don't mind if I do.' Gino loaded up a plate while Magozzi went to stand behind Tommy and McLaren, who were busy at the computer, files stacked precariously on both their laps because there was no room on the desk. Crime-scene photos were spread on a side table next to a greasy container of something.

'How's it going?'

'So far, it's not,' Tommy said as he shoved noodles into his mouth. 'We're running probability on the prison records Johnny pulled, but so far there are no red flags on a potential suspect. Weird as it seems, we don't have a single violent offender who went in after the first murder and got cut loose in time to do the second. At least in Minnesota.'

Magozzi picked up a fortune cookie and broke open the cellophane wrapper. 'Maybe he's from out of state. Theoretically, he could be from anywhere. Can you expand the search?'

'Sure, but from this end, with limited manpower and computing power, that'll take a lot more time than I think you want to burn. Say we get five hundred red flags nation-wide that fit your year-long time frame between murders – that's five hundred cases that have to be looked at individually so we can try to find a connection to Minneapolis. My opinion, if you want this thing done fast, go straight to Monkee-wrench. They have that monster computer, the Beast, that's already programmed for this kind of stuff, and they can link into any database in the world without leaving tracks. If you want fast answers, they're your golden ticket.'

McLaren finally retired his chopsticks and paper plate to Tommy's overflowing trash can. 'And there's always the possibility that this guy has never even done any time. Maybe he just took a year off to decide that he really likes the murder gig and he'd give it another go.'

Magozzi cracked open his cardboard cookie and pulled out the paper slip that revealed his fortune. *You will meet the man of your dreams very soon.*

He tossed the cookie and the fortune on top of McLaren's discarded chopsticks. 'I'll talk to Grace tonight.'

In the three hours before Malcherson's six-o'clock press conference, Magozzi and Gino finished their reports, followed up on every single tip and lead, and scoured initial lab reports that were mostly inconclusive. The single bright spot in the day was the blood on the thornbush Gino had pointed out to Jimmy Grimm – it was human blood, male, and Jimmy was putting the screws to the DNA lab for a high-priority analysis so he could run it through the CODIS registry of felons. If the guy and his genetic markers were in any system, they'd be able to track him down.

'Showtime,' Gino announced, turning on the old TV that sat on top of a file cabinet by their desks. The thing was a relic, and although everybody in Homicide had talked about replacing it with a new HD flat-screen at one point or another, nobody seemed particularly eager to discard an old friend that reminded them all of a more innocent time. Sure, they complained about it, but over the years, it had almost become a team mascot.

'I could paint my condo in less time than it takes that damn thing to warm up,' McLaren complained as he and Freedman went to stand beside Gino and Magozzi for a better view.

'It's your case, so why aren't you two out there with Malcherson?' Freedman asked Gino and Magozzi.

'It's just going to be a statement, not a real press conference,' Gino said, gnawing on the last fortune cookie that ominously didn't have a fortune in it. 'It's actually a good strategy – Malcherson's the slyest fox in the henhouse and he's used to this kind of crap, handling the press. We're just feet on the streets. More we stay off camera, more we can get done.'

Freedman laughed. 'And the less you can screw up. Good to know for the future.'

'Best lesson of all – keep your mouth shut at all times and let Malcherson be your voice box. Even though you have a really magnificent voice, Freedman. Still can't figure out why you never went to radio.'

'I'll be asking myself that very same question the first time I get my own nightmare case . . . Oh, here we go.'

They all watched the tiny screen as Chief Malcherson exited City Hall and stood in front of a cluster of microphones that amplified the din of reporters shouting questions. No surprise that Amanda White's shrill voice carried above the rest.

Magozzi smiled as the chief just stood there in total, stone-faced silence, his eyes calmly tracking his audience while he waited for them to shut up. And remarkably, they eventually did. It was like he had hypnotized them. Or at the very least, shamed them into silence.

'God, he's good,' McLaren said. 'Cool as a cucumber. Malcherson's the only guy alive who can get Amanda White to clamp her big mouth.'

'It's the suit,' Gino said. 'And that's a new one. Nice choice, too. Serious, authoritative, and the tie really takes it over the top.'

On-screen, Malcherson cleared his throat. 'Thank you, ladies and gentlemen. I will be making a very brief statement, and I won't be taking any questions afterward.

'As you know, a young woman – a wife and mother of two – was found dead this morning in Minnehaha Dog Park. It is far too early in the investigation to comment on this tragedy, and the victim's name will not be released at this time, however, I can tell you that this is a homicide investigation. All of our detectives are working around the clock to bring swift justice to the perpetrator, but until then, I implore every single citizen to remain vigilant, and take their personal safety seriously . . .'

The outburst from the reporters was instantaneous

and seemed endless, at least to Magozzi. 'What kind of cautionary measures should people be taking?' 'Do you have a suspect?' 'Are you saying our parks might not be safe?' Et cetera, et cetera. And then the real kicker, from none other than Amanda White: 'A young woman was similarly murdered in Powderhorn Park last year. Is there a serial killer operating in the Minneapolis parks?'

Gino pressed a palm to his forehead. 'Is this blowing up in our faces?'

'He's gonna be fine,' McLaren said, his eyes fixed on the TV screen. 'Guy's a rock star. Look at him. Body language is calm, assured . . .'

Chief Malcherson looked at Amanda White like he would look at a dead cockroach in his soup bowl. 'We cannot confirm with any degree of certainty that the two murders are connected. What we do know for certain is that there was a murder in that dog park last night, so for the time being, it would be wise to exercise caution and use common sense. If you run, or enjoy other outdoor activities, do it with a friend. Especially if you're a woman. Park patrol presence will be enhanced, but that is no sub- stitute for a vigilant public. If you see something or someone suspicious, report it. We have tip lines in place, both by phone and on our website. Now, we all have our jobs to do, and Minneapolis Homicide will be forthright with any new information. Thank you, and good night.'

The questions continued long after Malcherson had reentered City Hall.

Sixteen

There was something wrong this summer. Everybody in Minnesota knew it, because there were no mosquitoes. Sure, they were in the middle of a drought, but droughts, like deluges, were as regular as clockwork and had been for as long as they'd been keeping records. But there had always been mosquitoes. This was different, and Magozzi shared this observation with Grace, who was sitting in the Adirondack chair next to him, gazing up at the lush green magnolia tree in her backyard.

She looked at him with a bemused expression. Her dark hair was pulled back in a short ponytail against the heat and her cheeks were faintly pink, which made the blue of her eyes seem even more intense, even in the waning daylight. 'Mosquitoes breed in water. No water, no mosquitoes.'

'Minnesota has more water than land, even during a drought. There's something else going on. I think it's a portent.'

'Of what?'

'I don't know, but I was a kid in '87, during the last drought like this, and I'm telling you, the mosquitoes bred like drunken frat boys. Did you get some sun today?'

'A little. Harley dragged us all out to a country farm today.'

'You're kidding. Harley's been trying to get you on bed

rest since you were three months pregnant and then he drags you out to a farm in the heat and sun?'

'I think I've finally been able to convince him that I'm pregnant, not terminally ill.'

'That's progress. He's not talking about that ostrich thing again, is he?'

Grace shook her head. 'There's a farmer in southwestern Minnesota whose daughter disappeared. He and the local sheriff asked for our help.'

'Runaway?'

'Definitely not. She's mid-thirties, a devoted daughter, has a career she loves, and by all accounts so far, she's purer than Mother Teresa.'

'How long has she been missing?'

'Two months.'

Magozzi thought about the grim statistics on missing persons gone for even a few days. Happy endings were few and far between, and all too often, families lived in a hellish limbo for months or years, constantly searching for answers and closure they might never get. 'So you're taking it on.'

'It's worth our time. And it's interesting. There was blood on the road where they found her abandoned car. The good news is, the blood wasn't the daughter's. The kicker is that it rang bells on CODIS. It matched a felon with multiple drug convictions and ties to the Mexican cartels. They haven't been able to track him down, but maybe we can.'

Magozzi's eyebrows peaked and his mouth turned down all at the same time. 'A beloved farmer's daughter disappears into thin air, and a pool of blood next to her abandoned car belongs to a drug dealer? That is interesting. Any chance she was leading a double life?'

'Extremely doubtful. The most scandalous thing on her computer was a recipe for apple crisp with brandied whipped cream. But we won't know until we can input everything into our computers. There's a huge amount of paperwork on the case, a lot of information that needs to be streamlined, collated, and cross-referenced, and that's exactly what we designed our software to do. Harley and Roadrunner are packing up the Chariot tonight. We leave tomorrow.'

Magozzi loved the Chariot. It was Harley's moniker for his over-the-top RV that served as Monkeewrench's mobile workstation. It was outfitted with almost as much computing power as their home office, complete with a satellite uplink so they could literally work from anywhere without sacrificing technology. But it wasn't your average mobile computing lab – the interior was about as opulent as a room in Versailles. 'You're going to work on-site?'

'Faster and easier than a two-hour commute each way. If we need to access any additional evidence or files, it will be right there. I can't imagine we'll be gone for more than a couple days.'

'If you're taking on something new, I suppose it's not a good time to ask for a favor.'

Grace turned to look at him. 'I saw Malcherson's press conference. The woman in the park – that's your case?'

'It's going to be everybody's case if we get another one.'

'What makes you think there's going to be another one?'

'This wasn't his first. A woman was killed in Powderhorn Park last year. Same MO, down to every detail.'

'That's right. A reporter brought that up.'

'Amanda White,' Magozzi grumbled. 'But what she doesn't know is that our most recent murder may have been his fourth.'

Grace looked down – at her growing belly, at the ground, at Charlie snoozing on the Adirondack chair next to her, Magozzi didn't know. What he did know was that she was remembering a not-so-distant time in her past when she'd been pursued by a serial killer.

'You think it's a serial?' she finally asked.

'He leaves calling cards, literally, and that detail never left Homicide. The woman in Powderhorn Park last year had an ace of spades tucked into her shirt.'

'The death card.'

'What?'

'Mobsters used to leave the ace of spades on their victims as a warning, back during Prohibition. Lore has it that in Vietnam, American soldiers left it on the dead bodies of Vietcong to psych out the enemy. Psychological warfare.'

Magozzi took a sip of his beer, which fell flat on his palate. 'Our most recent victim had the four of spades tucked in her shirt. We're wondering if there's a two and a three out there somewhere.'

Grace reached over and touched his hand. She'd been doing that a lot more lately. 'How can we help, Magozzi?'

Seventeen

Katya Smirnova didn't run to keep in shape; she ran to stay sane, as if she could escape the bull's-eye she'd been carrying on her back for the first three decades of her life just by putting on a little more speed.

She'd been only three at the time of the Chernobyl disaster, and had no memories of the horrors that followed. Her family had been living near Minsk then, surely far enough away to be safe, but someone had forgotten to tell them not to drink the milk of the grazing animals that lived in the path of the fallout. She was one of four siblings, and the last one still alive.

As she finished her third loop around the lake, she was feeling the burn in her legs, and pushed herself harder, thinking of her favorite American movie, *Marathon Man*. She watched it twice a year, a month or two before her semiannual doctor exam, because in the movie, Dustin Hoffman's running saved his life in the end. Maybe she'd be that lucky, even though she knew it was foolish to think she could outrun death – especially when the threat was lurking inside her, waiting for just the right time to explode.

Or maybe it would never explode. The uncertainty was the worst part, and in the very darkest recesses of her mind, she often wondered if she wouldn't feel some twisted sense of relief to hear the prognosis she'd feared her entire life. At least then the fear would be gone.

Katya made one last loop around the lake just as the sun was setting, then veered off the paved path and onto the wooded terrain trail that was the shortcut to the parking lot. It was her favorite part of the run because the trail carved through elegant clusters of birch trees. It reminded her of playing in the famous birch forests of Russia, back when her parents and her brother and sisters were still alive.

She sensed the impact a split second before she felt it on her back, knocking the wind out of her and sending her down hard onto the ground. As she gasped to refill her lungs, she felt hands around her neck, felt herself being dragged into the underbrush, and she realized that all the uncertainty and fear of sickness she'd been living with was definitely not the worst thing in life.

An entirely new fear ignited Katya then, and she fought like hell in the little birch forest that represented a small piece of her homeland, praying to God she would make it to her doctor's appointment tomorrow morning to hear any kind of news, good or bad.

Eighteen

Magozzi and Gino were sitting in a booth at the back of Pig's Eye Diner. They served the best breakfast in town, and every table was full, even though it was just shy of six in the morning and the sun was barely birthing onto the horizon.

Gino, a talented and seasoned stress eater, had made a substantial dent in his double huevos rancheros platter with chorizo and a side of ropa vieja, which took up half the table; Magozzi, a stress starver, was content to push around his single scrambled egg while he chugged down his fourth cup of coffee and ignored his side of toast.

'God, this is great,' Gino mumbled, finishing the first of his two chiles rellenos, then chasing it down with a mouthful of beans.

'What's that brown stuff that looks like old rags?'

Gino gave him a surprised look. 'That's what it's called. Well, technically *ropa vieja* means old clothes. It sounds better in Spanish.'

'Why the hell would you ever eat something with a name like that?'

'Because it's fantastic. Help yourself.'

'No thanks.'

'You should be a little more adventurous with ethnic food, Leo.'

'Hey, I ate Indian food once or twice. I'm sticking with Italian.'

Gino returned his attention to his plate. 'Feels almost normal, you and me grabbing some chow before work, as if we're not going to be walking into a clusterfuck in about fifteen minutes.'

'Breakfast was a good call,' Magozzi humored him, even though food was the last thing on his mind.

Gino slugged down some orange juice. 'So Monkee-wrench is riding the Chariot down to the Iowa border for a missing persons case, huh?'

'Yep, but they're working on our prison records as we speak. Helping catch a serial killer trumps everything. I told Grace about the cards, Gino. It's one more piece of data they can put into the Beast.'

'Good. I hope it helps. We've got all the legwork done, all the feelers out there, but nothing came in overnight on the tip line or from the lab, and now we're just dieseling, waiting for something to pop, and dammit, I hate that. Twenty-four hours into this and we're stuck in neutral. Are we missing something?'

Magozzi crumpled his napkin and gave up on his plate. They were both frustrated by the slow forward plod and the waiting, but that was ninety-nine percent of the job. Reeling in a bad guy was the one percent that made it all worthwhile. 'Maybe we should take a step back, think about the perp and who he might be.'

'He's a seriously warped individual, is who he is. Like you said, we can't get into the mind of a crazy.'

'Yeah, I know, but he's also seriously ritualistic. The cutting with the same kind of knife, the cards, the strangulation, the archetype, no sexual assault – I could go on and on. This guy has a plan and he has a goal. It all means something, at least to him, and there has to be a clue somewhere in there we can figure out.'

'That's all fine and dandy if we had somebody to look at, but we don't. This guy works clean and stays in the shadows – no prints on the cards, no prints on the body, no murder weapon, and that little drop of blood on the thornbush I found isn't a solid connection to the murder. It probably doesn't even belong to him. And even if it did, how would we know? We're missing pieces. Big pieces. We might as well blindfold ourselves, open up a phone book, and poke our fingers on a random name.'

Magozzi sighed and poured himself more coffee from the carafe on the table. 'Do they print phone books anymore?'

'I don't know. Maybe.'

As their waitress made a courtesy stop and Gino threw out a credit card, Magozzi felt his phone vibrate against his hip and looked down at the caller ID. 'It's McLaren. Hey, Johnny, what's up?'

Magozzi's frown grew deeper as he listened, then he pulled out his notebook and pen and wrote down a number and a name. 'Thanks, Johnny. We'll catch you later.'

'Who the hell is Lon Cather?' Gino asked, squinting at Magozzi's notebook.

'Saint Paul Homicide. He wants a call back ASAP.'

Gino sagged back in his chair. 'Do not tell me they have a body.'

'They do. Phalen Park. Cather called our homicide unit because he saw some similarities with our murders. He wasn't giving it all up at first, but when Johnny told him he'd caught Megan Lynn last year and that he was working tandem with us on Charlotte Wells, he told McLaren about the card.'

'Shit. Angela and I just took the kids to that park last weekend.'

'Five of spades, Gino. You were right – he's trying to finish the suit.'

Nineteen

Saint Paul homicide detective Lon Cather was trying to stay cool in the shade of some birch trees while he watched shards of sun play tricks with light on the surface of Lake Phalen. Across the lake, on the public beach, kids were screaming, giggling, and thrashing around in the shallow water, looking like tropical fish in their bright suits.

He'd been that carefree kid once, spending most of his young summers on Phalen with his grandfather, swimming, fishing, and eating sandy peanut butter and jelly sandwiches on the beach. On calm, hot days just like this one, Grandpa would take him out in an aluminum boat to fish the deeper waters, and those were the only times he remembered him talking much, as if the water had the magical power to suddenly animate the stoic, mostly silent old man.

He told him tall tales about catching sunfish the size of his head and walleyes that weighed more than some dogs. He told him how Saint Paul had been founded by a French Canadian bootlegger named Pig's Eye Parrant, which explained how screwed up the streets were. And sometimes, he told him stories about life on those screwed-up streets as a cop.

And once – only once – as they rowed back to shore under a rainbow sunset with a pail full of fat panfish – Grandpa had gone way back in time, telling him how his great-grandfather had been Saint Paul's chief of police when Al Capone and his crew had been running rum along the Mississippi and setting up speakeasies in the caves along the river.

What's a speakeasy, Grandpa?

Kind of like Grundy's, where we go for hamburgers every Friday.

Oh. Okay. Who's Al Capone?

He was a bad man who didn't believe in following the law.

What's it like to be a policeman?

His grandfather hadn't really answered, he'd just gotten a faraway look and a little smile that curved up his mouth, making deep wrinkles around his eyes that looked like the furrows in Grandma's garden when she was just starting to plant vegetable seeds. And since his grandfather didn't smile all that much, Lon decided that being a policeman must be the greatest thing in the world.

With that single, defining memory of observing happiness in a mostly unhappy man, he'd entered the police academy after graduating from Hamline University with a criminal justice degree, and had never looked back. He'd had his detective's shield for three years now – still green, but smarter than most by his estimation, with a solid caseload under his belt. And yet for all the things the job had thrown at him over the years, he'd never imagined returning to this peaceful place of childhood summers that had formed his future to observe and record the aftermath of a serial killer.

He heard Detectives Magozzi and Rolseth approaching, escorted by a patrolman, and retreated from the shadows of the birch grove and back to Katya Smirnova's crime scene a few yards away.

*

Lon Cather was vegan pale and had a skin-and-bones physique that made Gino want to tie him down and force-feed him hamburgers. It's not that he had anything personal against vegans, but as a devoted carnivore who believed in the power of ingesting hemoglobin at every available opportunity, he thought they were all certifiably insane masochists.

As Cather led him and Magozzi into a wooded area of Phalen Park, his mouth running the clipped, fast dialogue of a highly caffeinated person, Gino began to rethink his initial assessment of the man. Maybe Lon wasn't a malnourished vegan after all, maybe he just lived on coffee and cigarettes and ate microwave bacon for dinner. He was about the right age and demographic for reckless living in this line of work – Gino estimated he had probably three or four years with a shield under his belt, and he wasn't wearing a wedding band.

'Thanks for coming, Detectives,' he fired off rapid-speed. 'Second I got here, I thought of your case in the dog park, figured we might be able to help each other out. After I talked to Detective McLaren, I knew we were looking at the same guy.'

'We appreciate the call,' Gino said, his eyes scouring the underbrush as they terminated their depressing journey at the body of another pretty brunette.

Katya Smirnova had the same telltale desecrations as Megan Lynn and Charlotte Wells – strangulation marks around her neck, knife slashes to her torso, and, of course, the playing card tucked inside her shirt. But if you looked at the woman instead of just the dead body, you saw the differences.

Katya was older than the others, for one thing. Gino saw his wife, Angela, in the more mature features, which was chilling, and there was something else behind the flat eyes. Not fear, not panic, but a remnant of sadness, as if she had seen pure evil and couldn't bring herself to believe it existed.

'Everything's been processed but the card and her personal effects. I had the ME hold the body in situ so you could take a look.'

Gino sucked in a quick breath. 'Oh, man.'

Cather winced. 'This looks familiar to you, then.'

'Oh yeah. It's a bad déjà vu in every way except one.'

'What's that?'

'He cut off her hand.'

Magozzi crouched down, looked closer, and swallowed hard. The work was butchery, the skin ragged around the stump where a hand should have been. 'Did you find the hand?'

'Not yet. So this guy takes trophies?'

'He hasn't in the past.'

Cather folded his arms across his chest and squinted off into the woods. 'Serials don't usually change things up.'

'No, but the smart ones adapt when things go off script,' Magozzi said. 'My guess would be she was a fighter and tagged him, and he felt like he had to get rid of the evidence.'

Cather swatted at a fly on his hand. Homicide cops were all squeamish about flies at crime scenes because you kind of knew where they'd been before they landed on you. 'If he cut off her hand to get rid of his DNA, he's gotta be in the system.'

'We're working that angle.'

'Still – no offense intended – that's pretty smart for a killer in my experience.'

'This isn't an ordinary killer. He's polished. And he's smart. Find that hand, and maybe you'll have something solid to work with. It's only a possibility, but it's all we've got right now.'

'We're working on that. I've got men hitting every trash bin in the park, divers in the lake already, and dogs on the way, but I don't hold out a lot of hope for any of that. He'd be crazy to leave the hand close to the scene.'

'Still a good call,' Gino said.

Cather gave him a wry look. 'All of us Saint Paul cops watch old *CSI* reruns so we know what to do. So what about your scene? Anything that could help us out?'

Magozzi stood up with a sigh. 'We have human male blood waiting on DNA tests so we can send it through CODIS, but it was just a few drops on a thornbush by the immediate scene. And it could belong to anybody. It's a busy park. We're not counting on anything being easy with this guy. I've never seen crime scenes this sanitized.'

Cather looked seriously irritated, and folded his arms across his chest. 'I like your cynicism, Detective Magozzi. What I don't like is the fact that we've got two murders in two nights. This guy is on fire. We've gotta stop him. And we've gotta work together. You have a problem with that?'

'No problem whatsoever. We'll get you copies of our reports and the surveillance footage from around the dog park and Powderhorn Park, for what's it's worth – nothing popped on them.'

Cather's posture relaxed a little. 'And I'll do the same.

So, you two have been on the job a long time. Any instincts about this one?'

Gino made a circuit around the body. 'Nothing you probably haven't come up with yourself. The ritual is the key here. He's telling us a story, and he's staying true to every detail. Except taking the hand, in this case.'

'The playing card angle bothers the hell out of me,' Cather agreed. 'It's bizarre. And why spades? Why not hearts or diamonds or clubs?'

'It all means something. If we can figure that out, then we've got him.' Gino slipped on a glove and gestured to the five of spades peeking out of Katya Smirnova's tank top. 'You mind?'

'Be my guest. I've been waiting to bag it.'

Gino carefully removed the card from the body and flipped it over. 'Same pattern as the other cards.'

Magozzi bent in for a closer look. 'Standard-issue Bicycle brand. You can buy them anywhere.'

Cather glanced at the card Gino was holding. His face went very still as if his mind was traveling somewhere else his eyes couldn't follow, and then he took the card in a gloved hand and looked up at Magozzi. 'Maybe he's not as smart as you think he is.'

'What do you mean?'

'I mean, I know where this card came from. It's a Bicycle, yeah, but not standard issue. See the top? Some of the white border is sliced off.'

Magozzi and Gino both took a closer look. 'Yeah, you're right about that. So what does that mean?'

'It means this card came from a casino.'

'How do you know?'

'You don't play?'

'Crazy Eights, and that's as far as I go.'

'Casinos only use decks for one deal at the table. Pretty expensive overhead if you have to replace every deck once somebody's touched it. So they sell the used ones for dirt cheap, but they don't want them coming back to the table to fill in a five-card flush or something, so they mark them before they let them go out the door. Some of them cut the corners off, some of them take a slice off the top or a side – either way, the dealer can see it or feel it in a heartbeat.'

Magozzi thought about all the random scraps of information and experiences people collected during a lifetime, and how sometimes they came into play in the most unexpected ways. 'So that card came from a casino.'

'Not just any casino. Eagle Lake is the only one I know that slices the top off.'

Magozzi raised his brows. 'You're a devoted gambling man.'

Cather shrugged. 'Kind of a semiprofessional hobby. Half the time, it pays better than the job.'

'I've never heard of Eagle Lake,' Gino said.

'It's new and it's small, in southwestern Minnesota near the Iowa border. I'll check it out.' Cather's phone rang and he lifted a finger and answered the call while Gino and Magozzi took the opportunity to make some notes and snap photographs of the scene.

A few minutes later, Cather hung up. 'Surveillance footage from the cameras around the park is ready to look at. You got some time to compare notes?'

'We've got time for that.'

An hour later, the three detectives were gathered around a computer screen at Saint Paul Police Headquarters, staring at a freeze-frame of surveillance footage from a traffic cam on the edge of Phalen Park. It was dark and grainy, but there was an unmistakable image of a man entering the park through a wooded area. The time stamp on the footage was four-forty in the morning.

'This could be our guy,' Cather said, gnawing on a toothpick like it was his last meal before his execution.

Gino craned his neck to get a closer look at the screen. 'Could be, but no way we can get an ID from this, and there's nothing from our footage for corroboration. But maybe you can drum up some new witnesses with the time frame and run with it. I sure as hell hope so, anyhow.'

Cather tossed his pulped toothpick into a trash can. 'Maybe I can do even better than that. Thanks for your time and your eyes. I'll keep you posted.'

Twenty

Detective Lon Cather had spent plenty of time in casinos, but those times, he'd been half in the bag and hitting the tables hard. Today, he was nursing a Diet Coke and sitting in the control room at Eagle Lake Casino with Sammy 'Junior' Liman, head of security. Ironically sweet nickname for the guy, because there was nothing junior about Junior – he was built like a tractor and had the demeanor of a contract killer. He also had an impressive chunk of gray matter lurking inside his thick, bullet-shaped skull.

Lon was resting his eyes on an enormous wall filled with security monitors that covered the entire floor of the casino from every conceivable angle while Junior clickety-clacked on his computer keyboard in focused silence.

Junior finally lifted his head and leaned back in his chair, his muscular bulk pushing it to its limits. 'So this is the guy you want me to run through our database?' he asked, pointing to the grainy surveillance shot from Phalen Park.

'Yeah, that's him.'

'Lon, the light is shit, the resolution is shit, the angle of his face is shit, and he's too far away. What the hell am I supposed to do with this?'

'Whatever you can.'

'You don't have any other shots of this guy?'

Lon sighed and sucked some lukewarm Diet Coke out of

a straw, thinking of the time his team had spent parsing three different cases' worth of park and park-adjacent traffic cam footage, hoping to find some images that corroborated this suspicious one. They'd come up zeros on the footage at Megan Lynn's scene last year in Powderhorn Park, same with Charlotte Wells's scene at the dog park; there was only this one shot from Katya Smirnova's scene.

'Sorry, Junior, this is all I've got. But there's a possible . . . no, a probable connection to this casino, and he's shorter than average, goes five-six at best.'

'You know that for sure?'

'I checked out this spot at the park after I saw the footage. Did the measurements, did the calculations. This trail marker here is approximately seven feet away from his entry point, the marker is four feet five inches . . .'

Junior held up his hands with a smile. 'I got it, Mr Math, and I believe you. So I've got some kind of a baseline. Still, this is going to be a huge pain in the ass, Lon. I'm going to have to run this image through enhancement before I even put it into facial recognition to compare with our casino footage, same with the biometrics. And there's no guarantee that anything that pops – if anything pops – will be even remotely accurate. The computer is learning with every face it records, but the whole concept of taking a blur and making a person is still in prepuberty.'

'I got it, Junior. I know it's a long shot, but it's worth the time, trust me.'

'I do. So you think this guy is your killer?'

'My gut tells me so.'

Junior sighed and looked back at his computer screen. 'I'll do what I can.'

'Thanks, friend.'

'No problem. Come down for some leisure time once this is all wrapped up and we'll call it even.' He frowned. 'You look like crap. You want a room, grab an hour before you head back up to the Cities?'

Lon pushed himself out of his chair before his butt grew roots. 'Wish I could, but the clock is ticking.'

'I don't envy you that.'

Lon shook his hand, gave him a solid clap on the shoulder. 'You ever miss the job?'

Junior gave him a crooked smile. 'I miss it like crazy, six days a week.'

'What happens on the seventh day?'

'I get my paycheck and see that extra zero on the end. Makes up for a lot.'

Twenty-one

Grace and Annie were in the third-floor Monkeewrench office, checking the Beast for any progress on Magozzi's and Gino's serial killer case before they left for Walt's.

'Look at this stack,' Annie complained, holding up a thick fistful of printouts. 'The list just keeps getting longer and longer. Who knew there were this many cons who went into prison right after Megan Lynn's murder last year and got out before the murder of Charlotte Wells two days ago?'

Grace pushed another inch away from her desk, thinking that pretty soon she wouldn't be able to reach the keyboard. 'Any homicide hits?'

'Not like our boy. Mostly people shooting home invaders, deaths by auto, that sort of thing.'

They heard the elevator rising, then the heavy tread of Harley's boots on the maple floor. 'All systems go, ladies. Remote access to the home office is online, satellite uplink is fully functional, and we are ready to launch. Button-willow, here we come.'

'Yippee,' Annie mumbled, rising from her chair and smoothing the front of her dress.

'You're wearing four-inch heels to a farm?'

'These are not four-inch heels, they're three-inch heels, and I have no intention of stepping foot outside the Chariot the entire time we're down there.'

'Think of it as an anthropological trip. You can learn all about where your food comes from.'

'My food comes from a grocery store, thank you very much. Speaking of food, did you stock the Chariot's pantry? Because Lord only knows if they even have grocery stores down there.'

'Nah, I thought we could butcher a hog if we get hungry. God, Annie, of course the Chariot is stocked. I am amazed by your constant underestimation of me.'

'Hmm. I suppose, in this particular instance, I could manage to be impressed by your planning ability, depending on what you stocked in the Chariot. We'll see.'

Grace started gathering her tote and laptop. 'Did you pack the salads I brought over this morning, Harley?'

Harley looked around the room in a decidedly evasive way. 'Salads?'

'The pasta salad. The potato salad, the green salad, the vegetable salad . . .'

'Oh. Yeah. Those. Well, I wasn't quite sure they were supposed to go in the Chariot . . .'

Annie dropped her head and let out a suffering sigh. 'You ate them.'

'Well, I may have sampled some of them . . .'

Grace was about to scold him, but then her phone chimed. She picked up immediately when she saw the caller ID. 'Hi, Magozzi. We're just about to leave . . .'

Annie and Harley watched her expression still, then darken as she listened. 'Send whatever you have, whenever you have it. We can access anything from the road and send it to the Beast remotely.'

Grace hung up and said, 'They have another one. Phalen Park in Saint Paul. The five of spades.'

Annie covered her mouth. 'Oh no.'

'Jesus,' Harley muttered. 'That's two women in two days. This guy is going nuts.'

'He's decompensating.'

'Right. That's what the profilers call it. I call it a fancy word for going nuts. So what can we do for Magozzi and Gino?'

'They're sending us some surveillance footage we can plug into facial recognition, and anything else they get along the way. They're fresh off the crime scene, so new information is coming in all the time. Let's get started from here before we head down to Walt's.'

Harley grabbed his phone. 'I'll give him a call, let him know we're going to be a little late. Annie, why don't you go get Roadrunner and Charlie?'

'Where are they?'

'Sitting in the Chariot, waiting to push off. Charlie's in the captain's chair. He thinks he's driving.'

Twenty-two

Minnesota was at the beginning of one of those summers farmers sat up nights worrying about. Five days of sun for every good rain was the formula for giving the crops a good start without making quagmires out of cow paddocks and dirt roads, but few of the old-timers had ever seen such a thing happen, and it certainly wasn't going to happen this year.

June hadn't blown the goodbye kiss yet, and already the corn plants were showing signs of drought stress that only the farmers noticed. For the most part, it was a tough crop. Corn loved heat and sun, and it took a long time for lack of water to visibly wither the leaves and dry out the stalks. Monday's hard rain had been cosmetic, washing the dust off the plants, but also damaging, pummeling dry soil balls away from the roots. On this morning, those who had spent a lifetime connected to the land saw the cornstalks starting to lean, just a bit; saw, too, the tiny petals on alfalfa blossoms curling in on themselves, and they worried. Those not connected to the land saw only the lushness of the landscape, never imagining how quickly things could change.

There was a gentle swell to the land here. Not so much that you'd call it rolling – hell, when the land rolled in Minnesota, they called it a mountain range – this was more like the lazy waves on the Pacific when it was bedding down for the night.

Walt had seen that ocean once when Mary had got it into her head to buy that broken-down old camper and see the U.S. of A. before they got tied down with kids and the farm. They'd made it all the way to California, looked around a bit, then hightailed it right back to the Midwest like a runaway horse heading for the barn. Maybe that was the mistake. Maybe the badness had been here all along, and they ran right back into it.

Walt was standing at the edge of his cornfield, where the runoff ditch butted right up to the June-young leafy stalks, and for a long time he watched, waiting. Eventually, the lion appeared, as he always did, and Walt felt the quick thump of his heart. The creature was enormous, his massive paws flattening the strip of quack grass the herbicide had missed. He moved to his usual place and settled into the dirt to bask in the sun. It was so damn wrong, this huge African lion with that big shaggy mane lying in the middle of a Minnesota cornfield, but by now, Walt was getting used to it.

'Hello, lion,' he said, and the lion chuffed his customary greeting.

'I had company yesterday. They're going to find out what happened to Marla.'

The lion chuffed again.

The beast appeared every spring, as certain as the first croaking of the peepers near the lake and the sparrows chirping in the cottonwoods. In a strange way, the lion was spring to Walt, but he was also the death of his son, the passing of his wife a year later, and now the disappearance of Marla.

''Course they may not be able to. No one else has. But I got a feeling. What do you think about that?'

Funny thing about how that lion turned his head to look at you and blinked real slow, like he knew just what you were saying. He was a polite beast, when it came to that. You asked him a question, he gave you his attention and then chuffed his answer. Except this time. This time he didn't chuff at all. He lifted his big head, closed his eyes, and roared.

A few minutes later, the big cat's head and ears perked up to full alert, his body tensed, and hc hightailed it back to the woods. He'd heard the car coming down the road, too. The animal was smart enough to stay far away from humans – the people at the game preserve over in West Grant had been trying to recapture this fella for over five years with no luck. But for some reason, he tolerated Walt's presence. Walt didn't know what that meant, but as long as he didn't eat him or any of his cows, the lion was more than welcome to roam free on his land.

Walt was a little surprised when he got back to the house and saw Jacob, not the Monkeewrench crew, settled on the porch glider, waiting for him. 'Good day to you, Sheriff.'

'Don't know why you keep calling me sheriff. For Christ's sake, Walt, what happened to Jacob?'

'Jacob grew up is what happened. Got a badge and a title and you got every right to wear both.'

'I used to ride on your shoulders all over this damn farm while you fed me cookies.'

'Mary fed you cookies. I just hauled you around until you got too heavy. I heard a car and figured you were the Monkeewrench folks.'

'That's why I'm here. They wanted you to know they'd be here a little later than planned, probably around four or five. They had some last-minute details to handle on another case they're working before they left the city. They tried calling to let you know, but you never answer the phone and you don't have voice mail. Or email.'

'I hate all that damn nonsense. It's just useless noise.'

'You're going to have to move into this century pretty soon.'

'Don't know why. I'm not going to be here that long.'

'Bullshit. You're going to outlive all of us.'

'I surely hope not. I just want to live long enough to see Marla come home one way or the other, and you to get a date. Damn, boy, you're climbing the thirties tree pretty near to the top and you never even had a sweetheart. I had it in mind to carry your kids on my shoulders one of these days.'

Jacob looked away. 'I always had my eye on Marla. You know that. We just couldn't figure out the right time to be together, I guess.' He slapped his hands on his knees and stood. 'I'd best get back to business, just wanted to give you a courtesy call.'

'I appreciate it.'

'Give me a jingle as soon as Monkeewrench gets here so I can bring over all the files they need to start their work. You're going to have a lot of company for a couple days.'

'Nothing wrong with that. This house has been too damn empty lately.'

Walt watched Jacob's cruiser roll slowly away down the dirt driveway, tiny rooster tails of dust pluming from the rear wheels. He wondered how different things would be now if Jacob and Marla hadn't waited for the right time to be together.

Twenty-three

Walt only knew how to cook one thing – a ground beef hot dish with noodles and mushrooms and canned cream soup thinned with a little milk. Mary had taught him how to make it in her final days, when she could barely lift her arms anymore.

Fry the meat and onions before you add anything else, then drain off the fat. Add some dillweed at the end. Some sour cream, too. It's not a company dish, but it'll keep you fed after I'm gone.

Maybe it wasn't a company dish, but Walt liked it, and he hoped his guests would, too. As he browned the hamburger and onions in a skillet just like Mary had told him to do, he heard a large vehicle coming up his road. He peeked out the gingham curtains at the kitchen window and saw a haze of dust rising in the distance, so he killed the burner and walked outside.

The scorching daytime sun had mellowed a little as evening approached, but it was still hot and humid enough to wither every living thing. Even his sturdy cows were sheltering in the shade of the loafing shed instead of grazing, staying close to the water tank.

He pulled out a kerchief and mopped his brow while he waited for the vehicle to crest the hill, and when it did, his jaw sagged in amazement. If he hadn't been expecting Monkeewrench, he would have thought he was looking at a mirage.

Harley was behind the wheel of one of those souped-up monster buses like the ones famous rock bands toured in. Walt and Walt Junior had seen such a thing driving up to the Cities once, but he certainly hadn't been expecting Monkeewrench to arrive in one.

Harley pulled to a stop by the house and opened his window. 'Hey, Walt. Sorry we're late.'

'No apology in order. I didn't mean to pull you away from your regular work. You sure you can spare the time right now?'

'We've got everything covered.'

Walt took a step closer and peered inside. The skinny Roadrunner fellow was riding shotgun, and sitting upright on the console between the two front seats was Charlie, who wriggled his butt and gave a soft woof in greeting.

'Hey, there, Charlie boy. You want to take a run?'

Charlie's answer was much louder than his greeting.

Harley chuckled and opened the hydraulic door of the Chariot. Charlie very carefully traversed Roadrunner's lap before he lit out and tore around the front of the RV to personally acknowledge Walt by licking his hands, then rolling around in the grass by his feet. 'You've got some kind of magic, Walt. That dog loved you from the second he met you.'

'Let's just say the feeling is mutual.' Walt stooped to pick up a stick, threw it into the yard, and watched Charlie bound after it like a puppy. 'Where are the women?'

'In the back, finishing up some things. Is there some-place relatively flat where we can park this thing?'

'You bet. Up there next to the garage. I scraped it flat and laid some concrete for my own camper back in the day. There's a power outlet there I ran from the barn. Takes a lot of volts to run the milkers, so it should be able to manage this rig.'

'Thanks, Walt, but we won't drain you. We've got an onboard generator that could execute a space launch.'

'Well, then pull on up to the garage and get the crank for me and I'll get busy leveling it for you.'

Harley looked at him blankly for a moment, then nodded his head in understanding. 'This rig levels itself, Walt. No crank needed.'

'No fooling. It levels itself, does it? Well, what will they think of next?'

Annie was the first one out the door when the rig settled to a final stop by the garage, and the first one to regret it. She and hot weather had never been friends, she and the sun were virtual strangers, and here she was standing outside in the middle of both. Lord, what if she got a tan? How long did it take for such a terrible thing to happen?

'Hello, Walt.'

'Afternoon, ma'am. Glad to see you.'

Grace followed her, regretting her wardrobe choice of black jeans and riding boots, but when she'd dressed, it had seemed like a necessary choice. There probably weren't any people who'd want to cut her Achilles tendons out here, but there might be a few genuine snakes in the grass on a farm. 'Hi, Walt.'

'Ma'am.' Walt moved his hands from one set of his coverall pockets to another. 'If you'll excuse me, I have some things to tend to in the barn. Why don't you get things settled here, then go on up to the house, get out of the sun and heat. I'll let the sheriff know you're here. He said he'll bring everything you need.'

Grace gave him a smile. 'We'll be up shortly, Walt. Thank you.' She watched as he walked away, and unbelievably, Charlie raced to his side and followed him into the barn.

'I don't think I've ever seen Charlie so besotted,' Annie observed. 'Do you think he might have been a farm dog?'

'No way of knowing. I found him in the city, but that doesn't mean anything.'

'No reason a dog can't have secrets in his past, just like humans. Lord knows we all do.' She fanned her face. 'Harley, Roadrunner, are you almost finished?'

Roadrunner stuck his head out the door. 'Couple minutes more.'

'All right, then let's get up to the house before I die of heatstroke.'

Monkeewrench all climbed the three steps, crossed the porch, and entered through the front door; the screen door slapped against the frame behind them with a sound Grace had heard in an old movie. The living room they stepped into didn't do anything to dispel the image.

Faded rose sofa in the middle of a faded rose room with carpet so worn it looked like paths led from one doorway to another. There was a lot of other furniture jammed up against the walls like an audience watching the sofa, waiting for it to do something special – several mismatched chairs, a stack of old metal TV trays leaning against one another, a big round-drawered breakfront with rose-patterned china behind the glass hutch on top, and a row of family pictures marching across a yellowed lace runner draped over wood that held the scars of a family. An ancient window-mounted air conditioner labored loudly, dribbling condensation into a plastic tray.

The whole room looked forlorn, as if it had been deserted by the occupants long ago, and had just been sitting here wearing out slowly, waiting for someone to come home.

Grace wandered to the breakfront and examined the photographic chronology of a happy family of four, preserved in tarnished silver frames. As things stood now, Walt was the only one left.

She heard him coming up onto the porch, stomping his feet on the bristly mat outside the door, slapping his feed mill cap against his thigh to get the dust off. *Strange noises*, Grace thought, totally unfamiliar to her. Funny how certain noises defined a place and a lifestyle.

'Hotter than a scorched skillet out there,' he complained, then noticed Grace by the breakfront. 'I see you found Mary's art gallery. At least that's what she called it. She was quite the shutterbug, taking pictures of this, that, and the other thing, but mostly the kids. Glad for it now.' He joined her and picked up a picture that showed two grinning blond children sitting in a canoe. 'We used to take them to Wisconsin Dells every year when they were little. That's Marla when she was eight and that's Walt Junior, going on eleven. He doted on his little sister something fierce.'

Grace didn't hesitate before asking, 'What happened to Walt Junior?'

'Lost him some years ago. Farm accident. Got caught up in some equipment while we were baling straw . . .' His voice trailed away as if he'd run out of breath. 'Mary died a year later, almost to the day. The doctors would tell you the cancer took her, but I think she died from a broken heart, corny as that sounds.'

Grace suddenly felt like a voyeur, witnessing an ongoing family tragedy that wasn't meant to be seen by a stranger's eyes. 'That doesn't sound corny at all. I'm so sorry, Walt.'

'Thank you.' He gave her a sad smile, then turned to look at the others. 'Anybody else want a cold one?' Without waiting for an answer, he disappeared into the kitchen and came back carrying five frosty bottles with the necks stuck between his fingers, saying, 'Here you go,' to each of them as he passed them out. 'Lemonade for Grace, beer for everyone else.'

Walt disappeared again, then returned with a big bowlful of water, which he set in front of an appreciative Charlie. He wagged his stub tail and started drinking noisily. 'What happened to this fella's tail?'

'I don't know,' Grace said. 'I found him that way. Thanks for the water.'

'He already thanked me, but you're welcome all the same.' He settled into an old recliner and took a pull off his bottle. 'The sheriff should be here within the hour. Not sure what all you can do with what he's bringing you, but I appreciate you trying all the same. This may well be a fool's errand, but I'll never stop trying to find Marla until the day they plant me in the ground.' He took another drink of beer. 'It's the not knowing that kills you.'

Grace watched pure agony distort Walt's features. He didn't seem remotely self-conscious about it, probably

135

didn't even know it was as plain as a Broadway marquee, playing out on his face for everyone to see.

She had always possessed a deep empathy for people who were missing a loved one, especially a child, but now she was beginning to understand on a very personal level what that pain might be like, and it tore at her heart in a way nothing ever had before. She was, after all, a mother herself now. 'We'll do everything we can, Walt.'

He met her eyes with his own piercing blue ones, then simply nodded and pushed up out of his recliner. 'I'll get to finishing dinner. We've got a little time to pass, so we might as well eat something.'

'We weren't expecting dinner, Walt,' Harley said.

'On a farm, everybody gets fed. There's plenty to go around, and it's the least I can do. Tell you the truth, it'll be nice to have some bodies around the table for a change.'

'That's nice of you. Is there something we can do to help you out?'

'If you can run a can opener, then that's a yes.'

Harley smiled. 'That's right in my wheelhouse, Walt. I'm damn good at it, too.'

Grace, Annie, and Roadrunner watched Harley trail Walt into the kitchen, then listened to the clanging of pans, the whir of a can opener, the muted conversation punctuated by an occasional chuckle. Happy sounds of everyday life in a house that had been in silent mourning for two months.

Roadrunner had been fidgeting for a while, completely out of his realm. 'I'm going to run out to the Chariot and check the sat link, make sure the computer is ready for input.'

'That's a fine idea,' Annie said, repositioning herself on the floral sofa to get a little closer to the air conditioner. 'And why don't you bring back a couple of those salads Grace made.'

Sheriff Emmet arrived just as Walt was bringing out a big dish of something brown with noodles. Grace didn't know what it was, just that canned goods had been involved, but it had flecks of dillweed on the top, which she thought was a nice touch for a man who probably hadn't spent a minute in the kitchen before his wife passed away.

'Didn't know we were having a dinner party, otherwise I would have brought a bottle of wine,' the sheriff jived Walt fondly.

'I got beer, or something stronger if you're in the mood.'

'A cold beer would be just fine, Walt, thanks.' He turned his attention to Monkeewrench. 'That's quite a rig you've got parked outside.'

Harley's face took on the warm glow of a proud papa. 'She's a beaut, and you'll get the full tour after dinner. That's our mobile computer lab, and Walt said you were bringing everything we need to get started.'

He patted his chest. 'Digital case files are right here in my pocket. Looking forward to the tour.'

Dinner was an experience unlike any Grace had ever had. It wasn't a Michelin three-star meal by any stretch of the imagination, but it was just the kind of food that would refuel people who toiled hard outside all day and needed something substantial to fill the void when they came in for the night.

The conversation was light and cordial, and the darkness in Walt seemed to disappear, at least temporarily. Circumstances had made him a lonely, desolate man, and this odd, impromptu gathering of strangers seemed to lift him up, and for that, Grace was happy. What made her unhappy was the strong likelihood that their work here wouldn't yield good news, if it yielded any news at all.

After dinner, Harley and Roadrunner took Sheriff Emmet out to the Chariot to upload all the data from Marla's case, while Annie and Grace stayed behind to help Walt clean up. It felt wildly chauvinistic to assume the traditional female role that was largely an artifact from the past, but Grace thought the gesture felt right at this time and in this place.

But Walt wasn't having any of it. 'I'll take care of the dishes, don't trouble yourselves. But if you don't mind, there's something I'd like to show you.'

'As long as it's not outside,' Annie said in her smooth voice, still tinged by a lingering Mississippi accent. 'I can hear those mosquitoes just waiting to feast on me, and they're hungry.'

Walt's face broke into a genuine smile. 'You're right about the mosquitoes, and I wouldn't think of sending you outside, ma'am. What I want to show you is Marla's room.'

The mood shifted to things more grave as Annie and Grace followed him up a narrow flight of wooden stairs to the second floor and led them to a closed door at the end of the hallway. He didn't even touch the doorknob, and Grace wondered if he'd been in this room since Marla had disappeared.

'Rummage around all you like. Everything from her apartment in Minneapolis is in there, mostly still in boxes. Dishes and clothes and so forth. But she did keep a hand-written daily journal, which I put in the center drawer of her desk, if you think it would help. Mostly she wrote about newborn calves and kitten litters and such, but she had a way with words, that gal, and she was funny. You can get to know her a little bit by what she wrote.'

Grace noticed that Walt had referred to his daughter in the past tense. 'We'll take a look. Thank you, Walt.'

He sucked in a breath, then blew it out hard. 'There's no way we can figure this out, I know that. She was in the wrong place at the wrong time and somebody bad and dark either took her or killed her. Happens all the time, doesn't it?'

Twenty-four

While Roadrunner and Harley uploaded the cache of mostly unproductive reports and seemingly meaningless photos of the woods and the base of the tree where Marla's ring had either fallen off or been intentionally left, Jacob sat motionless on a side sofa, looking down at his hands. He'd gone over those photos a million times himself, but seeing them enlarged and displayed on the enormous overhead computer screen amplified his memories of that horrible night and made them so much worse.

'There was no scent of Marla beyond where you found her ring, right?' Harley asked.

Jacob lifted his head, keeping his eyes averted from the screen. 'The dogs couldn't find one. Any trace of Marla stopped right there.'

Roadrunner rocked back and forth, heel to toe, watching the screen scroll at warp speed through the evidence Harley was uploading. The computer was programmed to mark and briefly freeze-frame anything that it determined was an anomaly, either in documented evidence or photos. It stopped on a shot of a littered area of forest floor. There were empty beer cans, a used condom, cigarette butts, a couple of balled-up fast food bags. 'What's all this junk?'

Jacob forced his eyes up to the screen. 'Party detritus. Teenagers, lowlifes, anybody who can't party in public finds somewhere private to do their thing. And they leave their sh . . . stuff behind. We ran every single scrap of it through the BCA. DNA tests on the used condom, the cigarette butts, the beer cans, the whole shebang. We were hoping something would match up with the blood we found on the road by Marla's car, maybe take us a step closer, but nothing matched him or anybody else in the system.'

Harley paused his work and looked over his shoulder at Jacob. 'Where did your search perimeter end?'

'Where we lost Marla's scent. Officially, anyhow. But volunteers and search crews were out all over the woods and surrounding fields for days. Their reports are all in what I gave you.'

Harley clapped his hands on his knees. 'You've given our equipment plenty to chew on, Jacob. If there are any missing links, we'll find them.'

'You have my gratitude. And Walt's.'

'You and Walt are close.'

'I've known him since I was a boy. Marla and I pretty much grew up together.' He stood up wearily, his shoulders stooped, just like any man carrying a heavy weight. 'I'll be in touch. Call me if you need anything, day or night.'

For the first half hour in Marla's room, Grace and Annie had been mostly silent. Annie finally pushed herself away from the desk she had been sorting through drawer by drawer, mostly because her stomach was sweating and that had never happened before.

'Lord, Grace, pretty soon I'm going to have to take

a break and go downstairs to sit in front of that window AC.'

Grace looked up from a framed picture of Marla in a high school cheerleading uniform, her arm around the waist of a handsome young football player in full regalia. 'Go sit for a while in the Chariot. Harley keeps the computer room at sixty-five degrees when all the equipment is working.'

'I don't think so. That poor sheriff is just about the saddest man I ever did see, and looking through all that evidence again is going to make it worse. I don't think I could bear to watch it.'

'I think I know why.' Grace handed her the photograph, and Annie's eyes grew wide as she examined it.

'That's Sheriff Emmet, isn't it?'

'I think so.'

Annie clucked her tongue. 'Well, that explains a lot. The pictures in this house certainly have stories to tell, don't they?'

'Pictures always do,' Grace said, thinking of the complete absence of any photos in her own house, which also told a story. It wasn't because she hadn't had time to get them framed and displayed; there were simply no photos to frame. Nothing from childhood and nothing from adulthood, save for a single picture of her with Harley, Annie, and Roadrunner from their college days in Atlanta that she kept in a locked drawer in her office. If she ever disappeared, investigators might conclude that Grace MacBride didn't exist at all. And she hadn't, until twelve years ago.

She stepped away from the dresser she'd been investigating, where many other photos were carefully arrayed, just like they were on the breakfront in Walt's living room – Marla as a toddler, Marla as a gap-toothed youngster, Marla with a mother and brother who had been lost before she was. It was a meticulous account of the lives that made up a family; a record that they had existed.

It suddenly struck Grace that if something happened to her during childbirth, her baby would never even know what she looked like. Just like she'd never known what her own mother had looked like. The realization horrified her, and as much as she shunned cameras, she was going to have to get over it.

'Grace?'

'Just thinking. Did you find anything useful in the desk?'

'Not really.' She held up a leather-bound journal. 'It's just like Walt said, this journal is filled with things about animals, Walt and the farm, her job at the vet clinic in Minneapolis. There are a couple entries about people at work . . . how nice, how compassionate, what a skilled vet Dr Swanson is, the summer softball league she was looking forward to joining. What a stirring homily about resurrection Pastor Van gave on Easter. No writings about a secret love affair with a bad boy. No writings about any love interest at all. I'm telling you, up until now, I hadn't completely dismissed the idea that Marla was a very good girl who'd gotten tangled up in something over her head, or maybe got tricked by some Web predator, but now I don't think so. Marla Gustafson was about as pure of heart as you can get.' Annie passed the journal to Grace. 'Take a look for yourself.'

Grace carefully leafed through the pages as if it were an

ancient artifact from which she could somehow decipher a mystical rune of truth. 'Wrong place at the wrong time,' she murmured, not even realizing she'd vocalized.

'What?'

'Sorry. I'm just repeating what Walt said earlier. Marla was most likely in the wrong place at the wrong time. Call it fate, call it bad luck, call it whatever you want.' She paused on a page near the end, then read it out loud. '"I thought I saw Angel today when I was grocery shopping, how crazy is that? I didn't say anything, though, it's been so many years. Besides, it couldn't have been Angel, probably just my mind playing tricks on me."'

Annie tapped a sparkly silver nail on her lower lip. 'Angel. Sounds like a stage name for an exotic dancer, if you were to ask my opinion.'

'It's probably nothing, but let's go ask Walt about it.'

Annie stood and unsuccessfully tried to smooth the wrinkled front of her dress. 'That's very cop-like of you, Grace, chasing after every possible lead, even when you know it won't go anywhere.'

'With all the time we spend with cops, something's bound to rub off.'

Walt was in the kitchen, elbow-deep in soapy dishwater when they came downstairs. He turned and gave them a nod. 'Find anything up in Marla's room?'

'Not really, but there is an entry in her journal that mentions somebody named Angel. Was that an old friend of hers?'

Walt frowned and a strata of lines creased his forehead. 'I don't think so. She did have a deaf white cat she named Angel when she was a girl.'

'She was talking about a person.'

'Huh. Nothing springs to mind, but I'll think on it.'

They heard the clump of heavy shoes on the porch steps, then the squeak of the screen door opening. 'Came to say good night, Walt.'

'Come on in, Sheriff,' Walt called out, drying his hands on a checked towel.

Grace noted the man's subdued demeanor as he strode into the kitchen. She'd considered Sheriff Emmet's face an affable one, but now it was stormy and morose.

Walt clucked his tongue. 'You look like you need a snoot of whiskey, and fast.'

'Wish I could, but I still have to drive back to the office before I head home.'

'I won't keep you, then. These ladies were just asking me about somebody named Angel. Does that ring a bell to you?'

The sheriff's eyes drifted from Grace to Annie. 'Ah, you took a look at Marla's journal. The best I could come up with was the migrant workers' kids. We used to swim and fish with them in Walt's lake during the summer. There were a few kids named Angel, it's not an uncommon name in Mexico. Maybe she thought she saw one of them. But that was twenty-some years back. Nobody looks the same after that amount of time has passed.'

Walt clapped him on the shoulder. 'Go get some rest, Jacob. We'll catch up tomorrow.'

After he left, Annie peered around the kitchen. 'You finished cleaning up.'

'I did, and now I'm going to settle down in front of the TV with some popcorn and watch the Twins game before milking time. You're welcome to join me.'

Grace nodded graciously. 'Thank you, Walt, but we're heading back to the Chariot to work.'

Walt got a funny look on his face. 'That's what you call that rig?'

'It's what Harley calls it. I guess the name stuck.'

'Fair enough. And just so you know, I do my milking late, around ten, so don't get spooked if you hear a commotion out by the barn, it's just me and the cows.'

Twenty-five

The evening shift at Global Foods had been frenetic – there was the first rush between five and six o'clock, when the after-work crowd came en masse to buy last-minute meals for their dinner, then a second rush between seven and eight. Global Foods had more than its share of difficult, demanding customers – the more people paid for things, the more they expected, which seemed reasonable – but at the end of a day, some of them turned downright nasty, channeling their own day's frustrations by venting on minimum-wage employees who didn't deserve the brunt of their grievances and didn't dare talk back.

In her normal life, Cassie would have made short work of these jackasses with a simple tongue-lashing, but her ruse didn't allow her the luxury. It was infuriating, but it also kept her mind off the things she would be doing once ten-o'clock closing rolled around.

Sarah, the yippy Chihuahua, seemed to be suffering the worst of angry customers' wrath, and Cassie found herself almost feeling sorry for her. But it made sense – as mouthy and judgmental as she was, she exuded a homing beacon of low self-esteem which made her a prime target for bullies who didn't want to pick a real fight. Darwin at work. The strong survived, the meek got crushed. Cassie didn't have a problem with survival of the fittest, but it was getting painful to watch. Besides, she had a new relationship to cultivate and nurture. Sarah was the senior employee here and Dalek trusted her. And if his paranoia ever found focus in Cassie, she needed Sarah as a defensive buffer.

After a particularly shrewish woman had chewed Sarah up and down for a leaky container of Castelvetrano olives before stalking off, Cassie gave her a sympathetic look, and not all of it was manufactured. 'Sucks, doesn't it? Somebody has a bad day, so they run around ruining other people's days like it's going to make them feel better.'

She watched Sarah bob her head woodenly. Jesus, was she on the verge of tears? 'Hey, you haven't taken your break yet. Why don't you take it now?'

'I can't, it's still too busy.'

'I can handle it. Besides, you had my back yesterday, so it's my turn.'

Sarah blinked a few times and looked at her. 'Are you sure?'

'Positive.'

'Okay. Thanks. By the way, I hope you're feeling better today.'

'Much better. There's always that one day of the month, you know?'

'Oh, yeah, I know. I won't be long.'

Sarah wasn't long, and when she came back from her break, Cassie observed a difference in her demeanor. Nothing major, but her stiff, guarded posture seemed to have relaxed just a little. Even more alarming was the fact that she would actually make eye contact with Cassie for more than the briefest second.

During an interview or an interrogation, that was a tell that the subject you were working on was starting to humanize you and was entertaining the idea of trust; and trust, even the flimsiest, made for cooperation and looser lips.

She didn't know if Sarah would ever be cooperative with anybody, but she sure loosened her lips. She started out tentatively, making innocuous comments here and there, and the more Cassie showed interest, the more encouraged she became, until she was chattering like a songbird.

During the last hour before closing, Cassie learned a lot about Sarah through idle chitchat and had begun to construct a preliminary psychological profile. Her initial assessment was that she was one of those people who had a persecution complex, perceived herself as a victim, and felt much better about herself when she could help another victim. She was lonely – her life outside Global Foods revolved almost exclusively around her two rescue cats, Butters and Sugar, who provided her with unconditional love. Her bitchy facade was just a protective mechanism.

By no means was the woman a total wreck, but when you broke down anybody like that, they seemed beyond hope. But in Cassie's opinion, if there was a single redeeming human characteristic, it was a love for animals, and Sarah definitely had that going for her. She might actually find her way in the world, probably running a rescue shelter.

' . . . and then Sugar made this weird, loud meow in my ear and dropped a dead mouse right on my pillow at three a.m.!'

Cassie was staring at the wall clock, which was ticking off the last four minutes before ten. 'You must have had a heart attack . . . Wow, I can't believe it, it's closing time already.'

'Thank God.' Sarah started cleaning and organizing her station and gathering her personal things in preparation to leave for the night. In a few minutes, Cassie would be totally alone in the store to do what she needed to do and get out. Focus, focus, focus.

But then Sarah paused. 'I can stay and help you close up if you want. It's not hard, but if it's the first time you've done it and you don't feel comfortable . . .'

Cassie's jaw tightened, but she put on a winning smile, desperately fearing her deceitful overture of friendship had backfired. 'Thanks, Sarah, thanks for everything, but you go home. I know you want to get back to your kitties. You had a long shift today and they must be so lonely by now.' Mentioning beloved pets languishing alone at home was manipulative gold. Cassie hadn't learned that at Quantico, it was just a fact of life.

'You're sure?'

'Positive. Besides, you already helped me with the hard stuff. All I have to do is set the alarm and lock up. No problem.'

Sarah looked genuinely cheerful for the first time since Cassie had known her. 'I'll give Butters and Sugar a kiss from you.'

'Why don't you grab a couple bags of those new organic cat treats on your way out? I'm buying.'

'Really?'

'Really.'

'Okay! I will. Thanks! See you tomorrow, Cassie.'

Cassie let every muscle in her body relax when she saw Sarah finally leave with her cat treats in tow. She locked the front door behind her, then remotely activated the sneaky little virus she had installed in the security system a few days ago to black out the store's main-floor security cameras temporarily without raising suspicion. She had five minutes.

She picked the lock on Dalek's door easily and let herself in. The office was dark, but she didn't need light. The laptop was gone, but the desktop was still there, so she took another flash drive out of her pocket and started uploading those contents.

She fought her nerves, fought the incessant prickling of adrenaline by staring at the monitor, watching the blue progress bar creep forward against a black screen as it counted down the endless seconds until the upload was complete. And then she sensed something that made the hair on the back of her neck stand up, made her stomach writhe and her breath stop.

On the screen, she suddenly saw the reflection of a man's face. He was standing behind her, a wire wrapped around the thick fingers of each hand, stretched taut. A garrote. Dear Jesus. She didn't have her gun, she only had her skills.

She took a deep, silent breath the way she'd been taught.

If you see or sense an assailant behind you, do not reveal your awareness. All you have is the element of surprise. If they sense they have been spotted, your only advantage is gone.

So Cassie continued to stare at the monitor, breathing through her nose, and when the words 'upload complete' blinked on the screen, she retrieved her flash drive and tucked it in her pocket, never taking her eyes off the reflection.

In the next instant, the wire started to come down over her head, but she was ready for it. She flung her arms over her shoulders and her thumbs found the man's eyes, pushing inward until he started screaming. She kicked her chair back into his stomach, jumped to her feet, and ran toward the loading dock doors.

Twenty-six

Magozzi felt a numb ache buzzing through every cell in his body as he crawled into bed after almost forty sleepless hours, a lot of it spent on his feet under a cruelly hot sun. He'd lost count of the days, and the details of the crime scenes had started bleeding together in the undulating plasma of his semimelted brain. McLaren and Freedman had finally kicked him and Gino out of the office at eight o'clock, begging for mercy.

You two smell like week-old gym bags, you've got worse tempers than a couple of wet bees, and your collective brain power is hovering somewhere between sea slug and plankton. Go home. Shower. Get some sleep.

McLaren had been absolutely right, there was a tipping point when it came to sleep deprivation – when you started making bad decisions, or none at all – and he and Gino had probably surpassed that hours before they'd finally left City Hall. Besides, with all the cases almost through the bureaucratic maze to get joint-task-forced between Minneapolis and Saint Paul and staffed around the clock, they had a lot of new information coming in and fresh eyes and brains to process it. Brains that wouldn't miss a gossamer thread of evidence that could break a case.

But as exhausted as he was, Magozzi couldn't push away the leaden sense of hopelessness. They were the first line of defense for the people they'd taken an oath to protect and serve, and so far, they were being outsmarted by a psychopath, albeit a very organized one. And beyond the hopelessness, there was white-hot anger that such a monster existed at all.

There was another monster in this mix, too, and that was the media. Amanda White had essentially led the charge on the evening news, upping the ante from speculation to unilaterally proclaiming that there was almost certainly a twisted serial killer on the loose and he was spreading his net to Saint Paul. He could still hear her annoying, shrill voice as she did her best to incite fear and uncertainty in the masses.

There is still no official confirmation that the murder in Saint Paul's Phalen Park early this morning is connected to Minneapolis's unsolved murder yesterday, which also occurred in a park. But the presence of Minneapolis homicide detectives Leo Magozzi and Gino Rolseth at the Saint Paul scene today is noteworthy and seems to speak volumes. What aren't they telling us, and why?

Magozzi rolled over onto his side in disgust, jamming another pillow under his neck, trying to get comfortable in his unfamiliar bed in a house he now hated. He tried to mentally transport himself to the lake, where his new bed and only wonderful memories resided, but there was too much pollution in his mind to quite make it there.

He should never have turned on the TV tonight. And what pissed him off even more was the fact that Amanda White was right – she was just putting pieces together that were out there for anyone to see. The problem was she was making damn good and sure she scared the shit out of everybody in the process.

It took him a while, or maybe no time at all, to fall into a scattered sleep, his turbulent thoughts becoming twitchy dreams that made no sense. At ten o'clock, he woke up to a howling stomach, reminding him that he hadn't eaten since breakfast.

He gave up on sleep for the time being, stumbled downstairs, and threw a frozen meal into the microwave. It smelled weird after the first minute, weirder after the second, so he wandered into his living room to let it complete its six-minute cycle, hoping it would smell better by the time it had finished cooking.

The living room, and the house for that matter, was not the same place it had been since his divorce from Heather. She'd taken most of the contents, but had happily relinquished the house after their divorce, and small wonder. Her salary as an attorney was so far above his he couldn't even see it from here, and easily paid for her downtown condo with a view of the river and muscular young personal trainers who serviced the on-site gym, and probably Heather as well.

Bad Magozzi. Not nice.

He didn't really harbor any ill will toward his philandering ex-wife, except when it came to her defending a lot of the dirtbags he broke his back to put in jail. They'd been a bad match, equally cheated by coming together, but Magozzi had come out of it smelling like roses, because Grace MacBride had come into his life.

Magozzi got up from the sofa when he heard the microwave ping, leaving his memories behind in the living room. His dinner still smelled weird, but he wolfed it down anyhow. Just as he was putting the last forkful of something pretending to be meat in his mouth, the phone rang.

Caller ID announced it was Gino. 'Oh, shit,' he mumbled, then answered. 'If this is anything other than a social call, I want you to hang up right now so I can go back to bed.'

'That's exactly what I told McLaren when he called me from the scene of a fresh one. Six of spades.'

Twenty-seven

McLaren was waiting for Gino and Magozzi outside the boarded-up storefront of what was once Suds and Suds – a long-defunct Laundromat that used to serve cheap beer to bored clients so they could enjoy a buzz while they waited for their socks and underwear to dry. According to a posted sign, a gastropub-slash-microbrewery would be occupying the space in the fall. My, how things had changed here.

When this neighborhood had started to fray around the edges back in the early nineties, Suds and Suds had closed up, along with most other mom-and-pop businesses, leaving nothing but cheap rental units, a couple of sketchy bars, and a church mission that served the homeless. The area had languished forgotten over the years, until hipsters discovered the neighborhood. They were charmed by the low rent so close to downtown Minneapolis and the slightly dangerous, dingy bars where they could drink Grain Belt beer side by side with people who didn't possess a philosophy degree, but did possess exotic jobs, like factory assembly line workers, janitors, and small-time criminals.

Now it was in full renaissance and a new bar, tapas restaurant, or boutique was opening up every month. There was even a shiny new CVS pharmacy and a high-end grocery store. There were still a few pimples on the rapidly clearing urban complexion, but overall it was a success story for everybody except the factory workers, the janitors, and the small-time criminals, who didn't like microbrews, tapas, or the associated rising rents.

Tonight, this city block was shut down and bathed in a kaleidoscope of flashing blue-and-red lights that advertised something very bad had happened here. Dozens of officers crowded the street, manning barricades and taking statements from onlookers.

McLaren threw up his hands in what was maybe a greeting, an admonishment, or general frustration. 'Jesus, it's about time you guys got here.'

'We were here in twenty,' Gino growled. 'Did you think we were going to teleport here or what?'

McLaren was unfazed by Gino's grumpy hibernating-bear impersonation. 'Yeah, well, twenty is about all it took for things to go downhill faster than a boulder. We're gonna have company soon.'

'What kind of company?' Magozzi asked, dreading the answer.

'The FBI.'

'What the hell business do they have with this? They're not in on our serial.'

'This has nothing to do with the possible serial angle, the Feds don't even know about it yet. See, the vic was robbed. No personal effects, no identification. So we ran her prints and got nothing. A little while later, I get a call from Chief Malcherson, telling me and Eaton to play nice with our new friends when they show up.'

'That's all he said?'

'That's it. Until I mentioned the fact that this was

maybe our serial and I'd called you guys in for a look, then he got quiet for a minute, said he'd get back to me.'

Gino wiped his bleary eyes, dragging the bags under them farther down his face. 'So the vic doesn't have a criminal history, no prints on any open file, and yet the minute you ran them, the Feds were all over you. What do you bet she's an agent?'

McLaren cocked his head. 'That's a decent assumption for a guy who hasn't slept in two days.'

'I'll do you one better, because I know exactly what's going on. When the prints red-flagged with the FBI, our fondest friend, Special Agent in Charge Paul Shafer, called Malcherson, said he was taking over the hand with a federal trump card. No pun intended. Nothing Malcherson can do about it. But when he found out about the serial angle from you, he had to call Shafer back and let him know he wasn't going to bend over on this without equal access to evidence, because we've got a butcher on the loose killing a woman a day and MPD's ass is on the line big-time. Bet you anything Malcherson and Shafer are negotiating right now for an interdepartmental love-fest where we can all share evidence nicey-nicey. I rest my case.'

McLaren folded his arms across his chest. 'You are one crafty, conniving fucker, Rolseth. You ever think about going into politics?'

'I'd shoot myself in the head first.'

'Johnny, you sound a little ambivalent about this being our guy,' Magozzi redirected.

'Right. I'll show you why.' He waved his hand for them to follow him past the crime-scene tape and led them around the back of Suds and Suds to an empty parking lot. Weeds sprouted up in cracks in the pavement, and a rusty shopping cart was jammed against a pile of broken wooden pallets where Eaton Freedman was standing watch over the body, a colossal guardian of the dead.

Eaton nodded a morose greeting and stepped back to reveal the body of a woman wearing a bloody orange smock with a Global Foods logo on the left breast – the high-end grocery store that had opened up nearby a few years ago. But the blood wasn't the result of any cutting on her torso, at least from what Magozzi could see. It looked like it had all seeped down from the precise, thin laceration around her neck. On the ground next to her was a six of spades.

'What in the hell?' Magozzi mumbled. 'Nothing about this jibes except for the card. And even the card doesn't jibe – it looks like it was tossed there as an afterthought.'

'Yeah, that's what Eaton and I were trying to figure out. If it wasn't for the card, I'd say hell no, this isn't our guy, because nothing about this scene reads serial killer fantasy. First off, we're clearly not in a park, and this woman wasn't out jogging, she was a clerk at Global Foods, maybe on her way home from work. She's blond, not brunette, she wasn't strangled, she was garroted. No cutting on her torso, but check out her left wrist.' He pointed a flashlight, which revealed a deep, ragged cut. 'It looks like somebody tried to hack it off. Just like Katya Smirnova, except Katya lost her hand, this one didn't.'

Gino went down on his haunches for a closer look. 'This is a damn mess, nothing planned or careful about it. It's like a badly botched frame job.'

'Could be a copycat,' Eaton said. 'We never leaked the card, but sometimes stuff gets out whether we want it to or not.'

'Two possibilities,' Magozzi said. 'Either the info about the card got leaked and it is a copycat, or this is our man and for some reason, he totally broke from his fantasy. Which doesn't make any sense. Serial killers are nothing if not predictable.'

McLaren shoved his hands in the pocket of his seersucker sport coat. 'Or this was a rush job. Maybe something scared him off before he could finish. This is a busy area. Pretty stupid place to kill anybody if you ask me.'

Magozzi chewed his lower lip, as if his lip were somehow connected to the improved functionality of brain synapses. 'Exactly. This kill was different from inception. So why here and why all the discrepancies in the MO?'

Eaton took a deep breath and looked away. 'Maybe he had to kill her, for whatever reason. Like she made him somehow. She's not his type, this venue isn't his twisted little paradise, but he has no choice but to chase her down and shut her up. He tried to preserve his fantasy the best he could under the circumstances.'

Magozzi raised a brow at him. 'I could buy that. Who found the body?'

'A guy who walks home from CVS every night after work. He's in a squad giving preliminaries until we can get to him.'

Magozzi looked toward the street and saw two notable things: an FBI Forensics Unit pulling up and a tall man in a suit getting out of a sedan and crossing the crime-scene tape without MPD escort. 'Malcherson's here.'

'Damn right he is,' Gino said almost cheerfully, giving Eaton a nudge. 'Listen up, greenhorn, that's a leader for you right there. Not afraid to get in the trenches, not afraid to get his boots dirty when his men need some backup. And trust me, when the FBI gets involved, you need cover from an authority figure. You'll need it other times, too, but just so you know, Malcherson's always your man.'

Eaton nodded studiously. 'Got it, Obi-Wan.'

The chief joined them with a curt nod and salutation, then studied the scene with a grim expression. Magozzi could only remember a couple of times when it had been necessary for the chief to be present at a crime scene. His demeanor never wavered from the unreadable stoicism that defined his personality, but beneath the cool exterior was a compassionate man and a former street cop and homicide detective who had devoted his life to stopping the kind of violence they were all looking at now.

He finally turned away. 'Please, let's step over here. I need to speak with you all in private before things get complicated.'

'Are we getting shut out, Chief?' Gino asked the minute they'd found a cozy little corner in the latticed shadow of a chain-link fence that separated the Suds and Suds lot from CVS.

'Not entirely. There will be full cooperation on this case between the MPD and the Bureau with shared and equal access to any related evidence. I assured Special Agent in Charge Shafer that he can rely on our full compliance, and he assured me of the same. We all have the same goal in mind, and that is to find the killer.'

'Sounds great,' McLaren said. 'So what's the caveat?'

'For the time being, you won't pursue anything other than the physical evidence provided by the FBI's forensic unit. Specifically, you are not to conduct any interviews or question anyone directly related to this case.'

Gino made an unpleasant sound. 'You've gotta be kidding me. So we are getting shut out for all intents and purposes.'

Malcherson looked irritated. 'It will be temporary.'

'Did Shafer tell you what's more important than trying to find a serial killer who also happened to kill one of their agents?'

Malcherson's expression remained still.

'Come on, Chief. Give us a little credit. The prints and the Feds suddenly storming the Bastille was a dead giveaway.'

'All I can tell you is this case relates to an ongoing, high-priority undercover operation. And Shafer had a very specific request – stay away from Global Foods.'

Twenty-eight

Amanda White was sitting in a CVS pharmacy parking lot, enjoying the view. From her position, she could see every vehicle arriving at the crime scene, and it was starting to get very interesting. She knew it was a homicide from the get-go, but when Detectives Magozzi and Rolseth had shown up later, she knew it was also connected to the serial killer. And just now, Chief Malcherson had shown up in person, along with the FBI. There was gold here, she just had to figure out how to mine it.

Her stomach growled and she reached into the greasy McDonald's bag on the passenger seat, then started shoving cold, limp fries into her mouth with an angry defiance directed at all the devoutly superficial people in her life who were constantly trying to repair her glaring imperfections. For her own good, of course.

Mom: You shouldn't eat fried food, dear. It's terrible for your complexion. Besides, it will make you fat, and where will you be then?

Bob, her producer: Love the new teeth, Amanda, but the camera adds ten pounds at least, so lose an extra five or so, 'kay?

Jenny, her hairdresser: What do you think about going blond, maybe add some extensions? You'll feel so much sexier, and it'll play great on TV. Have you gained weight?

God, the world was fucked up in so many ways. Childhood obesity was basically a pandemic now, so obviously not a lot of kids had moms anymore who told them they'd get fat and pimply and have no future if they ate fried food. At the same time, anorexia was still rampant. And what was worse? Diabetic kids who were too fat to run three feet without keeling over, or living skeletons who were too emaciated to run three feet without keeling over? And meanwhile, here she was, a skinny, neurotic, suggestible woman who was bingeing on fries in a car outside a pharmacy in a rugged part of town, watching the aftermath of somebody's tragedy, waiting to capitalize on it for her own benefit. The scales of common sense, her own included, needed a serious recalibration.

The funny thing was, this felt right, being here tonight. Her whole life, she'd dreamed of being a hard-core investigative journalist, somebody who solved mysteries by digging deep and working people. She'd never wanted to be a television personality, never even considered it. And yet she'd allowed herself to be misdirected onto a path that was becoming harder and harder to justify – an okay-looking Iowa girl transformed into a media paper doll who talked for a living but didn't have a voice.

Sometimes, as she spooled out preapproved, melodramatic speculations in front of the studio cameras, she felt marred, damaged, even. She felt that way when she looked at herself in the mirror, too. And maybe everybody around her felt the same way. Fake teeth and size two clothes didn't buy you respect.

She abandoned her fries when Magozzi and Rolseth exited the scene, along with Chief Malcherson. They spoke for a few minutes, then shook hands and went to their respective cars. After they parted, all three of them had cell phones glued to their ears.

Part of her wanted to call out to them, rush up, throw out some of her theories and try to get a thread to pull on. But the investigative journalist who'd been asleep for the past eight years asked the shiny news anchor who'd been born a few months ago what would come out of a confrontation now?

Nothing. No comment, Ms White. Have a good night.

No, she was going to play this one differently. Women were dying every single night. It was horrific and it had to be stopped.

Fortunately, she had a card up her sleeve. So to speak.

Twenty-nine

Jed was sterilizing his equipment in the back room when the shop's doorbell announced a visitor just before midnight. Goddamn Ginny had forgotten to flip over the closed sign and lock up. Again. She was a temperamental, scatterbrained bitch, but she was also the best tattoo artist he had, with a big clientele willing to pay two hundred bucks an hour for her skills, and he couldn't afford to shit-can her. She was a rising star and she'd break away soon to start her own gig, and he wanted to cash in for as long as he could.

He walked out to the front of the shop and saw a short guy in a baseball cap standing at the counter. 'We're closed for the night.'

'This is what I want.' The man slapped a sheet of paper on the counter with a drawing on it.

'Maybe you didn't hear me. We're closed.'

'The sign says you're open.'

Jed, who was six and a half feet of solid muscle and almost entirely covered in ink, didn't have to rely on anything but his appearance to intimidate. But this stupid shithead showed no fear, wasn't budging, and now he was getting mouthy. It happened sometimes, a drunk or a hopped-up highball wandering in late, chemical confidence clouding his judgment. Jed wouldn't get physical unless it was absolutely necessary, but there wasn't anything wrong with fantasizing about grabbing this scruffy little bastard by his shirt and tossing him out the door. 'I guess you're deaf. Maybe you know sign language.' He pointed to the door. 'Out.'

'I'm not deaf, and I don't think you're blind,' the man said, reaching into his pocket.

In a split second, Jed was crouched and about to launch a full-body assault, but he faltered when the man pulled out a wallet, not a gun, and carefully arrayed ten one-hundred-dollar bills on the counter. 'Maybe you're open now.'

It didn't take long for Jed to determine that this man wasn't drunk and he wasn't on drugs – he knew, because he'd been there himself ten years ago. That assessment, along with the thousand dollars in cash on the counter, helped him make his decision. 'Okay, let's go.'

But an hour into the tattoo, Jed was getting nervous. There was no conceivable reason, but something just seemed wrong. For one thing, his client was silent as a stone – most people talked at least a little to distract themselves from the pain. And he never made eye contact, just stared down at the needle gun stitching lines and swirls of ink into his flesh. The blood didn't seem to bother him, either. It was almost like he was in some sort of weird hypnotic state.

Although it was mostly silent in the shop, every tiny noise seemed to become more and more amplified as time passed: The wall clock behind him ticked away the seconds with increasing urgency. The buzzing of his needle grew louder and louder. His breathing started sounding raspy and his heart pounded in his ears.

Big, bad Jed, all bent out of shape over a guy you could snap in half like a pencil. Jesus Christ, get a grip, you're almost done . . .

'Finished.'

The man examined the work carefully, then nodded his approval and stood up.

'Let me get a bandage on that . . .'

But the man just turned and started walking out, pausing at the counter to lay down two more hundred-dollar bills. Then he disappeared out the door.

Jed let out a deep, shuddering sigh. He knew it was humanly impossible, but he felt like he'd been holding his breath for the past two hours. He quickly locked the front door, then looked around the shop, trying to shake the unnerving feeling that he was lucky to be alive.

Thirty

Grace was sitting on the glider on the front porch, slapping the occasional after-dusk mosquito when Walt came up from the barn. She watched him walk across the grass toward her with the stride of a much younger man. 'You smell like fresh hay,' she told him.

'Wouldn't think a city girl would know that smell.'

Grace smiled at him. 'I've slept in a few barns over the years.'

Walt's brows lifted, but he didn't say anything.

'It's pretty late for chores even by your standards, isn't it?'

'Cows are a trial in this kind of heat. I had to bring them in from pasture to cool off this afternoon, which means barn cleaning twice a day instead of once. Where are your friends?'

'They're all working in the Chariot. I took a break to take Charlie for a walk.'

Walt glanced down at Charlie on the porch floor, flattened on his side as if he'd spent the day on a treadmill. 'Must have been a long walk. You wore that dog plumb out. Where'd you go?'

Grace looked back into the living room windows as if she could see through the house to the fields. 'There's a fence on this side of the cornfield, and woods beyond that.'

Walt nodded. 'Giddings owned that place for four

generations. Martin's great-granddaddy homesteaded that land before Minnesota was a state.'

'Doesn't look like it was ever farmed.'

'Nah. They tried all sorts of things. Scottish Highland cattle – you know those midget cows with the long hair? Then buffalo, believe it or not, which was a big mistake. Goddamn buffalo is a plains animal. Needs grassland, not trees. They finally settled on goats, turned them loose in the woods and let them do what God intended, and holy moly, they were making goat cheese before you knew it. Never cared much for it, myself. Too sour. But they did a land-office business until Martin dropped dead stirring a vat of curds. Ethel went a few years later, and the kids sold the place off. Six kids, and not a farmer among them. Kind of a pity.'

Grace looked down at the dog collapsed at her feet. 'He was digging like crazy out there. That's what made him so tired. In all the years I've had him, I never once saw Charlie even think about digging a hole in the backyard.'

Walt shoved his hands in his overall pockets. 'Doesn't surprise me. Giddings buried the dead goats in the woods – some of them old, some sick, some stillborn. A dog would smell such a thing. Must be a hundred dead goats under the ground out there.'

Grace made a face. 'So it's a goat cemetery.'

'I suppose.' He looked down at Charlie's collars and tags and the smooth pads on his feet that hadn't seen a lot of rough ground travel. 'You know, you might want to keep this dog a little closer to home, especially after dark. There isn't much out here a country dog couldn't handle, but we do see the occasional bear and then there's the lion.'

Grace stared at him. 'Lion? Like a cougar or something?'

'Nope. One of those big ones with the mane, like you see in zoos.'

'An African lion?'

Walt gave her a crooked smile. 'Bet you're thinking I'm a crazy old man right about now.'

'The thought never occurred to me,' Grace lied.

'There's a wildlife preserve not too far from here. They rescue all kinds of exotic animals from bad situations, give them a second chance at a better life. One of their lions got loose a few years back, and they've never been able to recapture him.'

'How could it survive in this climate?'

'Animals are a heck of a lot more adaptable than people. There's a black jaguar still living free somewhere up near Washington County, and that's a jungle cat. They've been trying to trap him for years. You must have seen that on the news.'

'I don't watch television very often.'

'Good for you. But ever since they put those cameras in cell phones, people have been snapping his picture all over the damn place. Truth is, a lot of idiots lock up a lot of things that shouldn't be in cages, and occasionally one gets out and raises all kinds of hell. Goes after pets and livestock and the like.'

Grace thought about that for a moment. 'That has to be illegal.'

'Some exotic animals are licensed, some aren't. I called the Department of Natural Resources about it last year, but they haven't been able to track him yet. Not sure they've been trying too hard, truth be known. Wildcats will take down deer, and they're too plentiful here right now for a healthy population. Plus they've got their hands full with the zebra mussels in the lakes, and the emerald ash borer, killing trees left and right.'

Grace had no idea what he was talking about, and she wasn't about to ask.

'Invasive species, is what they call them,' Walt explained. 'Stuff from faraway places never meant to be here in the first place, wreaking havoc on native plants and animals. Kills the natural balance of things. Like the kudzu in the South.'

'Oh. I remember kudzu from my days in Georgia, strangling all the magnolia trees.'

'Yep.' He looked up as the crystalline, plaintive cry of a loon pierced the air. Grace thought it was one of the saddest sounds in the world.

'Loons down on the lake. Minnesota state bird, you know. They're raising young now, and they cry a lot, just like every parent doing the same thing.'

Grace felt a pull in her heart, thinking of Walt Junior, thinking of Marla, thinking of the hell Walt must have endured for the past two months and the years before that. She wondered what it was going to be like to have something so critically important in your life that it would shatter you completely if it was ever taken away, like blood or oxygen. Without thought or awareness, she crossed her arms over her belly, protecting the little person inside.

'This is your first child, isn't it?'

Grace met his eyes and nodded. 'Yes.'

'It's the best thing that'll ever happen to you. No matter what.'

'I hope we can help you, Walt,' she finally said quietly.

He turned his head and looked at her, the weak moonlight glancing off the sharp planes of his weathered face. 'You already have, just in the trying. And truth be told, it's nice to have people in and around the house again. I thank you all for your company, but I thank you most of all for asking the question everybody else pussyfoots around.'

'What's that?'

'You asked about Walt Junior, and it was good to share him with you. People don't want to bring up bad things like a child dying, and I guess that's natural. Afraid of stirring up bad memories, I suppose. But if you don't talk about the people you've loved and lost, they just fade away.'

Grace thought about the people she'd loved and lost and never talked about and wondered if she'd condemned them to anonymity. 'You have a healthy relationship with death.'

'No choice if you live on a farm because you see it almost every day in one way or another. Death is a part of life. Always has been, always will be. But I suspect you aren't sitting here because you want to hear an old man's philosophical ramblings about mortality.'

'I wanted to bring you up to date on Marla's case. Our computer is sorting through all the material we uploaded from Sheriff Emmet's investigation, and while that's working, we're going through everything by hand. I'm going to ask the sheriff to take me out to the crime scene tomorrow, and after that, we'll probably leave.'

Walt nodded. 'How long before you know it's a lost cause?'

Grace looked at him directly. 'Marla will never be a lost cause. Not to you and not to us.'

And that was the moment. Crickets and frogs and a

quarter moon in a starry sky, and then the gunshot. It speared through the peaceful country night like a knife through flesh, and Grace was in a crouch in a millisecond, the Sig miraculously in her hand and the safety off.

Walt watched the transformation sadly, wondering what terrible thing had taught her to dodge shadows like that. 'A shotgun,' he said quietly, trying to bring Grace MacBride off the ledge of whatever fears she lived with, back into reality. 'Corn's just coming in,' he said. 'This time of year, a lot of farmers bring in a few rows of young corn plants for silage, load them up in the corncrib, and the raccoons close in.'

Grace was frozen in place, her hand sweaty on the Sig's grip, barely aware of Walt's words.

'Even before the cobs form, the smell of the leaves brings the coons to the cribs, and you get a clear shot at them without losing too much of your crop.'

Something familiar registered in Grace's mind, something she'd learned as a child or seen on TV, and she flicked on the safety and looked at Walt.

'They ambush them?'

'Yep. Shotgun spray gets a lot of them at once.'

She slid the Sig back into its holster, making Walt take a deep breath.

'Sounds brutal, but it's kind of a war. Either the coons die or we starve. That's the way of the world.'

The Chariot was silent, except for the low, almost indiscernible hum of the air-conditioning. The only light came from the big back war room. The light was blue, and so was the top of Roadrunner's head as it was cradled in his arms in front of his computer. She didn't have the heart to wake him.

Harley's bedroom door was closed, but his snoring advertised a deep, healthy sleep she wouldn't disturb. Annie's door was cracked a bit to catch the night-light from the main corridor, and Grace could hear the rhythmic slosh of the ocean waves soundtrack she used every night of her life to block out city sounds and put herself to sleep.

But there were no city sounds here. She found her own bed and cracked a window to listen to the sounds of a country night, different from the sounds at Magozzi's lake house. Charlie was stretched into a long hot dog shape, pressed against her leg, his own paws jerking spasmodically every now and then as he chased a rabbit or a squirrel in his dreams.

Maybe Harley had been right after all, she thought, remembering what he'd said about doing something a little closer to home, something a little more personal.

Walt lost his wife a few years ago, and his son before that, and I'd like to help find out what happened to his daughter, give an old man some peace in his final years.

Taking a step back from the dark side of their work certainly offered another perspective. It was a sad venture, trying to find out what had happened to Marla, especially after you got to know Walt. It rarely happened in the course of the work they did. They were always tracking down killers, following digitized clues on computers that never really involved you in the tragedy and horror of the crimes themselves.

Cops were always deeply involved as they looked for

some nameless, faceless fiend, but it was all so antiseptic when you followed tracks through a computer screen instead of reality. This time they were getting an in-person look at the wreckage those fiends left behind, and that single connection was profound. It was the first time that Grace felt what she was doing was personal, and because of that, important in an entirely different way.

She wondered if that was what Magozzi felt all the time. There were women dying in the Cities at the hands of a madman, and he lived through the aftermath with all their loved ones he had to notify. The Beast would work on that case while she slept, and that was the level of detachment that defined their usual work. But out here there was a daughter missing from a farmhouse and a father and a community of people who had cared deeply about her. Families forever missed the members taken from them, but in a small community like this, the missing weren't just missing, they left a big hole in the world. You simply had to find them, no matter what.

She rolled onto her side and cradled her belly, feeling the tiny life inside; a perfect, innocent life, still safe from the world and all the horrors that lurked in the shadows, waiting to strike without mercy, without prejudice. She suddenly thought of Gino and his cherished family and wondered how he reconciled his job with his normal life once he was home at night. And how would Magozzi? How was it even possible?

Eventually, she fell asleep to the haunting cry of loons on Walt's lake, thinking that they, too, were mourning Marla, or maybe they were mourning all the lost souls.

Thirty-one

As Magozzi drove into City Hall the next morning, with a notably silent Gino – either ruminating or sleeping in the passenger seat – his weary mind meandered back to elementary school and the fitness test that always came at the end of the year. Of all the drills they had to complete, foremost in his memory were those long lengths of knotted rope you had to shimmy up to earn your stripes as a hard-core, fourth-grade athlete.

He'd hated those fucking ropes. You hit one knot, and then there were ten more to conquer, and all the while, your skinny, preadolescent biceps were already shaking, and the jeers of classmates below you crescendoed. It had only been the sheer terror of humiliation that had motivated him up to the top every time, beyond the ability of his strength. No way he was going to be the only loser who couldn't scale a stupid rope.

This case was turning out to be like that. He and Gino had reached the first couple of knots and now they'd hit the next goddamned knot, and then there would be all the rest of the knots to follow if they didn't get their shit together and figure this thing out. It was arduous, it was thankless, it was unrelenting, but instead of fourth-grade classmates jeering, it was the public and the media and the victims' surviving family members. Life kept sucking in all the same ways it always had; maybe he should at least be grateful for the consistency.

Gino finally stirred to life when his new phone groaned a faux foghorn from his pocket.

'Seriously, Gino? A foghorn? That's annoying.'

'Wasn't supposed to be a foghorn, it was supposed to be a steam whistle.'

'How is that any less annoying?'

Gino gave him a sour look, then passed the look down to his phone's screen. 'It's McLaren. He sent a text . . . and a picture.'

'Yeah? Of what?'

Gino fiddled for a few moments, navigating his new interface with chubby fingers. 'Two Siamese kittens in a basket full of yarn. Oh, man, and here's the caption – "SUPER CUTE!" All caps, by the way. Exclamation point. "Snowball and Snowflake want U at HQ ASAP! NEWS!"' He snuffled and pocketed his phone. 'Jesus, that guy is totally unhinged.'

Magozzi turned onto Fifth and headed toward City Hall. 'Never figured McLaren for a cat guy.'

'Are you kidding me? The guy's nuts for animals. He'd take in a Komodo dragon, then slap reindeer antlers on it and take a family portrait for his Christmas card . . . Aw, shit. Look at that.'

As they closed in on City Hall, they saw satellite vans gobbling up every spare parking spot within a three-block radius, which made sense. What didn't make sense was that there were no reporters, no camera operators anywhere. Not outside, on the nearly empty front steps, and not inside, where the hallways echoed. If anything, they should have at least been ambushed by the guerrilla warfare specialist Amanda White.

'Where the hell is everybody?' Gino asked. 'I mean, I'm not complaining, but this is weird.'

'Alien abduction, I hope.'

As they trudged toward the office with the verve of a couple of three-toed sloths, McLaren caught up with them in the hallway and paced them to their desks. 'Hey, guys, did you catch some sleep?'

'Probably more than you,' Gino said, transfixed by the sight of McLaren's paisley tie. It had swirls of lavender and green on a beige background, the kind of pattern that could trigger a seizure. 'How did it go last night after we left?'

'Pretty good, actually. The FBI forensics dudes were straight up, not arrogant pricks like some of their colleagues in suits.'

'So nobody messed with you.'

'Nobody messes with anybody partnered up with Eaton, he's scary-looking as hell. Come on, get your butts in your chairs and let me tell you a little breaking news.'

Gino rubbed his hands together and eagerly obeyed the command to sit down. 'Anytime, McLaren.'

'Okay. As of half an hour ago, the Feds and the DEA are crawling all over Global Foods, the media's not even there yet. The owner got dragged out in cuffs, and the FBI is pulling out box after box of stuff. There are a couple other raids going on across the city, too. Drugs.'

Gino looked truly alert for the first time in three days. 'No wonder the Feds didn't want us poking around at

Global Foods and spooking anybody. They were on the eve of a bust.'

'I called my inside guy, who told me the Feds think Global Foods was a storefront for one of the Mexican cartels – kind of a distribution center. Product came in on trucks carrying legitimate produce from south of the border. There have been undercover agents and surveillance in and around the place for the better part of a year. Our vic last night was an FBI agent, just like we figured, a plant inside the store. He thinks she got burned and somebody pulled the kill switch on her.'

'If this lady was a target and not a pleasure kill, that would explain all the anomalies at the crime scene last night,' Gino said. 'But it doesn't explain why there was a card at the scene, unless our serial killer has a day job as a hit man.'

Magozzi tried to ignore the exhaustion spots that were floating behind his eyes. 'The first guy I'd look at is the owner of the store, and he happens to be in jail right now.'

'Oh, man, wouldn't that be something if our serial was already in the can?'

Gino ran his hands through his blond buzz cut like he wanted to tear it out follicle by follicle. 'The Feds probably have him in a meat grinder right now – they lost one of their own and they're not going to show any mercy. But we never get that lucky. Besides, the owner of a big store like that, running drugs for the cartels on the side, he's a busy guy. I don't see him spending his nonexistent free time hanging out in parks all night, waiting for brunettes to jog by so he can kill them.'

McLaren conceded with a nod. 'Yeah, I don't like it,

either. And when you think about it, the card is the only thing that connects last night's scene to our others, and that's pretty thin without any other supporting evidence. I don't know – maybe we should revisit the idea of the card detail getting leaked. Somebody tried to cover a hit by framing a serial killer.'

Magozzi forlornly swirled his nearly empty coffee mug, regarding it as a barfly might regard his drained shot glass after last call. 'Maybe the card did get leaked. It happens, especially with the media getting so damned nosy and aggressive. Speaking of the media, Gino and I saw all the news vans when we came in, but this place is like a crypt. Where the hell is everybody?'

McLaren sucked in his cheeks and regarded his chewed-down fingernails. 'Somebody very brilliant and good-looking corralled them into the press room to wait for a statement from Malcherson.'

'Malcherson's going to make a statement?' Magozzi asked.

McLaren just shrugged. 'I'm sure he will eventually. Tomorrow, maybe the next day.'

Gino snorted. 'Does that somebody know the air-conditioning ducts in the press room have been off-line for a week?'

'No kidding? God, it must be hot in there.' Johnny looked up and waved when Eaton Freedman strolled into Homicide, carrying a manila folder and a sixteen-ounce bottle of Mountain Dew. He sank down into a metal folding chair next to Gino's desk that was at least five times too small to accommodate his frame, loosened his tie, and mopped the sheen off his dark brow with a handkerchief. 'This heat's gotta break pretty soon.'

'I sure as hell hope so.' Magozzi cocked a brow at the Mountain Dew. 'There was a dark and medieval time not so long ago when you couldn't buy one of those in New York City.'

Freedman took a swig and wiped his mouth. 'Sorrowful thing when a mayor thinks his people are too stupid to do the math and buy two eight-ounce bottles instead.'

'What's in the envelope?'

Freedman patted it. 'This very slim envelope contains what the FBI is releasing to us for now, but don't get all excited. It's mainly an inventory of trace found at the scene last night – the usual crap you'd expect to find in a city parking lot. I'll start slogging through it, see if anything compares from our lists of trace. Idle hands are the devil's workshop. You with me, partner?' he asked Johnny.

'Give me ten. I'm going to needle my Fed connection and see if there's any news on the real investigation going on behind our backs.'

After Freedman and McLaren went back to their desks, Gino pulled out a thermos from his satchel and poured hot coffee into Magozzi's mug, then topped off his own. 'Smells weird, but it tastes good. Angela's on these flavored coffees lately. I don't know why people want to put shit like vanilla and hazelnuts into coffee, but who the hell cares if it's got the same amount of caffeine?'

'Right now, I don't care. Thanks.' Magozzi started jotting down notes while he sipped the highly perfumed coffee. It wasn't half-bad.

'What are you writing?'

'Some thoughts. This cartel thing at Global Foods is itching me.'

'What about it?'

'The missing persons case Monkeewrench is working on. Grace told me there was blood at the scene that CODIS matched to a gangbanger with a cartel association.'

Gino shrugged. 'Yeah? The cartels are everywhere, Global Foods is a perfect case in point. Besides, any given homicide or violent crime, there's at least a fifty-fifty chance gangs and drugs are involved. Actually, it's probably more like eighty-twenty.'

'But we're talking two different criminal cases where cartel involvement is front and center, and that's unusual. They usually stay deep in the shadows with the other cockroaches and let local gangs do their dirty work for them. I don't like it.'

'You've got a point there. What do you know about Monkeewrench's case?'

'Not much. Just the basics.'

'Well, it's a place to go, and I'm all for following gut instinct. We'd never solve a case without it. Plus, it's better than sitting here dieseling, which is what we've been doing for the past couple days.'

'I'll call Grace. Check in with Lon Cather, give him a heads-up on the Global Foods situation.'

Thirty-two

Magozzi dialed Grace's cell phone before he tried the satellite phone, just in case whatever rural place Monkeewrench was situated in had a cell tower nearby. Apparently it did, because she answered on the second ring.

'Magozzi.'

'Hi, Grace, how are you?'

'Pregnant.'

Magozzi's mouth crooked in a smile. Grace had always possessed a light side, but it remained mostly obscured by the penumbra of her dark past. But pregnancy seemed to have lifted some of the shadow. 'You're kidding? How the hell did that happen?'

He heard Grace snuffle, which was about as close as she ever got to a chuckle. 'I don't know, I didn't pay attention in biology class. Listen, Magozzi, the Beast isn't kicking out anything on your serial yet and we're having the same bad luck with our missing persons case. Tell me you're doing better.'

'I wish I could, but we have another body. Six of spades.'

Magozzi heard a soft sigh on the other end of the line before Grace whispered, 'Oh, no. Tell me about it.'

Magozzi took a breath, pausing a moment to think about how odd this conversation was. How many other lovers and prospective parents chatted about bodies and serial killers? Shouldn't they be discussing plushy toys and whether or not the kid should be baptized? 'First, give me some good news, tell me about your ever-expanding waistline and the current disposition of our child. Still kicking?'

'Fighting all the time.'

'Taking after you?'

'Don't diminish your fifty percent contribution to the gene pool. So tell me.'

Magozzi was still smiling, which seemed absolutely inappropriate given the information he was about to deliver, but when had life ever been anything but a sketch in light and dark? Suffer the dark, go to the light whenever it's there. 'Our latest victim was a checkout clerk at Global Foods – or so we thought – but it turns out she was under-cover FBI working with the DEA on a cartel drug sting.'

'You're kidding me,' Grace interrupted. 'I shop there all the time.'

'Not anymore. Apparently, Global Foods was a distri-bution center, so the place is shut down and the Feds mostly locked us out. We're working tandem, but they're only sending us bits and pieces at this point.'

'Pass on whatever you have and we'll add it to our search.'

'I'll have a package coming your way soon. But we're not sure it's our serial. There are a lot of discrepancies in the MO.'

'Copycat?'

'Maybe. You said you had some blood at your scene that CODIS traced to a gangbanger with a cartel associ-ation, right?'

'Right. His name is Diego Sanchez. The last time he was on the radar anywhere before his blood turned up at our scene was three years ago, in Laredo, Texas. He was arrested on multiple drug charges and eventually got deported for the fourth time.'

'He obviously made a fifth return trip to the States. Do you think he's your perp?'

'The locals don't think so and neither do we. There was a lot of Sanchez's blood at the immediate scene on the road where our missing person's car was found – her name is Marla, by the way, Marla Gustafson – but dogs tracked Marla into the woods, and there was no blood trail. No blood at all.' She paused for a moment. 'Are you trying to pull this all together?'

'We're just covering every angle.'

'We can merge our searches if you want.'

'What does that mean?'

'Link up your search with ours and route everything to the Beast. It might slow everything down a little, but if you think there might be a payoff, then it's worth it.'

'We'd appreciate it. Thank you.' Magozzi's peripheral vision caught Gino's flailing arms as he tried to get his attention. 'Grace, I have to go, Gino wants to play charades.'

'Good luck, Magozzi. We'll be in touch.'

Magozzi hung up. 'Windmill.'

Gino dropped his arms. 'You can be one snide and annoying son of a bitch when you're tired, you know that? I've got Jimmy Grimm on the line.' He put his phone on speaker. 'JG, my man. Tell me you've got some love for us.'

'I've got all kinds of love for you. Are the Feds playing nice?'

'Oh, yeah. They shut us out of last night's crime scene and they're spoon-feeding us bullshit lists of trace like we're colicky babies. Other than that, we're working together really well.'

Jimmy snorted. 'Figured. They're busting everybody's rump. Listen, I just sent you some lab results on that blood from the thornbush at Charlotte Wells's crime scene, pull it up. Turns out it matched some fresh blood we sampled from Katya Smirnova's scene in Phalen Park. Still doesn't mean the blood belongs to your doer, but I'd say the odds just got a hell of a lot better.'

Magozzi let out a disappointed sigh. 'But that blood didn't get a hit on any database.'

'Right. Whoever bled in the dog park and Phalen isn't in the system. But his father is.'

Gino was staring at his computer screen. 'You've got to be shitting me. Jimmy, I'm looking at what you sent right now. It's alphanumeric soup.'

'DNA results. I called in a favor and bumped you to the front of the line to get a more detailed analysis, and bingo – they came up with a matching DNA sample from a knifing eighteen years ago. Long story short, the Y chromosome tests peg your blood from the dog park and Saint Paul's from Phalen as belonging to that perp's son.'

Magozzi rubbed his forehead, his mind riding a manic Tilt-A-Whirl. 'Are they sure?'

'Genes don't lie. If you can get a bead on the father and figure out who the son is, maybe you've got your man. Of course, there's no telling how many sons this guy has, but at least it's a starting point. Good luck. Call if you need anything else.'

Gino hung up and jumped back on his computer. 'This could be a break, Leo. We've got some flesh to gnaw on now.'

Magozzi pulled his chair up next to Gino's desk. 'Do you have to use food-related metaphors when you talk about gruesome homicide cases?'

'Everything in my life revolves around food, I can't help it. Okay, here we go. Ernesto Cruz. That's our bad daddy, and I'm running his case number right now. It's going to be a couple minutes, so tell me what Grace said.'

'She's merging our search with theirs in case there's some connection.'

'What about the blood on the road?'

'Belongs to a guy named Diego Sanchez. Career criminal with a rap sheet longer than the tax code. He got deported after a drug bust in Laredo three years ago.'

Gino ruminated for a moment, slurping his vanilla almond coffee. 'But he's not our guy, otherwise CODIS would have lit up like Times Square on New Year's Eve.'

'Did you reach Cather?'

'Yeah, I brought him up to speed and forwarded everything new we have. He's still working the casino angle.'

Magozzi tapped Gino's computer screen. 'Here we go, Ernesto Cruz's case file is loaded. Let's find out who this guy is.'

Thirty-three

Sheriff Jacob Emmet was sitting on the bed where his father had spent most of his last year on this earth, eating canned fruit cocktail and Jell-O and little else while his mind and body slowly faded to black. He'd moved Pop down here to his own childhood bedroom, the only one on the main floor, once the stairs had become untenable for him. Six months later, when things had gotten really bad, he'd moved him into hospice care, where he died a week later.

He smoothed the old coverlet, worn and frayed, then laid his head back on a pillow, remembering the many stages of youth here. There had once been posters of Michael Jordan and Brett Favre plastering the walls, along with a few super-models whose names he'd already forgotten.

He'd received some very harsh reprimands here from Sheriff Elijah Emmet back in the day, when he'd been a hormone-drunk, frisky high school football and basket-ball star, a little too fond of drinking cheap beer and wooing the girls in to see his room.

Marla had been the one girl who'd never given in to his clumsy advances, hard as he'd tried to convince her otherwise. And Jacob had taken that as a good omen – she was a gem, a real keeper, and he'd always seen his future eventually coinciding with hers, up until the day he first investigated her disappearance two months ago.

Good times and bad. In the same room. In the same house. He'd blown it with Marla in high school, he'd blown it with Marla later, when she was in college and he was at the police academy and their lives never seemed to sync in a way where a real relationship could form. But now he'd really blown it. She was dead, he felt it in his gut. The only thing he could do for Marla now was to find out what had happened to her, and he prayed that Monkeewrench could make that happen.

He jumped when his phone rang, as if to remind him that indulging in self-pity was unbecoming of an officer and a gentleman. 'Sheriff Emmet.'

'Good afternoon, Sheriff. This is Gino Rolseth out of Minneapolis Homicide.'

His heart stammered a little, thinking of Marla. Jesus. He wasn't ready. 'Detective. What can I do for you?'

'I'm calling about an attempted homicide case you had in Cottonwood County back in '95. Were you on the job then?'

Jacob let out a sigh of relief. 'Just barely. My father was sheriff back then, though.'

'Would he be available to talk?'

'He passed a few months ago.'

There was a slight lag in the conversation. 'Oh. I'm sorry to hear that.'

'Thanks. Listen, most of our files from back then are still on paper. What case are you asking about?'

'The perpetrator's name was Ernesto Cruz. He knifed a man half to death over some kind of scuffle and did some time. Does that name ring a bell?'

'Name doesn't ring a bell, but the case sure does. Back then you could count violent crimes in Cottonwood

County on one hand. If memory serves, it happened at a seasonal camp where the orchard workers used to stay during fall harvest. I can dig up the old files for you. My father kept copies of all his handwritten notes, too, if that will help.'

'I really appreciate that, Sheriff Emmet. What's the name of the orchard?'

'It was called Country Sun Apples, but it's long gone. Closed going on a couple decades.' Jacob left the bedroom and went into Pop's old office, where wooden file cabinets lined the walls, each drawer meticulously marked by year. 'Anything specific you're looking for?'

'Actually, we're trying to find out who Ernesto Cruz's son is, but there are no records of him anywhere. He's a person of interest in some pending priority cases up here.'

Jacob pulled open the 1995 file drawer and started ruffling through yellowed folders. 'The women in the parks?'

'Yeah.'

'Hang on, Detective, I'm looking at the file right now.'

Ten minutes later, Gino hung up with a flourish. 'Okay, buddy, here's the story. Ernesto Cruz was a seasonal laborer, here on a work permit from Mexico back in '95. And check this out – he got lit up one night during a poker game and took some deep swipes at his friend with a bowie knife, whacked up his torso pretty good and almost killed him. Sound familiar?'

Magozzi's mouth tightened. 'I see where you're going. What happened to him?'

'After he did his time here, he got deported back to Mexico. It's a blank slate after that.'

'Any mention of Cruz's family in the sheriff's records?'

'Nothing. No wife or kids on record or at his trial.'

'That doesn't mean much. Maybe they hightailed it back home when Cruz got into trouble with the law. Maybe they weren't even here at the time.'

Gino propped his elbows on the desk and folded his hands together to make a resting place for his chin. 'Cruz might not even know he has a kid, although the knifing over the poker game and our serial's MO makes me wonder. Bottom line is, we have to find Ernesto Cruz and question him, and that's going to be damn near impossible if he's in Mexico. You know what it's like trying to get fast answers out of the Federales. Their homicide rate is double ours at least, half of them are in bed with the cartels, and it looks like that's the beehive we're about to poke.'

Magozzi looked over at McLaren, who was busy at his desk, dragging his hands through his mess of red hair and making it stand up like a miniature fire spreading over his scalp. 'Hey, McLaren, is Spanish one of the forty-seven languages you speak?'

'That's a supreme insult. I was fluent in Spanish when I was five.'

'Are you tight with anybody in the Federales?'

'Everyone's tight with the Federales until they decide to ignore you. Or shoot you.'

'We need to locate Ernesto Cruz . . .'

'That's the father of our serial killer, right?'

'We're assuming, and we just found out he was deported back to Mexico after his sentence here.'

'I'm already on it.'

McLaren spent the next forty-five minutes on the phone, then retrieved a sheet of paper from his printer and slid it across the rugged, paper-littered terrain of Magozzi's desk. 'Ernesto Cruz is dead. He and a few of his friends got killed in Ciudad Juárez five years ago, execution style. And if you don't already know, Ciudad Juárez is the drug cartel version of Dante's seventh circle of Hell.'

Gino grunted. 'So Ernesto Cruz decided seasonal work wasn't his gig after all. How about family?'

'No wife or kids associated with him on any paperwork south of the border, either. And that's all I could get before the guy I was talking to decided he was too busy for me.'

'Touched a nerve?' Magozzi asked.

'That was my impression. When you talk to the law down there, it's even odds you're talking to somebody who's getting squeezed or paid off by a cartel one way or another. My best guess is the family business didn't end when Ernesto Cruz got killed.'

Gino tossed a pen across his desk. 'We've got cartels popping like flashbangs at a riot, but no solid connection to our serial except for Daddy's DNA, which wouldn't make it to a courtroom in a thousand years. Hell, we don't really know that the blood at the scenes belonged to our serial, or how many kids Ernesto Cruz had in the first place. The blood only proves that one of his kids enjoys the Minneapolis park system.'

'Let's send the DNA profile to Interpol,' McLaren suggested. 'Maybe Cruz Junior was operating somewhere internationally and we can track him that way.'

'Already done,' Magozzi said. 'Nothing popped on Interpol. They have about a hundred and fifteen thousand DNA profiles, and our serial's not one of them.'

Thirty-four

Lon Cather had just made his third loop of the major Saint Paul parks that had jogging or walking paths and a lot of tree coverage, hoping to see something he hadn't seen before.

He had no delusions of grandeur, imagining himself as the one who would collar the guy in the act, especially with the stepped-up heat from extra street patrols and park police. The pressure had more than likely chased their perp away, at least temporarily, which is probably what had happened in Minneapolis and sent their man east across the Mississippi River to Phalen Park. Tomorrow or the next day, he might be in Wisconsin or Iowa or Ohio, at some other park. This trip had an entirely different purpose, which was to look through a new prism to try to get inside a hunter's mind.

Think about your quarry, Lon, that's first. You have to know where to find it, then you have to figure out what their special spot might be, based on what you know about the animal. Once you stake out their position of highest vulnerability, you need patience, silence, and good cover. That's your only advantage, because prey can pretty much do anything better than a human except think and plan.

Words of wisdom from good old Uncle Rudy when he'd taken him up north for his first and last deer hunt. Rudy had gotten a big old buck that had looked a hell of a lot better browsing peacefully in the woods than it did plastered above Rudy's mantel that Christmas Eve, and Lon had never seen life or death the same way after that. But Rudy's perspective was universal – it was the way a serial killer thought, and it was the way a good cop hunting a serial killer should think.

As he wound his car back to his starting point at Phalen Park, his cell rang – Junior Liman calling from Eagle Lake. 'Junior, tell me you have something for me.'

'You sound desperate, my friend. Is all the media getting to you?'

'I could give a shit about the media. What I do give a shit about is four dead women and a freak still on the loose.'

'I hear you. Listen, I did what I could, plowed through all our casino footage from the past two weeks and compared it to the film you brought down. I found something interesting.'

Lon veered over to the curb and parked in front of a busy Dairy Queen where a Little League team was clambering out of a couple of minivans, trampling each other to get to the walk-up window first. Maybe he'd get an Oreo Blizzard for dessert when he was finished with his call. 'Give it to me, Junior.'

'Okay, by your calculations and mine, the blurry figure of the creep sneaking into Phalen Park was a shrimp – five-six at best. Right now I'm looking at a split screen of that footage compared with casino surveillance video taken eleven days ago. And I'm seeing another shrimpy creep about the same height, same stocky build, sitting at the highest stakes poker table we have. He's wearing a

Nike baseball cap and drinking a Budweiser. The guy never looks up, never shows his face, even when he gets up and walks away.

'My first thought was, big deal, you could walk into any casino in the country and find fifty guys who match that description. But I showed the footage to the dealer, and he remembered him, said he'd been in a couple times before. He also said he was spooky – kept his head down, never made eye contact with anyone, never said a word, always bought in with cash – a lot of it.'

'No paper trail, then.'

'No. But here's the real story – the guy had a tatt on his neck. The dealer recognized it and so did I. Three dots above two bars.'

'What the hell does that mean?'

'Mayan numerology for the number thirteen. It probably means this guy is Sureño – Mexican Mafia, aka cartel thug. I've got security on high alert in case he shows again.'

Lon leaned back in his seat and stared at a Little Leaguer shoving a chocolate-covered ice cream cone into his mouth. 'Jesus Christ, are you kidding me?'

'The cartels are in every major city in the U.S. and probably most of the minor ones, you know that. And talk about an incubator for sociopaths – these guys come up as kids and they're stone killers. After decapitating a couple dozen people and hanging them from a bridge, a few women in some parks are probably like dessert.'

Lon looked away from the Dairy Queen then, abandoning all hope of an Oreo Blizzard for dessert. 'Yeah, I know that, it's just that this is setting off all kinds of alarms.'

'I'm happy to hear that. I'll send you my casino footage to put in your book. Go get him and bring him down hard.'

'Thanks, Junior. Be in touch.'

'You, too.' Lon hung up and started dialing Detective Magozzi.

Thirty-five

Roadrunner was in the war room of the Chariot, which was a back bedroom he and Harley had retrofitted into a mobile computer lab that was fully linked to all the office hardware via satellite, including the Beast. There wasn't any task they couldn't perform from the road, and as he looked out at the shiny waving green leaves of young corn and the pastures dotted with cows, he began to wonder why they didn't chew up the asphalt more often, just for a change of venue.

As he flicked his sleeping touch screen to refresh it, the satellite phone rang and went to safety screening mode. No matter how many times he changed the protocol, it still occasionally got electronic intrusions, sometimes from foreign hackers trying to mine their software, sometimes from one government agency or another, trying to do exactly the same thing. The first and best line of defense was voice recognition, and right now, his screen was telling him that this was a legit call from one of the few outside friendlies the software recognized, specifically Magozzi.

He waited for the caller to enter the requisite password for connection, then picked up when the caller was verified as authentic. 'Magozzi?'

'Hey, Roadrunner. Is everything okay on your end?'

'Grace is fine. We're all fine. Actually, it's pretty cool out here in the sticks. I'm sitting in the war room, watching cows and cornstalks waving in the breeze. Sounds wildly exciting, right?'

'You don't have to convince me, Roadunner, I'm the guy who bought a lake house in the sticks and I get excited watching herons and wood ducks. Listen, we need to talk. Are we secure?'

'Totally secure.'

Magozzi hesitated. 'You're positive?'

Roadrunner smiled a little. Most people couldn't wrap their minds around an ironclad security system, let alone understand how it worked. 'I'm positive, Magozzi. The Chariot scrambles and destroys everything coming or going. I wrote the program specifically to fly under Big Brother's radar.'

'That's exactly what we need to do. Okay, here's the deal – Grace told you about our new case and that the Feds are involved now, right?'

'Yeah, of course. Global Foods. What are the Feds saying?'

'Not much, but we're suddenly up to our eyeballs in cartel connections, which includes your blood on the road at Marla Gustafson's scene. We'd be grateful if you could take a look, throw it into the hopper.'

'That's a given, Grace is already merging our cases, so send whatever else you've got. Anything specific you want us to focus on, or is this just a general data dump?'

'A name – Ernesto Cruz, deceased. Mexican national who did jail time in Cottonwood County back in the mid-nineties and got deported after time served. He was killed in a presumed cartel hit in Ciudad Juárez a couple years ago, and we've got his DNA profile matching blood at two of our scenes that says he's the father of our serial killer. We need to find his kid or kids, but as far as we can tell they don't exist anywhere.'

Roadrunner pressed his fingers hard against his temples as he sorted through the information Magozzi was throwing at him. 'Wow, okay, we've got something to work with. Did you talk to the Federales?'

'McLaren had a conversation with them, but when he started pressing about Cruz's family, they shut up.'

'Hmm. I think I have an idea . . . wait a minute. Did you say Cottonwood County?'

'Yeah, why?'

'Because Cottonwood County is exactly where we are right now.'

Gino eyed his partner worriedly as he hung up with Roadrunner. 'You went all tense there at the end, Leo. Is Grace okay?'

'They're all fine. You know where they are?'

'Buttonwillow.'

'Buttonwillow's in Cottonwood County.'

'Whoa. Things are starting to pile up . . .' Gino looked at his watch and cursed. 'Leo, I'm really sorry, but I've got to take an hour, I promised Angela I'd go to the Accident's kindergarten roundup.'

'Go, go, go, it only happens once in a kid's life. I'll handle this. Meet me at my house when you're finished so we can get the hell out of the office while we try to tie this together.'

'Sounds good . . .'

Magozzi's phone interrupted. 'Hang on, Gino, it's Lon Cather. Talk fast, Detective, Gino's on his way out the door.'

Thirty-six

An hour later, Gino was camped out in Magozzi's living room, eating a slice of pizza and drinking a beer while he scribbled on a big whiteboard he'd set up on an easel. Magozzi had casually wondered why Gino had a whiteboard and an easel in the trunk of his car when he'd pulled them out in the first place, but was afraid to ask for fear it had something to do with the Accident's kindergarten roundup today.

He poured himself a glass of scotch and brought out a bowl of tortilla chips from the kitchen. 'How's it going?'

Gino gave him a look of exasperation. 'Don't pull that crap. You want to know why I had this stuff in my trunk, you know you do.'

'Not really.'

'Sure you do. It's driving you crazy, so I'm going to tell you. This piece-of-shit whiteboard is exactly one-half inch too long for a regulation kindergarten whiteboard – one frigging half inch. Are you kidding me? We're not talking pro sports here, we're talking kindergarten, for God's sake. Are they afraid that extra half inch is going to send them over the edge, or what?'

Magozzi was a little shocked by how ludicrous it seemed, but he didn't respond; even a grunt would have been interpreted as encouragement.

'Nope, this just won't do, and don't even think about

mentioning chalkboards to those fascists, because you have to use chalk on chalkboards, and God forbid some kid gets dust up his nose and sneezes. And you wanna tell me what does a kindergartner need with three-ring binders? They can't even pick them up in their little hands yet.'

'You're supposed to buy three-ring binders?'

'Yeah, that and about forty other things. The schools don't pay for shit anymore. Next year, they'll probably ask him to bring his own desk and chair and charge him rent. I'd like to know where the hell my tax dollars are going, because last time I checked, they've gone up every year for a decade, and there's still a pothole in my alley the size of a moon crater that I've been complaining about for two years. I'm telling you, the world is falling apart one whiteboard at a time.'

Magozzi selected a slice of pizza from the greasy box that was sitting on his floor. 'Other than that, how's it going?'

Gino brightened. 'A helluva lot better than if we'd stayed at the office. I've got pizza, I've got beer and tortilla chips, and no distractions. And the best part is, every single scrap of evidence that comes in just puts another bow on my "serial killer with a day job as a hit man" theory.'

'I didn't know that was an actual theory, more of an offhand remark.'

Gino threw him an annoyed look. 'You know what people do when they're resistant to fresh new ideas? They start revising history. I put out that brilliant theory when we found out Cassie Miller was undercover and most likely a hit. It explains the anomalies in the MO and it explains the playing card. Even *you* thought it was brilliant at the time . . .'

'Actually, I didn't.'

' . . . and now you're pretending you thought it was just an offhand remark. Come on, Leo, you used to have an imagination. Work with me.' He grabbed a marker and wrote CARTELS in huge block letters. 'This is the thread I'm going to use to sew this up.'

'I'm listening.'

'Okay, this whole thing starts with our serial killer. We found matching blood in two parks at two separate murder scenes. For the sake of argument, let's say it's for sure our killer's blood.'

'Fair enough.'

'And that blood belongs to a son of Ernesto Cruz, a felon who got snuffed out in a cartel hit, a guy who did time for slicing up his buddy over a poker game. And now we've got Cather's surveillance footage of a cartel thug playing poker at Eagle Lake Casino, the only casino in the state that cuts the tops off their cards, the same kind of cards found on all our serial kills. And size-wise, that dude in the casino matches up with the surveillance footage from Phalen Park the night Katya Smirnova was killed. Enter Global Foods and Cassie Miller, who was working there undercover on a drug bust before she got killed.'

He started writing names and drawing swoopy lines between them, then drew an arrow that pointed to CARTELS. 'There are more connections here than a Wi-Fi hub in Tokyo. I'm telling you, our serial has a day job as a cartel enforcer. He had to kill Cassie Miller under circumstances he couldn't control, so he tried to frame himself the best he could to deflect attention from Global Foods.'

'His serial killer self.'

'Exactly.'

Magozzi took a sip of scotch, thinking that as preposterous as it sounded, Gino actually might be onto something. Cartels had enforcers – the bosses sent them up to watch their operations, make sure nobody skimmed money or product off the top. And operations as big as Global Foods would definitely have at least one enforcer keeping an eye on things. And it was a good bet that those enforcers wouldn't be model citizens or even remotely balanced individuals. They might even be serial killers in their spare time.

He thought again about Monkeewrench's missing persons case in Cottonwood County, where the Cruz family had a history, and about the blood on the road that belonged to another unsavory character with a cartel affiliation. 'You're right,' he finally said. 'Things are piling up. But a serial killer with a day job as a cartel hit man? That's pretty out there, even for you.'

Gino huffed impatiently. 'Are you kidding? It makes perfect sense. Growing up in that life? It's a frigging training camp for sociopaths and serial killers. If you kill for a living, it's not a very big leap to kill for pleasure. Just think about Ciudad Juárez, where Ernesto Cruz got executed and was operating in the drug trade, probably along with his son. Hundreds of women have been ritualistically slaughtered and dumped in and around there. And that doesn't include the hundreds of women still missing.

That's not the work of just one guy. That's not the work of ten guys. There's a reason why it got the nickname Serial Killer's Playground.'

Magozzi swirled his scotch, listening to the soft, calming cadence of melting ice cubes colliding with glass. There were people who thought it was a mortal sin to dilute scotch with ice, but he wasn't one of them. 'I got you.'

'I hope so. You were the one who started this whole thing, pulling out a possible cartel connection early. I just ran with it. So you're with me?'

'I'll keep an open mind.'

Gino chucked his marker into the whiteboard's built-in tray. 'That's the kind of bullshit you say to your kids when they ask you if they can do something stupid.'

'I'll remember that for the future.'

'Come on, Leo, look at the big picture. Sometimes you have to jump right from A to Z to see it.'

'I'm feeling the big picture, and this is all great fodder for speculation, but in the end, all we've really got is an imaginary suspect with imaginary motivations and zero hard evidence.'

Gino sagged into Magozzi's favorite and only recliner. 'You're sucking the oxygen right out of the room.'

Thirty-seven

When Grace returned to the Chariot after taking Charlie for a walk – on-leash this time – Annie was waiting for her up front.

'It's about time you two came back. Harley was about to send out a search party.'

'The rest of you should get away from your computer screens for a while and take a walk. It's a beautiful night.'

Annie folded her arms across her bosom. 'Not on your life. There are bugs and cows and God knows what else out there.'

'Frogs, crickets, a sky full of stars, a half-moon . . .'

'All sinister in my book. I just made some tea if you want some.'

'Thanks.' While Grace poured herself a cup of tea, she suddenly realized the Chariot was oddly silent. 'Why is it so quiet? This is usually about the time Harley and Road-runner start getting on each other's nerves.'

'They're making headway on Ernesto Cruz and it's keeping them out of trouble. Come on, let's see what they've got.'

Grace unclipped Charlie's leash and followed Annie to the war room, where Harley and Roadrunner were hunkered in front of a computer screen.

Harley looked up and waved them over. 'Come take a

look, ladies. We finally cracked into Mexico's national law enforcement database, and damn was it fun.' He nudged Roadrunner's arm. 'We should do this more often.'

Roadrunner scowled. 'This is definitely not something we should do more often.'

Grace pulled a chair between Harley and Roadrunner. It was getting harder and harder to fit her growing bulk into cramped spaces. In another month, it would probably be impossible. 'Show me.'

Roadrunner pointed to the monitor, which showed a split screen. 'On the left is the enhanced composite Harley worked up from the surveillance footage of Gino's and Magozzi's suspect at Phalen Park and Eagle Lake Casino, along with a physical description. We ran it through the Beast's facial and physical recognition database, which is basically every database indexed for search on the Web.'

'You tried that earlier and you didn't get any matches,' Grace noted.

Harley nodded. 'Right you are, that search didn't turn up anything on the surface Web. So we decided to dive into the sewers of the darknet, and we got this.' He pointed to the right side of the screen. It showed a shot of a man who closely resembled the composite, standing on a crowded street in front of a taqueria, speaking with an older man.

'My, oh my, that's a match, if you ask me,' Annie said.

'The Beast thinks so, too. This older guy is none other than Ernesto Cruz, and the guy who matches our composite is his son Angel – aka Angel de la Muerte.'

'Angel of Death,' Grace said quietly.

'Yeah, and he lives up to his name. He's got a reputation in the cartel world for dispatching enemies in particularly gruesome and memorable ways, and that's a pretty remarkable distinction in the company of raging sociopaths.'

'How did you find all this out?'

Roadrunner shrugged modestly. 'Once Harley and I got into the Mexican military database through the darknet, it was easy going, because the database lists all the top secret information on cartels, their operations, and their operatives. This shot was taken by the Federales in Ciudad Juárez a couple years ago. Father and son were under surveillance.'

Grace nodded slowly. 'Of course. A lot of governments and law enforcement agencies stash sensitive material on the darknet because it's totally anonymous.'

'Created by our own government for that very reason.'

'So how do we find Angel Cruz?'

Harley deflated a little. 'That's the problem, I don't know if we can. First of all, he's presumed dead, at least according to the Mexican authorities.'

'If he's really Gino's and Magozzi's serial killer, then we know he's alive and kicking and right here under our noses murdering women.'

Roadrunner bobbed his head. 'That's what Harley and I thought, so we did some more digging. There is no record of any Angel Cruz entering the United States. So he either jumped the border or came in on fake papers, which means we're up against a wall. But at least we have a possible ID for Gino and Magozzi, maybe they can do something with it from their end. But to tell you the truth, they might be looking at an old-fashioned manhunt.'

Annie touched Grace's shoulder. 'Marla's journal. She thought she saw somebody named Angel, remember? Now we know who she was talking about. And she was right.'

Grace nodded. 'I'll call Magozzi and let him know.'

Thirty-eight

Amanda White had ultimately chosen Pike Island Park for her last stop of the night and her shot at journalism greatness – after visiting eight different parks in the past two nights, she'd learned a couple of things. For instance, suspicious behavior truly stood out if you were paying attention, something most park visitors didn't do, making them perfect marks. They were either running, biking, picking up their dog's feces, or walking with their faces fused to their phones, absolutely confident that safety in a public space was an inalienable right granted by the Constitution and somebody else would take care of it.

She'd also learned that serial killers were a lot like real estate agents. It was all about location, location, location. That's why Pike Island had stood out after her first eight trips to less desirable parks – at least if you had killing in mind. First of all, it was still within the metro area, just on the fringes of Minneapolis, which offered easy ingress and egress; secondly, it was heavily wooded, surrounded by the Mississippi River, and didn't ever have much visitor or park police traffic, offering terrific privacy. Tonight, her Camry was the only car in the lot, which didn't mean there wasn't a serial killer out there somewhere, long shot though it was. Not that she really wanted contact with a serial killer, but after her self-taught crash course in human behavior, she had the grandiose notion that she'd be able to identify him immediately, just by the way he acted.

She double-checked her flashlight and phone batteries, her canister of pepper spray, then doused herself with a good amount of mosquito repellent before she hit the trail that circled the island.

She could hear the dark waters of the Mississippi River lapping the shoreline all around her; barred and great horned owls hooted softly in the tree canopy; jet engines roared as they lifted off the tarmac at Minneapolis–Saint Paul International Airport a mile away. It was a bizarre contrast, trekking through raw nature while the noise of the modern world encroached from above. And maybe that's how she would approach this piece.

Moonlight filtered down through the trees, lacing the trail with a filigree of light, so she clicked off her flashlight and let her eyes adjust to the shadows. Her hearing began to compensate immediately for the partial loss of vision, sharpening and picking out the tiniest sounds, like a rodent or an insect stirring up leaves. Behind her, a twig snapped and she felt her heart rate jump to double time as adrenaline zapped into her bloodstream.

Foolhardy. Careless. Stupid. Fearless. All adjectives that people had used to describe her throughout her life. She was maybe all of those things, but safety never got you anywhere. She knew that now, because she'd been on that route for too long.

When another twig snapped loudly behind her, she stopped and pressed her back against a tree trunk along the trail, doing a three-sixty scan of the woods around her. *It's a deer. Keep walking. Right back to your car, you idiot.*

There were moments in life when self-doubt and uncertainty came crashing through when you least expected it, and those were the moments to fight. She didn't have a gun, had never even shot one before, but she had pepper spray and a fourth-degree black belt, and also the additional advantage of being on high alert.

She finally left the false safety of the tree trunk she'd been pressed against, reminded herself she was chasing a story, and started walking again, not to her car as better judgment would dictate, but onward, to the tip of the island, pissed off at herself for being scared by woodland sounds in a woodland setting. *Animals did stuff at night, get over it, what are the chances your killer is here? Slim to none. Better off buying a lottery ticket.*

When she finally reached the tip of the island, she settled into a squat on the slender beach and watched the water flow south, wondering how long it would take it to get to the Gulf of Mexico. It was mesmerizing, thinking of the journey the water took, from the springs of Lake Itasca up north to the sea so far south – so mesmerizing, in fact, her temporarily distracted senses didn't register the presence of the man behind her who wrapped his arm around her neck and started dragging her backward, into the woods.

Her scream was stifled beneath his hand as she bucked her body furiously, scrambling for her pepper spray. As the pressure on her throat got tighter and she saw the flash of a knife in the moonlight, she felt one of her hands being yanked behind her back with an excruciating pop that made stars flash behind her eyes.

You lack discipline! Pain your friend! This is fight to death! You see end, end finds you!

Her sensei, a merciless bastard who was going to save her life tonight. Focus. Control. Calm. Discipline. She'd been in worse situations in class, except her sparring partners hadn't been wielding a bowie knife and a clear motive to kill and leave her for dead.

She almost went limp when she tore her attacker's shirtsleeve and saw the tattoos, felt and smelled his hot, rank breath on her neck, saturated with seething violence as he dragged her deeper into the brush, choking her air supply, twisting her arm to the breaking point. He was strong, too strong . . .

Almost. But suddenly, her black belt kicked in with a furious vengeance and she started thinking the right way – leverage, balance, the physics of martial arts. No pain. Reservoir of power. Survive.

She dug her heels into the loamy earth beneath her, launched her body backward, and threw him off balance enough that he instinctively released her neck to catch his fall with the hand that wasn't holding the knife. And that was all she needed – that, and a well-placed elbow and foot that crunched some bone audibly in the sick son of a bitch's body.

Her hands were slick on the pepper spray canister at her hip as she pulled it out of the holster, felt her racing heart sink as it slipped out of her hand.

Don't drop it, for God's sake, don't drop it . . .

The man lurched up with a grunt of pain and dove toward her, and the world turned to slow motion as she rolled away, grabbed the lost canister, and watched aerosolized capsaicin shoot into his eyes.

She wanted to hurt him. She wanted to kill him. But

more than anything, she wanted to run, run, run before her legs collapsed beneath her. And so she did, tears streaming down her face, partially from the cloud of pepper spray, partially from the terror, but most of all from the uncertainty that she had cheated death tonight, because she could hear him crashing down the trail behind her. It was a vague sound, nearly drowned out by the pounding of her heart and the ragged gasps of her breath echoing in her ears as she tried desperately to pull air into her lungs through a damaged esophagus.

Angel's rage always manifested as great, pulsating towers of ugly bruise-purple in his head, devouring his thoughts, his sense of his own body, and everything else around him. When he was swept up by it, he became impervious to pain, impervious to everything except exorcising the rage, which meant finishing off this bitch, punishing her while she was still alive instead of giving her the courtesy of killing her first.

He didn't feel his searing eyes or his throbbing foot, just pure fury and the electrifying flood of adrenaline as his legs pumped. He couldn't really see, but he didn't need to – he could hear her pounding footsteps ahead of him, could smell her terror sloughing off in intoxicating waves, which made him run even faster.

GODDAMN FUCKING BITCH! he screamed in his head because he didn't dare scream it out loud. She could not leave this park alive – his own life depended on it. She'd been close enough to see his face, even in the dark. That would be enough.

He felt his feet hit pavement, and realized she'd already

made it to the service road out of the park. Two hundred yards, and she'd reach the hill that crested at the main road. He could see blurs of headlights even from here. He had to close in now, or he was done . . .

And then she surprised him. Veered off the paved road and bolted like a jackrabbit into the adjacent field, scrambled up the embankment that shortened the trip to the highway by at least a quarter mile.

The purple pillars in his mind vaulted higher and he pushed himself hard, stumbling through the field and up the embankment behind her. He could see her blurry silhouette jumping up onto the berm of the road, windmilling her arms frantically at passing cars.

Fuck fuck fuck. He retreated into the weeds and watched, felt like his life was draining out of him. It was over. There was nothing he could do now but watch that bitch get rescued, then try to ruin his life with her eyewitness description. His only hope was that he'd strangled her hard enough that she'd never be able to speak again.

And then, a miracle happened. A car slowed down for her and as she bolted for the passenger door, it squealed away, left her standing there on the side of the road. He smiled in the weeds, held back an almost irrepressible shout of joy. Of course – she looked stark raving mad, flailing around – who would stop for a psychotic woman? He certainly wouldn't. And there weren't many cars on the road this time of night, he realized, inching his way closer. Once there was a break in the traffic, she'd be his. And this time, he wouldn't make the same mistake and save his knife work for later.

He was about fifteen feet from her now, his approach

obscured by the roar of a jet above. Just a few minutes more, once this SUV passed her by, which it would, because it was going fast.

He crouched, ready for his final takedown, then watched in horror and disbelief as the driver of the SUV slammed on the brakes, pulled over onto the shoulder, then backed up, gravel from the shoulder spraying from the tires.

The rage was still burning white-hot, but he felt it start to trickle away, and that didn't bother him so much – he could conjure it at will, save it for another day, when the time was right. Right now, he had to focus on survival. Which meant going to ground until things blew over.

Thirty-nine

Amanda White looked horrible – her face and neck were black with bruises, her right arm was in a sling, and her eyes were livid red from the pepper spray that in part had saved her life. For the first time since he'd met her, Magozzi realized how tiny she actually was and how vulnerable she seemed, especially injured and curled up on her living room sofa under a blanket, sipping tea from a mug that dwarfed her small hands. At this moment, she wasn't a brash and reviled thorn in MPD's side – she was just an innocent woman who'd almost been killed by a monster that he and Gino hadn't been able to catch.

And yet her spirit hadn't seemed to suffer – her voice was a harsh, raspy whisper from her near-strangulation, but it hadn't stopped her from giving exhaustive eyewitness testimony to the first responders, the MPD sketch artist, and now, to Magozzi and Gino. She cringed in pain from time to time, but there was passion and purpose beneath the badly banged-up exterior, which Magozzi found interesting, given her terrifying ordeal. Not a traumatized victim, which she had every right to be, but a woman on a mission. A woman with a fourth-degree black belt who'd kicked some ass tonight.

'I'll sleep after I see the sketch of that bastard on the news.' She finally finished her retelling, then amended: 'After I see that bastard behind bars.'

'You may have filled in a lot of blanks for us tonight,' Magozzi said. 'BCA is processing all the trace they collected from you as we speak, and there's a blanket APB out on your suspect description, which corroborates some of our surveillance footage. All the networks are airing the sketch within the hour, as you probably know.'

She nodded. 'National stringers are already flying in on a hunting expedition, so I'm going on air with this first thing tomorrow. No matter what my producer says.'

'You've got quite a scoop on everybody.' Magozzi looked out her living room bay window at the patrol car parked on the curb outside her house, wondering what her spin would be. Nothing good, probably.

Amanda took a sip of tea and winced. 'I know what you're thinking, Detectives. Yes, I went to Pike Island looking for an angle and a serial killer, for that matter, but I got way more than I bargained for. I'm no hero, and I'm not going to play it like that. I had a freak, one-in-a-million encounter tonight, and I'm lucky to be alive.'

Gino hadn't said much during the interview, but now he was leaning forward, elbows propped on his knees. Magozzi figured his uncharacteristic silence was mostly due to the fact that he held deep contempt for Amanda White on principle, which was in direct conflict with his empathy for women in general, women who were hurting specifically, and it was messing with his mind. 'You haven't asked us a single question or asked for a quote yet,' he finally said.

'This is all off the record, as I promised you. In spite of what you may think, I always keep my word. But I do have a question. Personal interest, not professional.'

Gino nodded.

'Do you believe in evil?'

'We've seen it. More than once,' Gino said without hesitation.

She looked down at her lap and started running her fingers through the loose weave of her blanket. 'I never did believe in it. Not until tonight.'

When Amanda finally looked up again, her red eyes looked haunted for the first time since Magozzi and Gino had arrived. 'There's something I need to tell you about tonight. Something I haven't told anybody else.'

Magozzi and Gino both waited for her to speak, expressions impassive.

She folded her hands together, as if she wasn't sure what else to do with them. 'He had tattoos on his arms. Playing cards. Lots of them. Spades, hearts, diamonds. One of the spades was fresh, just starting to scab over.'

Magozzi tried to stay on his chair and keep his jaw from dropping down into his lap. 'Are you sure? It was dark, and you were . . .'

'In a panic, fighting for my life, yes, but I'm positive of what I saw. He's keeping a running tally on his goddamned arms.'

Magozzi and Gino both gaped at her, the whole impassive thing out the window.

'I knew about the cards all along, Detectives, I just didn't report on it.'

'Why?'

'The same reason I didn't tell the sketch artist about the tattoos tonight. It might be your only piece of disqualifying evidence, and I don't want to open your case up to copycats. Serial killers are hard enough to catch because they usually never have any connection to their victims. Whether or not you want to release the information is your call.' Her eyes flicked between the two detectives, who were doing a poor job of trying to hide their incredulity. 'Believe it or not, we're both on the same side. At least this time.'

Forty

Magozzi was staring out the windshield of their MPD sedan, hypnotized by the obnoxious fluorescent lights of a convenience store in Uptown Minneapolis. He could see Gino at the checkout register, paying for two cups of crummy gas station coffee, which they desperately needed – their monster was still out there but now they had a name and some solid history on him, plus an eyewitness description from a survivor. They were getting close, so close, and sleep wasn't an option – it wouldn't be until Angel Cruz was in shackles.

It was late to be calling anybody, but he dialed Grace anyhow, more to hear her voice than anything. Maybe it was selfish, but he needed a tether to something good right now.

'Hi, Magozzi.'

'You sound bright-eyed and bushy-tailed. You're still up?'

'We all are. And you sound exhausted.'

'That's going to be the new normal for a while. There was another attack tonight.'

'Oh, God. No.'

'This one has a happy ending. She survived with minor injuries, thanks to some serious martial arts training. It should be plastered all over every media outlet right about now.'

'We'll take a look.'

'One thing you won't hear from the media — at least not tonight — the killer has tattoos of playing cards all up and down his arms, one for every victim, we think. Gino and I are following up some leads right now.'

'That's . . . sick. Horrifying.'

'Serial killers are. I guess the tattoos are his version of trophies.'

'I'm sorry, Magozzi. I won't keep you, you and Gino go do your thing and keep us posted.'

'I will. Take care of yourself.'

'You, too.'

Magozzi signed off, wondering if 'Take care of yourself' was their version of 'I love you.' He hoped so.

Gino finally emerged from the convenience store and hopped behind the wheel, brandishing burned-smelling coffee and a box of donuts, which smelled better.

'Coffee and donuts, Gino? Really?'

'Cliché or not, this is the only way we're going to stay standing. Who the hell knew there were so many tattoo parlors in Minneapolis? By the way, McLaren called while I was inside. He and Eaton hit ten parlors with no luck, and the rest on their list are already closed.'

'What about our list?'

'There's one still open, over on the North Loop. I talked to the owner. Name's Jed Hanlon. He's expecting us.'

Jed Hanlon was about six-foot-five by Magozzi's estimation, with an intimidating prison build and full-sleeve tattoos that continued up his shoulders to his neck, then made a detour and carried straight down to his legs. There was a life story in those images if you looked, but this was not the kind of guy you'd stare at for too long. In fact, most people would probably run to the other side of the street to avoid him.

If you were to judge a book by its cover, he was also not the kind of guy you'd expect to be comfortable around law enforcement, but he was calm and polite when he and Gino introduced themselves. 'What can I do for you, Detectives?'

Magozzi showed him the police sketch and a still image from Eagle Lake Casino's surveillance footage. 'We're looking for this man. We believe he recently got a tattoo.'

Jed stared at the sketch and then the casino still and his mouth opened a fraction, as if he was trying to draw more breath, or maybe he was just trying to let something out.

'You recognize him?' Gino took the cue.

'Maybe. This kinda matches a guy who came in two nights ago.'

The night Cassie Miller was murdered, Magozzi thought. 'Was that the first time he came here for a tattoo?'

'Yeah. Never saw him before that.'

'How about other employees? Maybe they worked on him when you weren't around?'

'No way. I own this shack, I'm always around. I open, I close, and I've got one part-time employee I watch like a hawk. I know all her clientele, and the dude you're looking for isn't one of them.'

'Do you remember what time he came in?' Magozzi asked, assiduously taking notes.

'It was late, past closing, but the door was still open and he walked in. I was about to kick him out, but he laid down some good cash money, so I inked him.'

'What was the tattoo?'

'A playing card. Six of spades, on his left lower forearm, down by his wrist.'

Magozzi had to remind himself to breathe. 'Did you notice any other tattoos?'

Jed rubbed his jaw. 'The guy was pretty covered up, pulled up his sleeve just enough for me to work on him, so I couldn't tell you one way or another. He didn't seem to mind the pain, so I'm guessing this wasn't his first rodeo.'

'He was covered up how?'

'He had on a black long-sleeve shirt and jeans, wore a baseball cap with a Budweiser logo on it, just like in your picture. Had a damn scarf wrapped around his neck, and it was ninety degrees that day. Figured maybe he was a head case. You know how some nutters don't have a thermostat and they're always cold?'

Magozzi did know, it was a common symptom of certain mental illnesses. 'Did you talk about anything?'

'He didn't talk. Period. Asked for the tattoo and that was it.'

'Can you give us a description aside from his clothing?'

Jed shrugged. 'Like I said, he was pretty covered up. He looked at me once, so I know he has brown eyes. Hair was black, I could see a little sticking out from under his cap. Definitely Hispanic.'

'Are you sure?' Gino asked.

'Positive. I've inked every race God ever created, so I'm intimately acquainted with skin color and tone. Plus, the few words he said to me, he had an accent. Sounded just like an old buddy of mine, Paco, who grew up near Puerto Vallarta.'

'How about surveillance cameras in your shop?'

Jed's mouth turned up in a rueful half-smile. 'Wish I had some, but the rent here is killing me, and I put what I could toward an alarm system. I'm trying to put together a Web camera thing on the cheap, but it's not functional yet.'

'And you said he paid cash, so no credit card transaction?' Magozzi asked.

'No.'

'Did you see him get in or out of a vehicle?'

'I was in the back when he came in, and when he left, he hit the sidewalk and disappeared. I locked the door behind him, set the alarm, and that was the last I cared to see of him. So this is some bad dude, or what?'

'We're looking into that,' Magozzi said casually.

Jed shook his head. 'I knew it.'

'How do you mean?'

'The guy made my skin crawl, you want to know the truth. Somebody who looks like me, I scare people, not the other way around.'

'He scared you?'

'There was something about him that hit me in the gut. I had a full foot on him height-wise, and he wasn't exactly bulked up, but I could tell there was something wrong with him. Something broken inside. Sounds like a stupid, movie-cliché thing to say, but I did some time in Yankton ten years ago, and that's how you size things up on the inside. There were guys in there like me who made some bad choices and ended up paying the price. A lot of us get out, stay clean, and start life all over again. But there's another demographic in the prison population, the really sick, warped ones. You could cut them open and watch black slime ooze out, you know what I'm saying? Rotten to the core. And that was the dude I inked, the dude you're looking for.'

Good instincts, Magozzi thought, *because this dude is most likely a serial killer.* 'We really appreciate your time, and if this man shows up here again, call nine-one-one immediately and consider him armed and extremely dangerous.'

Jed nodded. 'Damn right I will.' He jabbed his forefinger at the sketch. 'That's one cat I'm not going to tangle with.'

Forty-one

Greg Trask hated the overnight shift at the gas station, except on nights when Maddie was waiting tables at the Rainbow Café across the parking lot. Sometimes she'd come in after her shift, buy a bag of honey roasted peanuts or a candy bar, and sort of flirt with him. Unfortunately, tonight wasn't one of those nights, and he was so bored, he was ready to drown himself in the live-bait tank at the back of the station.

The last customer he'd had was an hour ago, a stoner who put two dollars' worth of gas in his tank, then tried to shoplift some munchies. There was nothing on TV, because the cheap-ass owner refused to put in satellite, so it was all network, which was wearing out a police bulletin and sketch about some psycho killer up in the Cities, presumed armed and dangerous.

He checked his phone, then risked a text to his friend Alex, even though personal phone use on the job was strictly forbidden by the management and there were surveillance cameras all over the damn place. Alex was usually up all hours on his computer, playing whatever the hottest new game was, because his family had money, and he didn't have to work night shifts during the summer to pay for college.

RU THERE?

There was only a brief pause before his text alert binged.

WHERE RU?

Greg typed. WORK. BORED.

ME 2.

Greg looked up when he saw headlights. Somebody in a pickup truck, pulling in at the pumps. He'd swipe his credit card, fill his tank, then drive off, unless he was another stoner who would come in and pay at the register, then try to shoplift a bag of chips.

CUSTOMER, BRB, he texted back to Alex, then turned his attention to the man limping around his truck to the gas pump. He looked like he was in pain. More out of boredom than sympathy, Greg decided to do a good deed for the night and help him out. He pushed open the door and walked out into a hot, steamy night that seemed more July or August than June. 'Hey, man, can I help you out?'

'No.'

Greg paused at the tone of the man's voice. 'Well . . . if you need something else besides gas, we've got it inside.'

The man shoved the pump nozzle into the side of his truck, but didn't say anything.

'Okay, man. Have a good night.' *Prick*, Greg thought, backing away a few steps before turning around and heading back into the station. The TV was still spooling the police sketch and bulletin of the psycho in Minneapolis, and he paused. When he turned his head to take another look, the man pumping gas caught his gaze and held it.

Greg suddenly felt icy cold cramping up his stomach, and he went back behind the counter, considered texting Alex back, then decided to call 911 instead.

Dispatch answered after a couple of rings, asked what his emergency was.

'Uh, I'm not sure it's an emergency, but that guy on the police bulletin up in Minneapolis? I think he might be here . . .'

And then suddenly, the man was inside the store, a smile on his face, a gun in his hand. 'I changed my mind. You got any aspirin?'

Forty-two

Jacob Emmet had been dreaming about fishing with Walt as a kid when the phone had startled him awake a few minutes shy of five a.m. Deputy Al Lucas, a solid, good man with ten years on the force and as many commendations, had given him the bad news: Greg Trask – all-American athlete and model student getting ready for his sophomore year at Mankato State – was dead. Robbery-homicide. Shot in the head during the overnight shift at Fulmer's Gas and More, where he worked summers.

Fulmer's was perched alone on a flat, nowhere strip of prairie land that hugged the Iowa border. It was the farthest outpost of Cottonwood County, and nothing ever happened there, except an occasional deer versus car accident. Until now.

The scene was as ugly as Jacob had ever seen – a fine, ambitious young man who was going places in this world, was lying in a halo of his own blood as it dried on the floor around him, along with shards of glass and shattered electronics. Every single camera and computer had been shot to dust. Pretty goddamned thorough for some early morning meth head trying to rob a till for a fix, which had been his first assumption.

Deputy Lucas walked up and stood next to him, whispering, as they both watched the crime-scene techs methodically parsing the scene. The ME had yet to arrive.

'Greg called nine-one-one, Sheriff. I just read the transcript. He said he thought the guy on that Minneapolis police bulletin was here. Then the call ended.'

Jacob closed his eyes and rubbed them. Jesus. All the coverage in Minneapolis had flushed out their serial killer and sent him out of town, straight down the interstate. He was on the run. Definitely in Iowa by now, maybe even farther than that. 'I've got to get a national BOLO out to Highway Patrol. Do we at least have a vehicle description?'

The deputy shook his head. 'He shot up the outdoor cameras by the pumps, too. We're trying to find out if the gas station routes surveillance footage to a backup server somewhere.'

'Work fast, Al. Every minute we lose, this guy gains another mile at least.'

'Yes, sir.'

Forty-three

Gino and Magozzi were standing in front of a window that looked out onto the light rail track that fronted City Hall. The sun was just barely lifting from its nighttime sleep, painting the city a pale gold that would eventually crescendo about an hour from now, splashing vibrant color against the planes of the downtown buildings.

The surrounding streets and sidewalks were jammed with satellite vans and reporters from all over the country, and international crews were heavily represented, too. They'd all been camped out around City Hall ever since the MPD sketch had aired last night, waiting for an ambush, an interview, a little piece of the serial killer furor, which could mean one more rung up the ladder of success. Magozzi wondered how many of them were truly cognizant of the fact that the rungs of the ladder they hoped to climb were made up of four dead women. And of those who did realize, how many of them cared?

Cynical, cynical, cynical. Don't burn out; not yet.

Gino shoved his hands into his pants pockets and made a new set of hips, looking at his partner circumspectly. 'You okay, Leo?'

'Yeah, I'm just pissed. Angel fucking Cruz. We should have had this bastard in the can by now. The tip lines have been on fire all night, and we haven't gotten shit.'

'Lots of people think they saw him.'

'Some of those same people saw Elvis last night, too.'

Gino checked his watch. 'Amanda White's airing her piece in an hour. Maybe that'll stir something up.'

Magozzi took a sip of cold coffee from his flimsy cardboard cup and suddenly felt a pang of nostalgia for good old-fashioned Styrofoam, a vilified product now akin to Satan. Styrofoam was as unappealing to drink out of as cardboard, but at least it kept the coffee at a drinkable temperature for more than five minutes. 'He probably already went to ground. Hell, he might even be back in Mexico by now.'

Gloria was manning her station at the front desk, looking as frazzled as any of them had ever seen her. She was swathed in her mourning outfit – black headscarf, black caftan, black nail polish – because Gloria had a heart as big as the rest of her and always grieved for homicide victims.

She was typing frantically as they approached, said into the phone, 'Please hold for a moment,' then leaned back in her chair with a sour expression. 'You've gotta get this guy. He's never going to stop.'

'We're getting closer, Gloria.'

'Then get closer faster. The tip line has been ringing nonstop since they started running that sketch on TV. Do you know how many nut jobs have called into the tip line since I got here this morning?'

'As many as last night?' Gino asked smoothly.

'Hmph. More. And what's worse, the media is trying every single little trick in the book to get past me. They want a piece of all of you, so watch your backs. There's only so much even I can do.'

Gino cocked a brow at her. 'You're our iron curtain, Gloria. You're setting yourself up for failure already? It's not even seven.'

Gloria pursed her bright red lips, then smiled a little. 'Iron curtain. I like that. Now, back to business – your emails are loaded up with every message I've fielded so far. Some might be leads, some are pure trash. You decide. But you did get at least one legit call from law enforcement, some outstate sheriff who wants a call-back ASAP.' She tapped on her keyboard for a minute. 'Jacob Emmet, down in Cottonwood County.'

Gino looked at Magozzi and shrugged. 'Maybe he's got a new lead. Let's go make a call.'

Every desk in Homicide was filled with the entirety of the force's detectives, all busy on the phones as they followed up on the tip line leads. The place wasn't just humming – it was downright loud, with multiple conversations and buzzing phones reverberating through the room. Freedman was at his desk, phone glued to his ear, but he waved them over and put his call on hold.

'Welcome to the jungle,' Gino greeted him. 'Hell of a way to start your career in Homicide. You have something for us?'

'I just finished looking at the traffic cam footage from outside your tattoo parlor on the night our perp was there. Saw the bastard walk in and walk out and he's a dead match with the footage from Eagle Lake Casino. It's our guy, and I think he just made his first big mistake. I saw him get into a late-model black Ford 150. There are probably a million of those on the road in Minnesota, but this one had a big dent in the driver-side door.'

Gino rubbed his hands together. 'Please tell me you got his tags.'

'No such luck. But at least we have a vehicle description.'

'Update the BOLO.'

'Jeez, Rolseth, do you think I lost my frontal lobe overnight or what? It's already done.'

Magozzi looked around the office. 'Where's McLaren?'

'He's knocking on doors in the neighborhoods around the tattoo parlor. We can always hope somebody will look at the police sketch and say, "Oh, yeah, I see that guy every morning at nine a.m., sipping a macchiato at the Starbucks around the corner."'

'Wouldn't that be a dream come true,' Gino lamented. 'Why aren't you with him on the canvass?'

'He wanted me to stay here and keep plowing through all the trace evidence.'

'Any luck with that?'

'No. The only thing remotely interesting and totally irrelevant is lion hair at Charlotte Wells's scene, if you can believe that. But I suppose zookeepers and circus trainers take walks in parks, too, just like everybody else. Anything hot cooking on your stove?'

'We got a callback message from the Cottonwood County sheriff, but if he has anything to say, we're not going to be able to hear it in here. Let's go find a room, Leo.'

They settled in an empty conference room and Gino started dialing. Magozzi's eyes wandered up to the ceiling, where a spider lurked in a corner. It was big. And kind of fuzzy.

'Sheriff Emmet.'

'Sheriff, this is Detective Gino Rolseth and my partner, Detective Magozzi. We've got you on speaker.'

'Thanks for the callback, Detectives. Did you get the files I sent you on the Cruz case?'

'We did, and we thank you for that. Did you get something new?'

Sheriff Emmet sighed audibly into the phone. 'This is a courtesy call, mind you. I know how things go when you put out a sketch of a perp and open a tip line – suddenly everybody and their brother sees the bad guy next door, on the street, in a store, whatever, and I'm sure you're sorting through a hundred of them right now. But I just wanted to let you know that we had a nine-one-one call early this morning from a gas station attendant who reported a sighting of your perp there, then the call cut off. I'm just finishing up at the crime scene now . . .'

'Crime scene?' Magozzi interjected.

'Yes. Greg Trask, fine young man, sharp as a tack. Working his way through college. He was shot at least three times, according to the ME. He was dead by the time our first responder got here.'

Magozzi lowered his head and pinched the bridge of his nose. 'We're very sorry to hear that.'

'Thank you. It's a tragic thing.'

'Did you get any surveillance footage, a vehicle ID?' Gino asked, scribbling in his notebook.

'Nothing. The gas station's computer and all the cameras inside and out were shot up. We checked for data backup on an outside server, but the owner had a pretty remedial system, mostly all show and no go. Right now, I've only got boots on the ground, and they're going to scour every single inch of this county with your sketch.'

'We just got some footage of our suspect getting into a late-model black Ford 150 with a big dent in the driver's door. No way to be sure he's still driving the same vehicle . . .'

'But it's more than we had before you called. Thanks, Detective, I'll let my men know right away. But my guess? He's halfway to Missouri or Kansas or California by now. The gas station is close to the interstate, so he could be anywhere.'

Magozzi heard the sadness and frustration in the sheriff's voice, felt it himself. 'Sheriff, any chance you found a playing card on the body?'

'No, why? Is that a tell your killer leaves behind?'

'Yeah. That's one of the things we've been able to keep under wraps so far. But you might want to tell your men in the field that he has tattoos on his arms.'

'Everybody has tattoos on their arms these days.'

'These are playing cards.'

Jacob was silent for a moment, making the connection. 'Jesus. He's keeping score.'

'Maybe.'

After they'd gotten some more details about the scene and finally hung up, Magozzi and Gino fussed with making notes as they both drifted down the murky river of the case and all the weird tributaries it was taking them on.

Gino finally threw down his pen and looked up. 'I don't like the way Cottonwood County keeps creeping into our case.'

'I don't like it, either. Let's take a ride. We've got all

hands on deck here chasing the city leads, so let's go follow a new one.'

'Yeah, I'm with you . . .' Gino's eyes caught a sudden movement on the wall above his head. 'Jesus! There's a tarantula climbing down from the ceiling, Leo.'

'I saw that earlier.'

'And you didn't say anything? You didn't kill it?'

'It's not a tarantula. I think it's a wolf spider.'

'What the fuck is a wolf spider? Are they poisonous?'

'I don't know. Let's ask McLaren. It's probably one of his rescue animals.'

'Fucking McLaren.'

Forty-four

Grace was sitting on Walt's ramshackle dock, watching the sun creep above the eastern horizon and bedazzle his lake with flashing diamonds of light. If she squinted, it looked like a million tiny fires were burning on the water's surface, flaring, then extinguishing, then reigniting over and over again.

She leaned forward for a closer look as a massive gray bird suddenly lifted out of a marshy spot just to the west, flapping its enormous wings and rising into the sky as reluctantly as a 747, long legs dangling awkwardly behind. A heron, she remembered Magozzi telling her when she'd first seen one from his dock.

Turtles poked their heads up randomly, fish jumped to snatch bugs, making the water shimmy. She could hear the chirping of birds, the rasp of insects, the low of cows; smell the rich sweetness of earth and grass.

Before Magozzi had bought his lake house, it had never occurred to her that the country would hold any kind of appeal for her, but more and more every day she was considering what it would be like to wake up there every morning, not just a couple of mornings a week. To hear the melodious symphony of nature instead of the city's cacophony of sirens, car alarms and horns, chattering humans, traffic.

She looked over her shoulder and saw Charlie leaping

up and down like a pup, chasing a butterfly. He was happy here, in the same way he was happy at Magozzi's lake house. On one level, it was deeply disturbing to imagine a different way of life, but on another level, it was exhilarating.

Nothing's permanent, just remember that. One of her disengaged foster mother's words of wisdom. What she'd really meant to say was, 'You're not worth the government check, so back to the orphanage you go.' That had instilled an unhealthy need for sameness and stability in her life, whether or not it was good.

But maybe they actually had been words of wisdom, albeit delivered cruelly. You could make changes, and if they didn't work, then go to plan B. Or C. Or D.

She heard soft footsteps behind her, the rustle of tall grass, and turned to see Roadrunner awkwardly negotiating the alien terrain, his bony knees lifting high.

'You fell asleep at the computer last night.'

Roadrunner sank down next to her. 'Yeah, I know. My back is killing me.'

Charlie greeted Roadrunner, then ran off toward the woods.

Grace stood and slapped her leg. 'Come back here, Charlie.'

'What's the matter? He's just exploring.'

'No, he's digging up the woods, looking for dead goats. I had to drag him back last night.'

'Dead goats?'

'Yeah. Walt says there's a goat cemetery out there. Then again, Walt also said there's an African lion living somewhere out here. I know it sounds crazy, but . . .' She stopped when she saw the expression on Roadrunner's face. 'What?'

'I was just going through the list of trace evidence from Charlotte Wells's scene at the dog park. The techs found lion hair. Under normal circumstances, I wouldn't give that a lot of weight, but when you factor in all the connections to Cottonwood County that have turned up in Magozzi's and Gino's cases . . . I don't know. It's probably just a coincidence.'

'But maybe it's not. Come on, let's go call them.'

As they walked through the tall grass, Roadrunner chuckled.

'What is it?'

'I was just thinking that this is something the Beast never could have found, because the Beast can't talk to people, it can only process information. And I thought the Beast was the be-all and end-all.'

'The Beast is amazing, but there's no substitute for good old-fashioned cop work, and that should make you happy – humans aren't obsolete yet.'

Harley and Annie were sitting at the dinette table in the Chariot, drinking coffee and sorting through computer printouts from the Beast. Occasionally, one of them would scrape a neon-green line with a highlighter through a paragraph as they looked for orphan bits of information the computer hadn't pulled together.

'Stop looking at me, Annie,' Harley mumbled, keeping his eyes on the page he was reading.

'Don't flatter yourself. I was looking at that tree outside the window, which happens to be right behind your big head.'

Harley turned around. 'It's a tree. You hate trees.'

'The leaves are curling and the wind's picking up. A storm's coming.'

'Yeah, right. The sun's shining and there's not a cloud in the sky.'

'Shows how much you know. If you want a real weather forecast, look at the trees. Just ask Walt, he'll back me up.'

They both looked up abruptly when Charlie suddenly bolted into the Chariot, Grace and Roadrunner following close behind.

'I'm going to go call Magozzi and Gino,' Roadrunner said, retreating to the war room at the back of the rig, leaving Grace to tell the other two about Walt's lion.

Forty-five

Gino and Magozzi hung up the phone after Roadrunner's call and looked at each other.

'Well, the lion hair tears it for me,' Gino said. 'Cottonwood County is in this big-time. What if our guy isn't on his way to California or Kansas, what if he's shacking up down there?'

Magozzi was gathering his notes and stuffing them into his laptop bag. 'I'll Call Sheriff Emmet and give him a heads-up that we're on our way down. You pass the word on to McLaren and Freedman and we'll meet at the car.'

'Gotcha. See you in five.'

Magozzi redialed the sheriff's number and waited several rings before he finally answered.

'Sheriff Emmet, this is Detective Magozzi again.'

'What can I do for you, Detective?'

'We've got a pile of weird coincidences stacking up too high. We just got a call from a friend of ours working a missing persons case somewhere in your neck of the woods, for a Walt somebody, he's missing a daughter . . .' Magozzi heard an intake of breath on the other end of the line.

'Are you talking about Monkeewrench?' the sheriff finally asked.

It was Magozzi's turn to be surprised, and his hand tightened on the phone. 'You know them?'

'I'm the one who asked Monkeewrench for their help. What's this about, Detective?'

Magozzi closed his eyes and leaned back in his chair, wondering where to start. He finally decided the beginning would take too long, so he jumped right to the present. 'This is going to sound like a weird question, but is there an African lion on the loose down there?'

'There sure is. He escaped from a game preserve about four, five years ago.' The sheriff cleared his throat. 'That is a weird question.'

'It'll make sense when we tell you more. What about that old apple orchard and migrant camp you told us about, where the stabbing took place in '95 – any chance it's near Walt's place?'

'Sure. It's right across the lake on his property.'

Magozzi felt a sour sear of acid flooding his stomach as he jumped to his feet. He was amazed that he could move so fast on so little sleep, even more amazed that his galloping heart hadn't crashed through his chest. 'There's no time to get into details right now, Sheriff, but can you get some men out there and do a search?'

'You think your killer is here?'

'I think we need to make sure he isn't. My partner and I are on our way down.' Magozzi hung up abruptly and dialed Grace.

Annie was rinsing breakfast dishes in the Chariot's sink, eavesdropping on Grace's one-sided conversation with Magozzi. He was doing most of the talking – fast and panicked, she gleaned from the faint, muffled voice that was still loud enough to escape the phone. And when Grace did get a few words in, they were disturbing: 'You think he's here?' 'Of course we're all armed.' 'Don't worry, Magozzi.'

When she hung up, Annie abandoned the dishes and sat down next to her at the dinette table in the front of the rig. 'Not that I was eavesdropping or anything, but from the sound of things, Magozzi's got himself plumb up into a lather over something. What's going on, sugar?'

Grace sighed and laid her phone on the table. 'He and Gino are on their way down here. He thinks there's a possibility that their serial killer is here. Maybe even in that abandoned camp on Walt's lake.'

'Oh, my. Well, that is deeply distressing news, and if Magozzi's worried, then I am, too. I never did like the way a gun interfered with my wardrobe, but I won't let it bother me today.'

Grace shrugged. 'Serial killers don't go around randomly killing people. They're not a threat to the general population.'

'Serial killers are still killers, and if their back is up against a wall, taking a life that's in their way is like swatting a fly.' Annie regarded her curiously. 'For a woman who used to empty magazines into shadows, you're being pretty dismissive.'

'I've still got a gun in my holster, don't I? I just think Magozzi is overreacting. He's been doing that lately.'

Annie gave her a patient smile. 'Darling, Magozzi has always overreacted when it comes to you, and it's got nothing to do with that beautiful new life we're all going to meet in a few months. Maybe you never saw it, but anybody on the outside who didn't see it from the get-go is either blind or a flat-out fool. Whether you want one or not, you've got yourself a knight in shining armor.'

Forty-six

Walt forked and fluffed the last flake of straw into Bessie's stall. The younger heifers could handle the cement floors of the stanchions, but Bessie's joints had grown sore over the years, just as his had, so he had quite a bit of sympathy for her. Besides, after the countless gallons of milk she'd given him, he figured she'd more than earned a comfortable spot in a safe shelter to call her own. And she would probably need it today.

When he was finished, he slipped off his leather gloves, shoved them in the hip pocket of his overalls, then walked to the open tractor door for some fresh air, but there wasn't much of that to be had. It was like Mother Nature had decided to swaddle this piece of the earth in a sopping wet blanket, then light a fire under it.

Walt squinted at the barometer Mary had tacked on the wall by the door twenty some years ago – it was dropping fast. Not that he needed any fancy instrument to tell him what he already knew instinctively. In spite of the sun and heat right now, or maybe because of it, a storm was rolling in, and it was going to be a doozy.

Already, the leaves on the trees were curling up just so, shivering with the faintest of breezes, a tiny portent of the something bigger that would be coming next. Animals told you such things, too, if you weren't bright enough to figure it out for yourself. Weather like this, a herd of any kind was torpid. You had to move them with a stick and a few shouts if you wanted them to relocate, because all they wanted to do was lie in the shade of a tree. But they were restless now. They knew.

He wondered about the lion and where he might be taking shelter right about now. Being an undomesticated animal, he was a lot savvier than the cows, so more than likely, he was already hunkered down in a hollow somewhere, or maybe he'd even fixed himself a den over the years he'd been roaming free. Mary would have dismissed that notion, telling him homemaking was a female's purview, but bachelors had to make do, and that was something he and the lion had in common.

Walt walked out into the barnyard and primed the water pump so he could top off the stock tank just as two squad cars pulled up into his driveway, leaving a haze of dust behind them. They parked in the turnaround, and Jacob and three deputies piled out and started walking toward the barn like an Old West posse, guns and gear jangling in the belts at their waists. Walt stuck the hose in the tank to fill it and went to greet them.

'Morning, Sheriff, morning, Deputies. If you mean to haul me in, it's gonna take a lot more than you four.'

Jacob smiled and touched the brim of his hat. 'Morning, Walt. Never known you for a joker in all these years.'

'Who said I was joking?' He looked from one deputy to the other, giving them all nods. He recognized one of the men, broad and blond and built for farming, but equally suited to a uniform. 'You're Pam and John Larson's boy. Karl, is it?'

'Yes, sir.'

'I hope they're well.'

'They are, thank you for asking.'

'Your pop still running a full herd?'

'He sold off half last year. Arthritis, you know?'

'I'm sorry to hear that. You give them my best.' Walt looked up at the sky and took a deep breath of steamy air. 'Storm's coming.'

'A dangerous one, from what I've been hearing,' Jacob said. 'Keep an eye out. You might want to gather the Monkeewrench folks and bring them into the house later, just in case you need the storm cellar. That's quite a rig they've got, but it's still nothing but a trailer on wheels.'

Walt often assigned color to people's voices. Jacob's was black right now, and it had nothing to do with the storm. 'We've got some trouble, then?'

'The Trask boy was killed early this morning at Fulmer's station and some Minneapolis detectives think it might be connected to a killer they've been chasing for the past couple days.'

Walt looked off to the side, lips pulled together to keep emotions inside and private, but oh, Lord, the news of another family with a lost child cut close.

'Walt? You okay?'

He cleared his throat. 'Of course I'm okay. Just ruminating. Heard something about that killer on a news bulletin when I was listening to the crop report this morning. So I should be worrying about a maniac on the loose on top of the storm?'

'There's some kind of a tie-in to that old camp across your lake, Walt. We're going to do a search of the area right now, just to make sure your property is clear. And two Minneapolis detectives are on their way down here, just so you know, in case you see a strange vehicle pulling up in the driveway. They know Monkeewrench.' He turned to his men and whirled a finger in the air. 'You know what to do. I'll catch up.'

Once the deputies had trotted off, Jacob walked up and put a fond hand on Walt's shoulder. 'I woke up remembering fishing with you on the lake when I was a kid.'

'Good times, those.'

Jacob looked down, nudged a toe against a dying clod of grass next to a new fence post in Walt's paddock. 'Never did like fishing much.'

Walt raised a brow. 'You went with us every time.'

Jacob nodded. 'That was because Marla was there.'

Through the windshield of the Chariot, Grace saw Walt walking down the driveway. He didn't seem like the type of man to take leisurely strolls, and there was purpose to his stride. She waved through the windshield, then opened the door for him.

'Good morning, Walt.'

'Morning. I just talked to the sheriff, and there's some trouble afoot, so stay sharp. Your two Minneapolis detective friends are on their way down here to help sort it out.'

'We know. We just talked to them.'

He looked at the gun in her holster. 'That might keep you safe from trouble, but it won't help with the storm that's coming. I'd feel a whole lot better if you and your friends came up to the house, just in case we need the storm cellar. We're just under a tornado watch now, but with the size of this system, things can turn on a dime.'

Grace looked up through the windshield at the darkening sky that had been perfectly blue not too long ago. 'Annie was saying the same thing earlier.'

'You've got some time, but keep your eyes on the sky. When you hear thunder off in the distance, that would be a good time to pack it in and come on up to the house.'

'Hey, Walt,' Harley greeted him as he emerged from the back of the Chariot. 'You and Annie are right about the storm. Roadrunner and I were just checking out the radar and it looks pretty bad out West. It's still in the Dakotas, but it's moving fast.'

'Looks like we've got two kinds of storms brewing.'

'I hear you. Walt, is there anything Roadrunner and I can do to help you out? Batten down the hatches, help you close up the barn or something?'

'Thank you kindly for the offer, but I just have to get the rest of the herd inside and that's a one-man job with my gals. They're a little shy around strangers.'

Forty-seven

If you live most of your life in a place where the next person is always within eyesight and earshot, that press of humanity becomes comforting. New Jersey had plenty of open green spaces where you could catch a breath, and there was the Jersey shore, where the vast expanse of the Atlantic Ocean hissed and pounded or sometimes just lay there looking empty and restful, but it never made you feel alone.

This place was different, and Deputy Vince Cavuto didn't know if he'd ever get used to it. For instance, now he and his partner, Karl, were walking a field road with woods on one side and cornstalks taller than he was on the other, and there was no comfort there. It felt more like being isolated in a trap. No people, no comfort, no backup if you needed it. Just plants and trees and an unfriendly sky. You could suffocate in a place like this, especially with the air as hot and heavy as a weighty quilt.

The air wasn't moving. Not a breath of wind. No sound of the ocean, no smell of salt, just the sweet, cloying aroma of cornstalks that had been cooking in the sun, and the smell of other things that were dank and earthy and somehow sinister.

And then, a quick puff of breeze that smelled chemical and made the green stalks rustle, just a little. The sweat on his forehead prickled like it wanted to dry but couldn't, and there was a far-off rumble you could feel in your gut like something was calling out a warning. He didn't feel good. It wasn't nausea, exactly, but it was close. 'This place gives me the creeps.'

Karl was ahead of him, head swiveling this way and that, eyes busy, walking slow and heavy, like the air. 'This place is God's country. You'll get used to it.'

'Feels more like the Devil's playground.'

Karl turned around and smiled. 'That's the weather reminding us we can't really control much of anything. Slapping us down a little when we get too cocky.'

'Thanks for the reassurance. But take a look that way.' He pointed west. 'There's a wall cloud bearing down on us, and it's wearing Nikes.'

'What do you know from wall clouds, Mr New Jersey?'

'The first week Theresa and I got here the news kept harping on something called tornado awareness. Non-stop film clips of fucking wall clouds and crushed houses and barns. We almost turned around and went home.'

This was Karl's country, born and bred, and by now he didn't pay a whole lot of attention to tornado watches and warnings. Last year, Sarah Farmington had panicked, raced home with her two kids in the car, and went off the road and into a tree. Karl had been first on the scene, and all he could think of was that those three lives hadn't been lost to a tornado – that particular funnel never touched down. It was the warning that killed them.

But transplants took a while to get jaded and learn to trust their own senses over the radio. He could hear the apprehension in his new partner's voice, so he looked west, just so he could reassure him.

Lord. No wonder he was scared. The wall cloud damn near stretched across the whole horizon. It was black, ruler straight on the bottom, sagging close to the earth, leggy stripes of cloud to cloud lightning flashing inside it like hungry, gnashing teeth. 'We get a few really nasty-looking wall clouds every summer, Vince. Doesn't mean a funnel's gonna drop down.'

'Doesn't mean it won't.'

Karl shrugged, feigning nonchalance, but he felt that little squiggle in his gut every animal on the planet got when the barometric pressure took a tumble. Come to think of it, he hadn't heard a single birdsong since they'd started walking, and Walt's cows weren't complaining, which they always did this close to milking time. Animals went silent when something bad was coming, trying to hide. 'Let's put on a little speed, Vince. I'd just as soon be under some cover when this thing hits.'

'You feel it, too, don't you? Something pushing down like a big hand.'

'Nah. It's going to rain, that's all,' Karl lied.

'This is just excellent. We're out in the open, looking for a serial killer in the middle of a tornado outbreak. Guess the only question is which one is going to kill us. I should have stayed in New Jersey with the mobs and the gangs and the crazies.'

'Oh, for God's sake, relax,' Karl told him, but he picked up the pace a little more and actually started to jog around the lake. The old migrant camp was close now, on the other side of the water where raindrops started to hit the smooth surface. It looked like it was simmering.

The camp was nothing more than a collection of decaying

one-room cabins and a barracks building, perched on a small hill overlooking the lake. They were barely visible through all the overgrowth until you got right up into the camp yard itself, which was little more than a flat place with an old stone fire pit and a couple of collapsed picnic tables. Two of the cabins had been stripped of their front doors, and all the windows were broken out, littering the ground with shards of glass. Empty beer cans and booze bottles were nestled in the tall canary grass – it was like walking through a derelict's Easter egg hunt. It was a sad place; but it was also spooky as hell, with the sky turning dark above them, swallowing up the sun.

Vince toed a crushed Miller can. 'Kids' paradise. Empty cabins in the middle of nowhere.'

Karl nodded, feeling an uneasiness bearing down on him. 'This place has seen its share of shenanigans. Come on, let's clear the buildings.'

Vince unholstered his weapon and his flashlight. Clearing buildings, especially vacant buildings like these, was one thing that he hated about being a cop. Even though he didn't expect to find much of anything but more party litter and maybe some rats, it was what might be in any given vacant dump that made the hair on the back of his neck prickle.

The first cabin was dank and completely stripped of everything, including the sink. The beam of Vince's flashlight coursed across a thick coat of dust on the floor where there were more beer cans, a few candy bar wrappers, and a moldy pillow. 'No footprints. Doesn't look like anybody's been here in a while.'

Karl wiped his forehead with the back of his hand.

Goddamn, it was hot, and the air was getting heavier as the rain started coming down harder. 'One down, three more to go.'

In the second cabin, they found more remnants of forgotten parties. But the third cabin was different, and they both dropped to crouches on either side of the door, rain splashing down on the brims of their hats.

'Police!' Karl shouted, but his voice was swallowed up by a sudden crash of lightning that temporarily blinded him. Somewhere in the near distance, he heard a tree go down – a big one. He could feel his heart beating in his throat as his eyes followed the jittery beam of Vince's flashlight, piercing the gloom inside the cabin. One room, nowhere to hide. Thank you, Jesus.

Vince rose to his feet with a shaky breath. 'It's clear.'

'It is now, but it sure as hell wasn't.' Karl looked at all the footprints on the dusty floor, the stacks of supplies, the camp stove with an old metal coffeepot on the burner, the sleeping roll neatly tucked in a corner.

Vince crouched next to the camp stove and placed his palm against the coffeepot. 'Still warm.'

'Jesus.' Karl made a circuit of the room and stopped at a duffel bag stuck underneath a wooden bench.

'Still could be kids.'

Karl unzipped the duffel and just stared. 'I don't think so,' he finally said, turning to look at his partner. 'Guns. Lots of them.'

They both looked up when they heard the first pings of hail on the corrugated metal roof.

Forty-eight

All cars, possible murder suspect in the vicinity of Cottonwood County, presumed armed and dangerous. Exercise extreme caution. Repeat, extreme caution. Hispanic male, approximately five-foot-six, one hundred and fifty pounds, tattoos of playing cards on his arms. Last seen in a late-model black Ford 150 pickup truck, large dent in the driver-side door . . .

Holy shit, had that been music to Deputy Ryan Nagle's ears. In the three years he'd been patrolling Cottonwood County, the most exciting call he'd ever gotten was on a suspicious individual on Gravedale Avenue in Button-willow. It had ended unceremoniously, putting bracelets on some half-conscious meth head who pissed himself in the back of the squad on the way to the hospital. Ryan had heard later that the guy coded in ER three times before giving up the ghost.

The only problem with today's potential shot at a little glory was the fact that he'd been halfway across the county when he'd gotten the call-out. If there really was an armed and dangerous suspect somewhere out by Walt Gustaf-son's farm – which he doubted – Ryan was never going to get a piece of the action driving like a grandpa.

He squeezed the steering wheel, goosed the gas, and felt an intoxicating rush as he picked up speed along the serpentine road, accelerating at just the right moment into a curve, then launching onto a straightaway, building up as much speed as possible before the next twist in the road.

Ryan had aced his driving skills, but still, this road was a bitch, with more hairpins than a beauty salon. Even if he'd been a Formula One driver, there was only so much time he could make up on this route. It was time to change strategy, time to use a shortcut.

He braked hard, pulled to the side of the road, and cranked the wheel to reverse course. His tires slipped and squealed, then finally caught and propelled him forward to Lentz Road at seventy miles per hour.

Deputy Nagle, there's a note in your file from your time in Kansas. Seems you're a bit of a thrill seeker and we don't hold much truck with that here.

I was young and wild, Sheriff Emmet. But they took that out of me in a hurry.

That had been a line of bullshit, but Sheriff Emmet had hired him anyhow, and he'd been a good and loyal cop ever since. But the truth was, the adrenaline rush had always been his lure to a life in law enforcement, and Cottonwood County was a ho-hum place. Most of the cops not born and raised here moved on pretty quickly to big cities that promised high-speed car chases and TV time, and lately, he'd been thinking about doing the same thing.

Lentz Road turned to gravel after the first mile as roads tended to do in the Midwest, so Ryan slowed his squad, but not by much. He liked to see the gravel spewing a tumbling cone in his rearview mirror and he liked the rear-end fishtail when he swerved around the only curve on this nowhere road. Surely the single exciting moment he'd experience on this ride.

His radio crackled. 'Dispatch to all cars. Upgrade of tornado watch to warning. Touchdown reported by spotters in Haversfield. Heads-up, guys and gals. Be careful out there.'

Ryan looked in his rearview mirror. The sky was getting black and clouds were starting to boil in the distance. He'd spent some time with storm chasers in Kansas, and he knew something about tornadoes and how to avoid them, so he put on some more speed.

He only slowed down when he hit a patch of loose gravel and almost skidded into a deep ditch, which would have probably been the end of his tenure as a Cottonwood County deputy. Keeping his job was a hell of a lot more important than feeding his inner daredevil, especially now that he had a real sweetheart and a down payment on an engagement ring.

Besides, this was probably an exercise in futility. No way that guy was still anywhere near Cottonwood County after killing Greg Trask, a favorite son. So he'd drive these country roads all day long, looking for a truck that had either been dumped or was already out of state. What killer in his right mind would kill someone and hang around so close to the murder scene? Christ. He liked Sheriff Emmet, but this was just plain pointless in his mind.

The rain began gently, just a few drops on his windshield, but in a matter of minutes, it started coming down in heavy white sheets, forming instant puddles on the parched dirt road. Since the thrill of speed was definitely out of the question now, he amused himself by doing a few practice pit maneuvers, all the while imagining heroic scenarios if he ever caught the guy.

Ryan's fantasies were always detailed, well plotted, and rich with thrilling action and scintillating dialogue. At the core of it, he was a good cop – aced every test, scored tens at the range, and laid down every instructor in self-defense class – but Ryan was made for better things than driving aimlessly around, looking for an actor long gone. He had a much grander destiny. So he let his imagination run loose.

He'd see the black Ford parked on this very road, pulled off to the side, and he'd ease the squad up behind, run the plate, call it in, clear his weapon from his holster, and walk casually up to the driver's door; ready, so ready to shoot the bastard if he didn't buy Ryan's excellent acting.

Good afternoon, sir. Trouble with your truck?

Overheated, the perp would say.

He was Hispanic, with tattoos of playing cards clearly visible, of course – obviously the killer – but Ryan would not be afraid and would not break character.

Sorry for your trouble. I can give you a lift to Fulmer's gas station, it's not too far from here.

How clever he would be to mention the gas station where this monster had just murdered Greg Trask. He would watch carefully for his reaction . . .

Ryan had been so deep in his fantasy, he almost missed the stark reality of a black Ford 150 pickup truck stopped on the side of the road just ahead. It was parked slightly off center, just enough to show a large dent in the driver's-side door.

He hit the brakes and rolled his cruiser up slowly until he could see the plate number. As he punched it into his onboard unit, he felt sweat carving a path from his brow down his face, slicking his hands, drenching his uniform. He suddenly realized that there was a very big difference in adrenaline: there was the good kind you got from pit maneuvers, driving fast, and tornado chasing, and then there was the bad, sickly kind you got when you just happened upon a vehicle that potentially belonged to a deranged killer who might be inside, waiting for you.

Forty-nine

Gino and Magozzi were thirty minutes from the Cottonwood County border when things started looking ugly. Thick, dark clouds were eclipsing a sky that had been clear not so long ago, and a fierce wind churned up out of nowhere, buffeting the car.

'Jesus,' Gino muttered. 'Would you look at that sky? It's black. What the hell are we driving into?'

'Check the radar on your phone.' Magozzi had been maintaining a steady eighty-five miles per hour since they'd left the city limits, but he took it down a little because the wind was making the car squirrel around.

Gino started scrolling his phone for weather just as the first raindrop hit the windshield with a loud splat. Magozzi heard the sound first, thought it was probably a big, hard-shelled June bug, until he looked and saw spidery tendrils of water creeping across the windshield in all directions. It had been one big raindrop.

'Oh, man, Leo. There are severe thunderstorm warnings and tornado watches for the whole lower half of the state, and we're driving straight into a big, red blob, according to radar. Right into the eye of the storm.'

'It's supposed to be calm in the eye of the storm.'

'That's hurricanes,' Gino snapped. 'The eye of a thunderstorm is where you get washed off the road. Or blown off the road. Or killed by lightning. Or impaled by flying debris.'

'How many thunderstorms have we lived through? It's nothing to worry about. Look, there's blue sky over there . . .'

And then suddenly, the sky opened up and sheets of pounding rain started hammering down on them. It steamed as it hit the hot surface of the freeway, which was collecting pools of standing water at an alarming rate. Magozzi tightened his grip on the steering wheel and slowed down to fifty, then forty, then thirty, because visibility was almost down to zero. It was like driving into a white curtain. He dodged taillights as the few cars ahead of him started pulling over to the shoulder.

The rain was deafening on the metal shell of the car, and suddenly the sky started flashing like a strobe, forks and filaments of lightning chasing one another across the horizon.

Gino grabbed the dashboard when the car hydroplaned, bringing them perilously close to the ditch. 'Pull over, Leo, like every other sensible person on this road. This is some serious shit.'

'Our exit is only two miles away. We can make it. We'll stop there.'

Gino punched on the radio and put it on auto-tune until it finally found a local station.

' . . . tornado reported on the ground in northeastern Sylvester County. If you are in the area of Franklin, Chippewa, or Haversfield, seek shelter immediately . . .'

'Goddamnit,' Gino huffed, punching at his phone. 'Where the hell are we? I think I just saw a sign that said Chippewa.'

And then, as soon as it had started, the rain stopped.

Magozzi took a deep breath and punched the accelerator. 'See, nothing to worry about. We got through it.'

'Oh yeah? Oh yeah? The sky is fucking turning green. You know what a green sky means? It means there's a tornado. And that's a wall cloud.' He poked his finger against the windshield. 'Jesus, we have to stop somewhere . . .'

Magozzi saw his exit sign and pushed the car hard to the ramp so he could get off the freeway before Gino had a heart attack. He pulled onto the gravel shoulder of a two-lane country road just as pea-sized chunks of ice started battering them, pinging and thunking against the roof.

Gino was looking as green as the sky. 'Hail. You know what happens before a tornado? It rains like hell, then it stops and the sky turns green, and then it starts to hail. When this hail stops, we are fucked, because that's when the tornadoes move in.'

Magozzi was a little concerned himself. He'd lived here his whole life and he knew, just like Gino, that there were storms, and then there were storms that birthed tornadoes. By all accounts, this was one of the latter, especially in the flat farmland they were in now.

The radio chatter crept back into his conscious, punctuated by the beep-beep-beep that always preceded a doomsday weather warning.

' . . . two more tornadoes have reportedly touched the ground in the vicinity of Waterville and Chippewa. Seek shelter immediately. This storm is moving northeast at a speed of thirty-five miles per hour, accompanied by damaging winds, hail . . .'

Magozzi slammed the car out of park and hit the

accelerator. 'I'm going to keep driving until we find some-place to shelter. We're still in the wide open here.'

Gino squinted through the torrent of hailstones boun-cing off the windshield and road. 'Looks like there's one of those blue informational signs just up ahead. Maybe there's a McDonald's that's in a concrete bunker.'

There was no McDonald's in a concrete bunker listed on the sign. Just Fulmer's Gas and More – 2 mi. Dairy Queen – 15 mi.

And Eagle Lake Casino – 24 mi.

Fifty

Grace, Annie, and Charlie were sitting on the faded rose sofa in Walt's living room, which he'd explained was a front room if you were under seventy, a parlor if you were older than that. Charlie had commandeered most of the sofa and his wet nose was pressed against Grace's leg.

'Tell him to get down, Walt,' she'd said the first time the dog had staked his claim next to Walt on the sofa. But Walt had simply smiled and stroked Charlie's head.

'This is an excellent dog, leave him be. I've missed having a dog. Didn't know how much until now.'

It was quiet in the house, dim, and breathlessly close, and Annie reached over the sofa arm to turn on a side table light. 'I don't like the looks of things outside, Grace. It's as still as a cat out there and the sky is getting blacker by the minute. Harley and Roadrunner had better hurry up. And for that matter, Walt. How long does it take to get cows in a barn?'

'A question for the ages.'

Annie stood up and started pacing nervously. For all the years they'd known each other, Grace still marveled at her ability to navigate any terrain in high heels as if she were wearing track shoes. 'I think we should go down to the storm cellar to check out the accommodations. If we get stuck down there for any substantial amount of time – God forbid – I want to make sure it's well stocked. Men think of flashlights and storm radios but they don't think of water and food.'

Suddenly Charlie's head shot up out of a deep sleep, his neck corded with tension, his eyes focused out the door. He made a little sound deep in his throat, then bounded from the sofa to the floor.

Grace wouldn't have been surprised to hear the rumble of thunder that preceded most summer storms. What she heard was somehow more sinister. Tap, tap, tap, like little marbles timidly hitting the roof. And then just like that, it stopped. The leaves on the oaks still hung motionless, and there was no sound at all.

Suddenly, without any warning, the world seemed to take a deep breath, sucking the air from the house, and the screen door exploded outward, banging against the siding.

Walt had just gotten the last of his herd into the barn and was closing up the tractor door when the rain started. It was slow at first, but it didn't take long for it to start coming down with a vengeance. Rain was a blessed thing, especially in the kind of drought conditions they'd been enduring in this part of Minnesota, but the sky had a devilish look to it; suddenly day had turned into night and the heavens were angry.

He started jogging toward the Monkeewrench RV, rubber paddock boots squeaking and splashing in the puddles that were instantly forming on top of the dry, thirsty earth. Their rig was a fair distance away, and somewhere in the back of his mind, he wondered if he'd have to carry that Annie woman to the house, or if he even could carry her, because apparently she didn't have any sensible footwear, not that he'd seen.

The lightning and thunder were starting now, and it was close, flaring in the sky with blinding brightness, crashing in the woods, sending percussive waves through his body. There were no better fireworks, unless you were out in it, which was when it stopped being theater and started being life or death.

'Walt!'

He slowed, then stopped, wondering if he was hearing voices, because it was too damn loud to hear anything but Mother Nature raising hell in all kinds of ways, and all at once. He looked around, felt cold rain sluicing off his cap and down his shoulders, but he couldn't see anything through the curtain of water in front of him.

'Walt!' Jacob appeared out of the tree line near the cornfield, rain-drenched, muddy, and pale in the darkness of the storm.

'Jacob?'

'Get Monkeewrench inside,' he panted. 'We've got tornadoes on the ground southwest, moving up toward Buttonwillow.'

'I'm on my way. Where are your deputies?'

'Searching the whole damn county, which is where I'm going after I call in an all-units, damn radios aren't working out there . . .'

'Hell if you're going back out there, Jacob. Get down to the storm cellar.'

'We think he's here, Walt, and close. Deputy Nagle found his vehicle broken down and abandoned on Lentz Road. You take care of things on your end, I'll take care of things on mine. And make sure you have your shotgun at the ready, just in case.'

Walt was taking a battering from the wind and the hail that was turning his yard white as he held open the screened porch door for Harley and Roadrunner, who were making a last mad dash up the steps. They looked like a couple of drowned rats, shivering and dripping rainwater on the wooden floor. Thank the good Lord the two women had had the good sense to get safely to the house earlier, before all hell had broken loose.

'Down to the cellar,' Walt shouted over the howling wind just as a fierce gust pulled the door from his hands, ripped it off its hinges with an unholy screech, and tossed it out into the yard like a toy.

Annie suddenly appeared in the dark rectangle of the storm cellar door and started waving her arms. 'Hurry up!'

Fifty-one

Magozzi had pulled over in a gravel turnaround by a wicked S curve and a foaming creek, hoping the over-hanging tree limbs would protect them from the gargantuan hail that was pouring down out of the sky. Or maybe one of those overhanging tree limbs would snap off and crush their car with them inside – there just weren't a lot of choices at this point.

Gino had his face in his phone, giving minute-by-minute updates courtesy of the National Weather Service feed. 'Goddamnit, Leo. We've been following this thing the whole way. We drove into it, and we're still driving into it. If we'd stayed on the exit ramp, we'd be getting a suntan right now.'

'So we stay put until it passes.'

'Yeah. I guess, and hope to hell we don't get sucked up into a funnel cloud while we're cooling our heels.'

Ten minutes later, the hail slowed, then stopped, and the black sky lightened, just slightly. Gino's face glowed in the ambient light of his phone's screen. 'I think we dodged a bullet, Leo. Looks like this thing is breaking up and veering north.'

'Great. Then we can drive through it again on the way home.' He pulled back onto the road, which was littered with shredded leaves and twigs that the wind had ripped off the trees. A mile up, a big toppled oak blocked most of the road and had taken power lines down with it. They were still live, throwing sparks.

'Jesus Christ,' Gino muttered, bracing his arms against the dashboard. 'Can you get electrocuted in a car?'

'I hope not.'

'You hope not?'

'I can get around it if I ride the shoulder, it's clear.'

Gino pinched his eyes shut, so Magozzi saw the lights first, pulsating red and blue just beyond the crest of a hill on the other side of the fallen tree and the spitting power lines that were dancing erratically across the tar. 'Cops,' he said, tapping Gino on the arm, and he opened his eyes.

'Fire up ahead.' Gino pointed to a boiling column of smoke rising above the farmland.

Magozzi stared at the smoke for a minute, and then simultaneously, he and Gino both realized that they weren't looking at smoke rising – they were looking at a descending tornado, coiling and twisting across the horizon like a sidewinder rattlesnake headed right for them.

'Ditch!' Magozzi shouted.

If you find yourself in a vehicle without immediate access to a proper shelter when there is a funnel cloud within sight, or a tornado has been reported on the ground in your general vicinity, do not attempt to outrun it, and do not seek safety beneath bridges or freeway overpasses. If you have no other options, immediately exit your vehicle, find the lowest spot available, such as a ditch, lie flat . . .

And kiss your ass goodbye, Magozzi thought, feeling the cold, muddy water soak into his suit. He and Gino had been lucky – the ditch was deep, and there were no live power lines supercharging the water they were lying in facedown. Which didn't mean they were safe, it just meant they had avoided electrocution for the time being.

And then he heard a crashing in the woods, and a deafening, all-encompassing roar. Every eyewitness report of a tornado he'd ever heard over the years played like a broken record in his mind. 'It sounded just like a freight train.' That had always puzzled Magozzi, because he'd never once thought of a tornado when he'd heard a train.

But by God, all of those eyewitnesses had been right, and he lowered himself farther down into the ditch, praying to God he and Gino would miss this particular train.

Fifty-two

Grace had never heard anything like it – the angry scream of wind was deafening, even in Walt's subterranean stone cellar, and loud crashes that sounded like exploding bombs seemed endless. The power had gone out ten minutes ago, and now they were all huddled together in a tiny, windowless room lit by a single flashlight. Annie gasped and covered her mouth when a loud, unearthly groan sent a shower of mortar crumbling down the wall.

Buried alive, Grace suddenly thought, then tried to push the evil from her mind. She'd faced a myriad of terrors in her lifetime, but this was of an entirely different magnitude. Walt had been right – her gun was useless here and now. All any of them could do was cower in this tiny space and pray the house above them didn't vaporize in a vortex of wind.

Her grip tightened on Charlie, who was quaking against her leg. She wanted to soothe him, tell him it was going to be all right, but she just didn't know at this point, and she never lied, not even to her dog. Besides, any words she spoke now would be swallowed up by nature's roar.

She felt the baby kick and placed a defending arm across her belly, horrified as she imagined the precious life growing inside being drowned in her stress hormones. Since she was helpless to do anything else, she started humming a lullaby. The baby would hear her.

At some point – minutes later, an hour later? – Grace became distantly aware that the world had grown quiet again and everybody around her was beginning to stir.

'Is it over, Walt?' she heard Harley ask.

'Things like this don't last too long, though it seems like a lifetime when you live through them. I'd say so, but let's wait a few minutes before we go back upstairs.'

Grace felt the press of her friends circling around her, then Annie's plump arm around her shoulder. 'Everything okay, sugar?'

'Everything is fine. We're all still here, aren't we?'

Eventually, they all followed Walt up the worn wooden cellar stairs to the main level of the house. Annie couldn't stop shaking, because she had lived through tornadoes before down in Mississippi, and when you were cellared up and heard god-awful crashes like the ones they'd heard, you never knew what you were going to find when you finally opened up the cellar door.

She breathed a great sigh of relief when Walt finally pushed open the door, revealing an entirely intact house. They crept through the dark living room like a human train, hands on the shoulders of the person in front of them, as Walt led them through the unfamiliar territory of his house.

He trained his flashlight on the front porch that no longer existed. In its place was an enormous tree trunk. Rainwater dripped off the leaves and onto the living room floor, and mosquitoes were buzzing all around, eager to feast on bare flesh.

'That's what all the ruckus was about,' he said quietly, swatting his arm. 'Knew I should have felled that oak last summer, when it was starting to hollow out.' He folded his arms across his chest. 'I need to go out to the barn and check on the animals. Why don't you all go check on your rig, make sure it weathered the storm. We'll go out the back door, hopefully there isn't a goddamned oak tree there we'll have to climb over.'

He showed Harley, Roadrunner, and Annie the way, but held Grace back as she and Charlie were about to follow. 'Want you to know, my wife, Mary, and I lived through something as bad as this a few decades ago. Sheltered in the very same storm cellar and rode it out, just like we all did today. She was about six months pregnant with Marla. Mary told me she knew the baby was scared, so she hummed to her the entire time, trying to comfort her. That baby girl turned out to be a gem, and I've often wondered if that storm didn't have something to do with that.'

Grace looked at him curiously. 'You heard me humming?'

'I hear all kinds of things.' He looked down and busied his hands adjusting the straps on his overalls. 'You've got yourself some good people.'

'I do.'

'I'm glad, you deserve it.' He looked up at the quickly lightening sky and pointed. 'Sun comes out fast after something like this. It's going to steam up like a sauna with all the moisture in the air.'

'I can already feel it.'

'Keep your eyes on the sky, there's a rainbow coming, mark my words. Ironic, isn't it? Go on, now, catch up with your friends and get to your business and I'll go check on the barn and the herd.'

He watched Grace MacBride and her fine dog walk away, then took his own path out toward the barn, assessing the storm damage along the way. The yard was littered with downed trees and limbs, and part of his new paddock fence had been swept away. The old barn was still straight and true, just missing a few pieces of siding here and there. He'd lived through storms like this before, and he considered himself lucky, only losing some trees and a front porch this time. Some other folks may have lost everything, including their lives.

You could plant new trees and rebuild a porch or a house. Life was what mattered, and it was a damn shame that the Monkeewrench folks, for all they'd given him and all they'd been through down here, couldn't bring Marla back.

He paused at the tractor door of the barn in time to see the rainbow he'd predicted, arching over his cornfield. He'd seen hundreds of them during his lifetime – they were all a sight to behold, but they weren't anything special, just light and water particles – but he let it put a little hope in his heart, foolish as it was.

Fifty-three

Deputy Vince Cavuto had been pissed as hell when his partner, Karl, had suddenly and inexplicably dragged him from the shelter of Walt's cabin just as the storm finally hit with a vengeance.

'What the fuck, Karl!?'

'No time, get down!'

By then, Karl had pulled him through the woods to a low spot and shoved him facedown into a muddy hollow. Vince's fists had been ready for a fight and his mouth was rifling off all kinds of expletives, but then the tornado sucked the life out of the world just above, and Vince willingly breathed in mud while he prayed for his life as hell on earth grazed over him, just barely.

Looking at the cabin now, he understood – the damn thing was nothing but a flattened pile of rubble. If Karl hadn't had the good sense to get out, they would both probably be dead.

'Son of a bitch, Karl,' he breathed. 'You saved our asses.'

'We got lucky.' He looked around at the fallen trees and pieces of buildings scattered around the campground. A big swath of the woods had been completely stripped of trees. 'God, this is as bad as I've ever seen it. It looks like the tornado cleared a path straight toward Walt's farm.'

'Go do a welfare check. I'll stay here and preserve the

scene. Or what's left of it. Besides, who knows? This scumbag might come back for his guns.'

'Eyes wide open, Vince.'

'You, too. He could be anywhere.'

Karl started jogging through the woods toward Walt's, but his progress was hampered by the ugly, destructive mess the tornado had left in its wake. The path they'd taken down here before the storm was now littered with debris of all kinds, from toppled trees to sharp, nasty-looking pieces of corrugated sheet metal that had probably been ripped off somebody's outbuilding roof. He even stumbled across a car tire and a muddy stuffed animal, which wrenched at his heart. That stuffed animal had an owner somewhere, and what had happened to them?

He cleared another fallen tree, this time a mature maple, then stopped dead when he landed in a small river of watery mud sliding down from a high point on Walt's property. The muck was like quicksand, creating a suction that almost pulled his boots off.

'Son of a bitch!' he shouted to himself, then backed out of the quicksand and circled around the maple, heading for higher ground.

When he'd made it halfway up a small hill, he heard a strange sound, a low, loud sound, then watched in horror as a liquefied sheet of mud poured down the hill toward him. If he'd been a second too late jumping backward, he would have been buried alive in a mudslide.

His shoulder unit crackled and he heard Vince's voice. 'You okay, Karl? I heard you shouting. Over.'

'I'm fine, but there's a mudslide out here, a big washout, and it's . . .' Karl felt the earth go soft around his feet, then give way, and he fell and started sliding downhill with the mud and water and sodden clumps of dirt mixed with loosened rocks. He clawed at the moving ground, trying to find purchase, and finally latched onto something semi-squishy, but solid beneath. Maybe a rotted tree root.

As liquid soil sluiced around him in its relentless pursuit downhill, he finally saw what he was hanging on to. It was a human leg, and it sure as hell didn't belong to somebody who'd just been killed in the tornado. He recoiled and scrambled backward as he watched a badly decomposed man slide down the hill.

'Karl? Karl!' Vince was barking into his shoulder unit, but he didn't answer, because the horror show didn't end with the dead man. His sense of time and place halted abruptly the moment he'd seen the second body slide down the hill, and then the third. Their limbs flopped and tangled on their descent to the bottom of the incline, giving the lurid appearance of reanimated corpses struggling against the current of mud.

When he felt a hand on his shoulder, sheer panic vaulted him upward and out of the muck, because he was certain some bloody swamp zombie had come to claim him. But when he turned around, it was only Vince.

'Karl, come on, get out of this shit . . . Oh, Jesus. Jesus, Mary, and Joseph.' Vince's hand went limp on his shoulder, then dropped away when he saw what Karl had been seeing for a long time. 'Jesus, Mary, and Joseph,' he repeated as they both watched tiny human bones tumble down to mingle with the adult dead who still had some flesh.

'It's a goddamned graveyard, Vince. A goddamned graveyard. The storm flushed them out.'

Fifty-four

Magozzi and Gino were finally standing upright in the ditch that had saved their lives, drenched, covered in mud, and dumbfounded as they looked at the decimated forest on the other side of the road. It looked like Godzilla had blazed a trail through the old oaks and pines, tossing them aside like toothpicks to make room for the rest of the debris he'd collected along the way. Magozzi saw lots of metal, a couple of cars, pieces of houses.

'Jesus.' Gino let out a shaky breath. 'Jesus.' He looked up at the sky – the sun was starting to peek out, as if nothing had happened. 'There's a fucking rainbow, Leo.'

But Magozzi wasn't listening, he was frantically punching the speed dial to Grace's phone. He held his breath as her phone rang once, twice, three times, four – and then nearly collapsed back into the muddy ditch when she answered. 'Grace, are you okay?'

'Magozzi, where are you?'

'I'm standing in a ditch with Gino and I think we're close to Walt's farm. Are you okay?'

'We're all okay. Listen, before the storm hit, Walt told us one of the sheriff's deputies down here found a broken-down, abandoned vehicle that matches your description. They think he might still be down here.'

Magozzi looked up the hill they'd never crested, still seeing the red-and-blue lights pulsing. The rainbow was bizarrely arching over the flattened forest like it was frowning down on the devastation below. 'Thanks for the warning. We have to go, but . . .'

'Be safe, Magozzi. Be safe, both of you.'

Magozzi hung up. 'Gino, they found his truck down here.'

Gino narrowed his eyes. 'Huh. I want to be excited about that, but the truth is, he could have dumped it and gotten a ride or stolen another vehicle . . .'

'It was broken down.'

'Or he could be on foot.'

'Exactly. Let's go.'

The squad was parked behind an uprooted tree, which looked like it had just missed the car by inches. As they jogged up, they saw a deputy getting out. 'Minneapolis PD,' Gino announced as they approached. 'Are you all right, Officer?'

The man's head jerked back in surprise. 'Detectives Magozzi and Rolseth?'

Magozzi was finally close enough to see the star on his chest. 'Sheriff Emmet.'

He shook their hands and looked at their muddy, wet suits sympathetically. 'Sorry you got down here just in time to ride out the storm in a ditch. Glad you're okay.'

'We appreciate it, and we know you've got a lot on your plate with this storm, but Monkeewrench told us about the abandoned truck. Tell us what we can do to help.'

Sheriff Emmet puffed out a frustrated breath. 'I'd just assigned a search grid for a manhunt before the storm hit, but half of those men are already dealing with emergency response. I just called in support from other counties, but they're digging out themselves. We don't even know the half of what we're dealing with yet, but initial reports are bad. Resources are going to be scarce for a while.'

'Whatever manpower you can spare, we'll join them, just tell us what to cover,' Gino said.

'You sure about that?'

'Sure as anything. Tromping through woods in horse-shit weather, chasing down homicidal maniacs – it's nothing new to us.'

The skin around the sheriff's eyes crinkled. 'Yeah?'

'Hell, yeah. Except the last time we did this, we were on an Indian reservation in northern Minnesota in the middle of a blizzard, and all the bad guys had AK-47s.'

'Now that's a story I'd like to hear someday. Come on, jump in my car and I'll show you a map of the search grid and where we've got some holes. I've got a spare shoulder unit I can give you, but I don't have any spare body armor.'

'No problem,' Gino said. 'We've got that covered.'

'I'm glad to hear that.' The sheriff excused himself while he took a phone call. 'Deputy Cavuto. Are your radios on the fritz again?'

While he listened for a few minutes, his posture tensed and Magozzi literally saw the color drain out of his face. 'I've got to ask, Vince, is one of them Marla?' He closed his eyes while he listened to the answer, but Magozzi couldn't tell if the sheriff was listening to good news or bad. 'I'll be there as soon as I can. Call BCA.'

'What's happening?' Magozzi asked after he'd hung up.

The sheriff took a moment before he answered. He looked hollow and lost, like a man looking into a void. 'The rains unearthed at least four dead bodies near Walt's and washed them down a hill.'

Little pieces started clicking together in Magozzi's mind. Serial killers often buried multiple bodies in one location. And their serial in Minneapolis had a connection to Buttonwillow. Buttonwillow also had a missing woman. 'Marla. She's the missing woman Monkeewrench is trying to find.'

'Yes. Marla Gustafson. Walt's daughter.'

'Is she there?'

'My deputy wasn't sure. He thought they looked like men, but there's some decomposition. There are also some small skeletal remains. A child. He doesn't know if there are more, but I sure as hell hope not.'

Gino dragged his hands across his mouth and looked at Magozzi. 'Sticking with the theory that our guy is a serial killer with a day job, then that could be his dumping ground for his cartel hits. It might even be where he started.'

'You think this is connected to your serial?' the sheriff asked.

'It's looking like a good possibility. Sheriff, go do what you need to and we'll get out in the field.'

'I'll get you a map and let my men know you'll be out there in plain clothes. Right now they have orders to stop and question anybody who isn't in uniform.'

'We appreciate it. Just tell them not to shoot the guys in the muddy, wet suits.'

Fifty-five

Harley and Roadrunner were all over the Chariot, walking around it, climbing up to the roof, running their hands along the metal skin, smearing mud and water and leaves into a mucky collage. Grace didn't have to do a tactile inspection – the dents the hailstones had left were obvious.

'Is it bad, Harley?'

'It isn't good, but it's mostly superficial damage, nothing major. How did the rest of Walt's place fare?'

'I don't know yet. He's down at the barn now. If everything is all right here, I think I'll take a walk out there and see if he needs any help.'

Harley brushed off his hands. 'Roadrunner and I will take a walk with you.' He looked down at Charlie, who was sitting at Grace's feet, his tongue lolling out against the burgeoning heat. 'You need a leash, young man. Can't have you bolting off into the woods when there's a manhunt in progress.'

Annie popped her head out the door. 'I've got the generator back online, and just in time – dear Lord, it's getting hot again.'

'We're all taking a walk down to the barn if you want to join us,' Harley needled her.

'Well, you know how much I love tromping through mud in high heels and fraternizing with barnyard animals, but if you don't mind, I'll just stay here and get the computers back online.'

Walt was resetting his paddock fence posts and nailing boards when he saw Jacob slogging up the field road, looking like death warmed over. He stopped his work and watched him approach, a knot of dread forming in his gut. He'd known Jacob since he was a child, and he knew all his looks and all his tricks to hide his troubles. Something was very wrong.

'Jacob?'

'Is everything okay here, Walt?' he asked, swiping one cheek, then the other, wiping away mud streaked with the white lines sweat had cleared.

'There's some damage, but nothing that can't be set right in a day or two. But from the looks of you, I'd say I'm one of the lucky ones.'

'It's bad out there. Two fatalities reported already, roads all over the county are blocked by fallen trees and downed power lines, and a lot of homes in East Grant got leveled.'

'I'm very sorry to hear that. What about your men in the field, looking for a killer?'

'I've lost a lot of them to emergency calls, and a few have family they haven't been able to reach, so it's a skeleton crew now. The Minneapolis detectives are out there now, helping.'

'I'll give you a hand . . .'

'No, Walt, you stay and take care of things here. This is a law enforcement issue.'

'If there's a killer on my property, then it's my issue. I

know these woods better than anybody, and I've hunted all my life. As far as I'm concerned, there's probably no real difference between hunting a human or an animal, except for the fact that humans are generally dumber than animals, at least when it comes to hiding. But that's not what's stuck in your craw right now, so tell me straight up.'

Jacob let out a tortured sigh, something that sounded more like a cry of grief to Walt. 'Vince and Karl stumbled across a graveyard out in your woods. The storm stripped a hill and all the bodies slid down in a gully washer.'

Walt nodded. 'The goat cemetery.'

'No. No.' He looked down and cleared his throat. 'Not goats, people. Four of them so far. We don't know how many more and . . .' He raised his head and looked directly at Walt. 'I can't help thinking . . .'

Walt started twisting the simple gold band on his left hand that he hadn't taken off in fifty years. 'Is Marla there? In that godforsaken graveyard?'

Jacob looked away and saw three of the Monkeewrench people and their dog coming down the field road. 'We won't know until the Bureau of Criminal Apprehension gets down here. We can't touch the scene, do you understand that, Walt? If we go poking and prodding, we could destroy critical evidence.'

Walt looked up at the sky and saw the rainbow fading, disappearing into blue sky, gone just like that. He couldn't help equating that with Marla, thinking it was some heavenly pronouncement of an end to things, which was stupid nonsense. Rainbows didn't last, he knew that.

And neither do people.

'Dammit, I can't just sit here and fix my fence when Marla might be rotting away in that graveyard.'

Jacob winced. 'I know. Let's go up to the house and sit for a while.'

'No, Jacob, you have a job to do, and I'd be grateful if you let me tag along, because I don't know what else to do with myself.'

'You know I can't allow that, Walt. Besides, the BCA is going to be coming here – it's the fastest way for them to get to the site, and I can't stay here to wait for them. I was hoping you could give me a call when they arrive and direct them down the field road so I can meet them there.'

Walt nodded. He knew damn well that Jacob was giving him make-work, something purposeful to keep him occupied, and right at this moment, he was okay with that. He glanced up as Grace, Harley, Roadrunner, and Charlie approached.

'Sheriff, Walt,' Harley greeted them. 'We came to see if you need help with anything around the farm.'

'That's kind of you. Just got some trees and a fence down, nothing more than that. Is your rig okay?'

'Some cosmetic issues, but that's about it. I guess we all got lucky.' He looked at the broken fence. 'Let Roadrunner and I give you a hand with that.'

'I'd appreciate that. Normally, I wouldn't ask for help, but I'd like to get this fence fixed up so I can let the herd out. They're panicky and they need to get outside and figure out the world hasn't ended. That's the funny thing about animals – they'd rather be outside in a damn tornado than confined inside. They don't always know what's best for them, but I guess that's instinct.'

'Tell me what tools we need and Roadrunner and I are on it. I've got everything but a backhoe in the Chariot.'

'Got all the tools we need right here in the barn.' Walt crouched down when Charlie started whining and straining at his leash. 'Hey, boy, what's the matter?'

Grace gave the leash some slack and watched Charlie trot up to Walt and start licking his hands. She'd known something was wrong the minute she'd gotten close enough to see the somber expressions. Apparently, Charlie knew it, too.

'Good boy,' he murmured, scrubbing the ruff of Charlie's neck for a long time before nodding to Grace and the sheriff, then leading Harley and Roadrunner to the barn.

'What's wrong, Sheriff?' Grace asked as soon as Walt was out of earshot.

'We found some bodies in the woods near that abandoned camp. Some of them have been there awhile. Your Minneapolis detective friends think it might be connected to their serial killer.'

Grace felt a dark pall of sadness settle over her. 'Is Marla one of them?'

'Don't know yet. BCA is on the way, just so you know to expect them.'

Without any cognitive thought, Grace placed a hand on her belly, once again feeling the comfort of movement within. Life and death, coexisting just as they always had, just like Walt had said. 'Thank you for telling me, Sheriff.'

'Thank you for being here. Whether you know it or not, you're all going to help Walt get through the worst few hours of misery he's known since the night Marla disappeared.'

Grace nodded solemnly, knowing that Sheriff Emmet wasn't just speaking for Walt.

Fifty-six

Magozzi and Gino were absolutely silent as they coursed the section of woods Sheriff Emmet had assigned them to cover, their heads pivoting back and forth as they looked and listened hard. Every crack of a twig or wet rustle of leaves sent them into adrenaline overdrive, intensifying their senses and making the world around them seem even more surreal than it already was.

Magozzi felt like he was walking in a post-nuclear wasteland. Fallen trees were everywhere, their monstrous rootballs poking up from the sodden earth; runnels of brown water poured through shredded foliage on the forest floor; water dripped off the leaves and made gentle plopping sounds that somehow seemed ominous.

Occasionally, a weary tree the tornado hadn't quite managed to vanquish would creak and groan, then tumble down with a crash as its loosened roots finally gave up. Magozzi had channeled Gino's thoughts the first time it happened, just ten feet from them.

Jesus Christ, it's bad enough worrying about getting ambushed by a vicious sociopath and now we have to worry about getting crushed by a fucking tree?

Suddenly, Gino stopped and cupped his hand to his ear.

Magozzi stopped and listened. He heard the plop-plop-plop of raindrops falling from the tree canopy, the distant wail of sirens, but nothing more. He upturned his hands in question.

Gino shook his head. 'Thought I heard a voice,' he whispered.

It wasn't unusual to hear or see things in these types of circumstances, when you were straining so hard to watch and listen. That's when your mind started playing tricks on you. Magozzi had learned that on his first stakeout. He gestured to Gino to keep moving.

Angel wasn't afraid of much in this world. Every year, he fully expected to die before his next birthday, so fear of death didn't hold him back. Life expectancy in his line of work was short, and when you promised your services and your life to a cartel, you knew that. He'd lasted longer than most because of his unique talents, devotion, and tireless work over the years, and he'd risen through the ranks, had earned the trust of some very important people. That had kept him alive so far, but things were starting to unravel now. How in the hell had it gone so wrong, so fast?

It was the women's fault, he decided – the stupid bitch at Global Foods, the stupid bitch on Pike Island who'd gotten away and had obviously given the police a description, since he'd seen a sketch of himself on the TV at the gas station. He hadn't really wanted to kill the kid, there was no fun there, but he'd had no choice. And then there were the cops, crawling everywhere after this fucking tornado, in the one place he'd always considered a sanctuary. At least he was safe out here in the woods.

Women will always be the death of you, his father had told him with a bloodied face and a grim smile, his hand still on the knife he had driven into Angel's mother's chest again and again. *So you kill them before they kill you. Kill them over and over again. Remember that.*

He leaned against a tree trunk to rest, thinking his father hadn't known everything. There were exceptions to every rule and not all women were bad. Most of them, but not all.

'Freeze! Police!' He heard a voice shouting behind him, which was troubling. Why was there a cop in the woods when the whole county had probably been leveled? And why would he threaten a man from behind, walking through the woods after a disaster? He could have been a stranded traveler, injured in the storm, looking for help. He could have been a property owner assessing damage or looking for lost family or friends.

It took his mind only a split second to run a litany of possible scenarios before coming to a conclusion and making a choice. Without hesitation, he turned around calmly with a smile, then fired his gun and watched the man drop. It wasn't particularly satisfying, but it served its purpose. He spun and started jogging farther into the woods toward his backup car, waiting for him just a half mile away. As he cleared a fallen tree, he was startled by an answering gunshot and felt a searing pain in his leg as he crashed down into the muddy mire of the forest floor.

Gino and Magozzi crouched and froze when they heard gunfire. Magozzi listened to the echo and pointed south. 'Not far,' he whispered, and Gino nodded.

They couldn't run full-out in the woods, but they moved as fast as they could without breaking an ankle or twisting a knee, dodging underbrush, branches, and downed trees.

Gino was the first to see the fallen deputy and dropped to his knees beside him. He tore off his suit jacket and fashioned a makeshift tourniquet, tying it around the man's bloody upper arm.

Magozzi was already on his borrowed shoulder unit, putting out an 'All units, officer down.' He didn't like the pallor of the deputy's skin, and he hoped like hell the bullet hadn't hit his brachial artery.

'Deputy . . .' Gino looked at his name plate. 'Deputy Nagle. Help is on the way, stay with us.'

'I think I hit him . . .' Deputy Nagle said weakly, and his good arm flailed, trying to point. 'Ran . . . north . . . toward Walt's . . .'

'Stay with him until help gets here, Gino,' Magozzi barked, then took a northerly route, heading into the woods, gun drawn.

Fifty-seven

Grace and Sheriff Emmet jumped when they heard gun-shots, and a split second later, the sheriff was on his radio reporting shots fired. Harley, Roadrunner, and Walt came running out of the barn. 'That was close,' Walt said breathlessly. 'You folks get to your rig and stay put.'

'Come with us, Walt,' Grace said.

'I'll just go to the house, my shotgun's there.'

'We've got plenty of weapons in the Chariot.'

The sheriff got off his radio. 'Walt, she's right, go with them. I want to keep you all together and out of harm's way.'

Suddenly, Grace heard Magozzi's voice coming from the speaker on the sheriff's shoulder. 'All units, officer down!'

She looked at Harley and Roadrunner, whose expressions mirrored her own fear, offering no solace.

'All of you, go!' the sheriff commanded, then started running toward the woods.

Magozzi's pulse started pounding in his ears when he saw blood. There was a lot of it. If Deputy Nagle had hit an artery, then the killer wouldn't get far. He paused and listened. The woods were silent. That meant the son of a bitch was probably hiding because he couldn't run anymore. He swiveled his head around and every tree was suddenly a mortal enemy, potentially hiding a monster with a gun.

He followed the trail of blood, all the muscles in his body taut to the point of physical pain.

Then he heard it – a faint moaning just ahead. He crouched behind a tree, his eyes scanning the woods, his ears straining, then he crab-walked to the next tree, swallowing his heart, which had somehow climbed up into his throat. The moaning grew louder, then he heard a weak, raspy voice.

'Help me.'

Magozzi pressed his back against the tree. Would a brutal killer who was possibly mortally wounded want to take out one last person before he met his maker? It was a valid assumption, so before he moved forward, he thought of Grace, thought about their baby, because if things didn't go well here in these woods, he wanted those to be his final thoughts.

He peered around the tree trunk and saw more blood, then crept forward on his belly and saw a motionless man on the forest floor through a tangle of brambles. He waited for any movement and saw none, but that didn't mean it wasn't an ambush. 'Don't move!' he shouted, then clambered through the cover of the brambles, head low, waiting for a reaction. When it didn't come, he cleared the brush and came face-to-face with a monster.

Magozzi felt his stomach cramp when he saw the tattoos on his bare arms. *Do you believe in evil?* Amanda White's voice echoed in his head.

But he didn't look so evil now. His eyes were glassy and his skin was a dreadful shade of gray. Magozzi kicked away the gun on the ground next to him, then got down on his knees, stripped off his suit coat and tied it around the gaping wound in the man's thigh to staunch the gout of blood.

And that was the great irony and torment of his job – he couldn't calculate the many ways he'd imagined killing this man with his own bare hands over the past couple of days, and yet here he was, trying to save him in the hopes he would live to face justice.

He reached up and felt his neck. The man's carotid pulse was barely there and Magozzi knew he was looking at a dying man.

'Angel Cruz?'

The man's eyes fluttered open in surprise, then closed again. 'Marla,' he whispered.

Magozzi caught his breath. 'What about Marla?'

'Four-fifteen . . .' The man retched, then went still as his eyes closed.

'Angel! What about Marla?!'

'Four-fifteen . . . Lilydale Way . . .' Then the man let out a final, shuddering breath.

Magozzi checked for a pulse, but it was no longer there. Neither was the low-level current of electricity that every living creature emitted. Most people didn't know they could sense it unless they'd been with a person as they died. Angel Cruz was definitely dead, and if he even had a soul, it was on its way straight to hell.

He stared down at the man's fully inked arms, exposed by a short-sleeved T-shirt; it was a chronology of wickedness, at least the spades were. If there were indeed bodies to go with the other suits on his arms, then there were a lot of dead people unaccounted for somewhere out there, maybe even at 415 Lilydale Way.

Thirteen cards to a suit, four suits in a deck, do the math, that's fifty-two.

Magozzi let out a sharp breath, feeling something tightly coiled inside loosen, then stood and called it in. Immediately after that, he called McLaren.

Fifty-eight

Shock and exhaustion had drained all the adrenaline out of Magozzi and Gino, and that was before they'd had to tie up their most recent scenes with the injured deputy and their dead serial killer. They were damn near lobotomized at this point, completely mute as they trudged in surreal silence up Walt's mucky, rutted field road in filthy wet suits that were now splashed with other people's blood.

Magozzi wasn't used to Gino's silence under any circumstances, but today was different, and they were both privately replaying the day's horrors and anticipating the new horrors to come. It wasn't over, not by a long shot. They still hadn't seen the graveyard in the woods, still hadn't heard from McLaren about what he and Freedman had found at 415 Lilydale Way.

They saw the jumble of BCA vehicles and squad cars as they approached Walt's yard and a garage beyond, where the Chariot was parked. A rotund BCA tech was trotting awkwardly toward them with a kit in his hand, having obvious difficulty negotiating the inhospitable terrain.

'Hell's bells, Jimmy Grimm?' Gino finally broke the silence.

Jimmy stopped in his tracks, his eyes traveling up and down their gory attire. 'Oh my God, are you two okay?'

'We're fine, a couple others aren't.'

'I'd ask what you're doing down here, but I already know. Sheriff Emmet said you pulled some things together. I was going to call you the first chance I got, but now I can tell you to your faces – when we started excavating in the woods, we found cards, including the missing two of spades. I'm thinking, you've got your guy, right? But what doesn't sync is that the two of spades is a male, and there are at least three other vics with cards who are male, which doesn't jibe with your serial.'

'Actually, it does. We think he was a cartel heavy sent up to clean shop at Global Foods. The men were business, the women were pleasure.'

Jimmy grimaced. 'So you're thinking he stashed his hits down here to protect operations up in the city?'

'Makes sense. How long has the two of spades been in the ground?'

'By my estimate, a couple months.'

He looked at Gino. 'Diego Sanchez?'

Gino nodded. 'Timeline works. Jimmy, how bad is it?'

'Pretty bad. So far we've got eight in varying stages of decay. Some go back years. We have a forensic anthropologist coming up from Des Moines to sort those out.' He shook his head morosely. 'It's a burial ground down there. I'm hoping we're at the end of it, but we're not sure yet.'

'Get to it, Jimmy, we'll catch up with you later.'

'Yeah, but first tell me this, did you find the bastard?'

'He's on his way to the morgue.'

'Just what I wanted to hear. Great job, guys, catch you later.'

After Jimmy left, Magozzi saw a mirage in the distance. It was a terrific mirage – Grace MacBride was jogging down the road toward them, mud flying up from her boots. Charlie was pacing her, his fur a mess. He only realized it wasn't a figment of his weary, messed-up mind when he felt her arms around his shoulders, her swelling belly pressed up against his, and then everything became real again in the best possible way.

'Magozzi,' she whispered into his ear. 'Are you all right?'

Magozzi wrapped his arms around her as he felt Charlie pawing at his leg, then rested his chin on the top of her head. 'I am now.'

'Is he still out there?'

'He's dead. One of the deputies returned fire and he hit the bastard in the femoral artery with the luck of the saints. Angel Cruz bled out before we could do anything.'

'Good.' Grace had no compassion for people who killed innocents. None of them did. 'You said the deputy returned fire. Is he all right?'

'He's in the hospital now, he's going to make it. There's something else, Grace. Our killer said Marla's name before he died and gave a street address.'

Grace's arms fell away from his shoulders and she looked up at him, her eyes fogged with sadness. 'Alive or dead?'

'We don't know yet. McLaren and Freedman are on their way there. We're waiting for their call.'

'Oh, God. What are you going to tell Walt?'

'Nothing for now. It would be a cruelty to get his hopes up when we have no idea what they're going to find.'

'Does Sheriff Emmet know?'

'He does.'

She let out a stuttering sigh and looked at Gino, who had gained Charlie's affection by dragging his fingers through his muddy coat. 'Come on, let's get you two cleaned up while we wait.'

Fifty-nine

Johnny McLaren slam-parked in front of a small brick rambler with blooming flower beds and a birdbath in the front yard – not the kind of place you'd expect to conceal a horrific monster, but this was the address Magozzi had given him. Eaton Freedman was unbuckling his seat belt while he pushed his door open, anxious to get out.

Johnny laid a hand on Eaton's arm. 'Listen, Eaton, we don't know what we're going to find in there, so be prepared for some serious ugliness. We're talking about a twisted fuck.'

Eaton paused and looked up at the house. 'Ever since Magozzi called, I've been wondering if we're finally going to find the missing two and three of spades.'

'You might be right. He knew he was dying when he gave Magozzi this address, so maybe he didn't want any of his extra-special handiwork to go unnoticed before he cacked.'

The radio crackled. It was the sergeant running their hastily assembled backup team. 'Detectives, we're in position, we've got the back of the house covered. No sign of movement from inside.'

'Copy that, we're going in,' McLaren answered, then looked at his partner. 'Let's go, careful, careful, just like we talked about.'

As they jogged in a zigzag pattern up the front walk,

guns drawn, McLaren listened to the disturbing cadence of his heart pounding double beats while his mind played an endless loop of worst-case scenarios. His inherent Irish melancholy and his cynicism about the wretched state of the human race wouldn't let him think otherwise.

He'd seen too much carnage during his tenure as a homicide detective, but he'd eventually learned to manage the nightmares and the depression. But walking into the lair of a serial killer was different, and it filled him with a dark, onerous sense of dread, because this might be the one time his imagination couldn't anticipate the horror show waiting for him behind the front door.

An eternity seemed to pass as they knocked, announced themselves, and waited for any response or sign of movement from within. McLaren finally gave Freedman a nod, then stood back while he easily rammed through the hollow-core door with one massive shoulder.

They entered the gloom in half-crouches, flooding the small space with flashlight beams as they moved through to clear it. The place looked uninhabited. There was no furniture, just a futon in a corner and no signs of life. *A stash house*, McLaren thought.

For drugs, cash, dead women . . .

The place had central air, and it was turned way down. McLaren felt like he was in a meat locker. And maybe he was.

'Johnny?' he heard Freedman call out from the kitchen.

McLaren took a walk from the empty living room to a corner in the kitchen where Eaton was standing, flashlight trained on a door. There was a board across it, set in two braces fastened on either side of the frame, and there was a hasp with a padlock and a chain in place of the doorknob.

'MINNEAPOLIS POLICE! IS ANYBODY DOWN THERE?' McLaren shouted, pounding on the door, praying for an answer. He thought he heard something, but he couldn't be sure. 'Get the cutters, Eaton!'

'Fuck that,' he said, smashing the door to splinters with his fists and clearing a man-sized hole in the door.

McLaren ducked under the board barricade and descended the stairs slowly. It was the longest walk he would ever take in his life. There was an overhead light on and his heart fell when he saw acoustic baffling on the walls and boarded-up windows.

But as he emerged from the stairwell, he saw a different picture from the torture chamber he'd been anticipating. There was a small kitchenette generously stocked with food and beverages, a microwave and mini-fridge. A small dinette table was stacked with books and magazines. Sofa with a blanket, a bathroom, a treadmill.

'Minneapolis Police! Is anyone down here?' McLaren cocked his head and was answered by soft sobbing. 'Marla Gustafson? We're Minneapolis detectives. We're here to help.'

They found her huddled and trembling in a corner, arms wrapped protectively around her shoulders, and it took all of McLaren's strength to swallow his emotion.

'It's okay, ma'am,' Freedman said in his deep, soothing baritone, crouching down where he stood a few feet away. 'I'm Eaton Freedman, and my partner's name is Johnny McLaren. You're safe now.'

She looked up and tried to wipe tears from her cheeks

with limp hands, but the tears kept coming like they would never stop. Some of the terror was gone from her eyes, but she was still wary. 'How do you know who I am?'

'Because there are a lot of people who have been looking for you for a very long time. I'm going to get you a blanket and call the medics, okay, Marla? Johnny will take care of you.'

She put her face in her hands and sobs racked her body. 'Did you catch him?'

McLaren crouched next to her, but he didn't dare touch her. She was in a place he couldn't imagine, possibly in shock, possibly ruined beyond any comprehension, so he choked back his instinct to hold her, comfort her. 'We caught him, Marla. Did he hurt you?'

She shook her head. 'He wanted to, but he couldn't. Maybe he would have eventually. How did you find me?'

'He gave us this address before he died.'

McLaren felt his soul shatter when she looked up at him with impossibly sad, wet eyes, then reached over and wrapped her arms around him and wept, her tears soaking through his jacket down to his shirt.

'We played together when we were kids. I think Dad and I were the only people who were ever nice to him his whole life. He couldn't kill me.'

Johnny tried to blink away the sting in his eyes as he held her and patted her back. 'It's okay, Marla, we're going to take you home.'

Sixty

Walt was sitting at his outdoor picnic table with a cold beer, giving his aching arms and shoulders a break from the chainsaw. He'd pushed himself too hard, too long, because when he was working, he wasn't thinking about anything but the task at hand. But now, in the quiet aftermath of chaos, his thoughts were meandering off on dark roads as his eyes kept drifting toward the woods where Jacob and all the crime-scene folk had disappeared. It was a waiting game now, and if that didn't kill him, nothing could.

Harley and Roadrunner were sitting with him at the table, and he was grateful for the distraction of their company. Their presence didn't entirely still his troubled thoughts, but it was some relief having other places to visit in his mind. For instance, to his great surprise, they'd turned out to be fine farmhands, even though they didn't look the part. They'd helped him fix his fence, repair the downed siding on the barn, and clean up most of the debris in his yard that the tornado had left behind.

'I thank you for your help today,' he finally said quietly.

Harley dismissed him with a flip of his hand, like he was casually swatting off a gnat. 'No problem, Walt. Just let us know if there's anything else we can do. I've got the brawn, Scarecrow here has the brains. Well, actually I've got both.'

Roadrunner rolled his eyes. 'That doesn't even dignify a response, especially after I had to show you how to use a hammer.'

Walt was surprised to find himself smiling even a little. Their banter was natural and real, but it fell a little flat, and he couldn't help but think they were putting on a show on his behalf. They knew what was going on. They knew about the cemetery and they had some skin in the game, too. They'd come down here to help him find Marla one way or the other, and they were waiting it out just like he was.

'I think I've got a handle on things now. Another hour with the chainsaw and the oak that took out my front porch will be next winter's firewood.'

Walt turned around when he heard the Chariot's door open and close. Annie Belinsky, wearing some crazy, fancy getup, a lot of makeup, and silly high heels that punched holes in his yard, was approaching with a big platter of sandwiches. She plunked it down on the table and settled next to Walt.

'Nobody's eaten a thing all day, and I'm assuming that wrestling cows and chopping wood and whatever else you all were doing uses calories.'

'That's kind of you,' Walt said, helping himself to a sandwich, even though food was the last thing on his mind.

'And uncharacteristically domestic,' Harley added.

'I am a woman of untold talents. Making peanut butter and jelly sandwiches happens to be one of them.' She lifted her head suddenly and Walt followed her gaze.

Grace, Charlie, and two men in muddy suits were

coming up the field road, headed for the picnic table where they all sat. Walt felt a lump form in his throat as he swallowed his bite of sandwich. There was a torment to the way they walked real slow, like they didn't really want to get up here and join the rest of them, and Walt knew there would be bad news at the end of their walk. And he knew the badness was headed straight for him. They'd finally found Marla in that cemetery – that's all it could be. 'Are those your Minneapolis detective friends with Grace and Charlie?'

Annie nodded. 'Detectives Magozzi and Rolseth.'

Walt took in a breath and couldn't seem to let it go. The past two months of waiting suddenly flashed by in jagged fragments and he didn't realize he'd been clutching the edge of the splintered wooden table until Annie put her hand on his, like she wanted to hold him together. He wondered where Jacob was, and if he knew, why wasn't he here telling him in person?

One of the detectives suddenly stopped and pressed a phone against his ear. He listened for a long time, talked a little, then consulted with Grace and his partner before they continued their walk, a little faster now.

He didn't remember how much time had passed before Grace and her bedraggled companions finally reached the picnic table. But he would always remember Grace smiling at him and giving him what they called a phone nowadays, some flat, weird contraption like the one Marla always used to carry with her.

'There's somebody who wants to speak with you, Walt.'

He took the phone and fumbled around with it. 'Who wants to talk to me and how the hell do you use this thing?'

'Talk into that.' She pointed at a tiny pinhole at the bottom of the phone. 'And you listen here.'

Walt eyed the phone with deep suspicion but followed her instructions. 'Hello?'

'Daddy?'

Walt swallowed hard, thinking it was a damn good thing Annie's hand was still on his, holding him together, because otherwise he would just fly apart.

'Daddy, it's me. I'm coming home.'

Epilogue

Walt and Marla stood at the edge of the cornfield. The tall stalks had lost their emerald hue and were drying and withering now as autumn settled in to put things to rest for the winter. Harvest wasn't too far off, and Walt anticipated a good crop this year in spite of the stress of an early drought.

'By the looks of things, I figure another couple weeks.'

Marla smiled. 'And you'll be out on that old combine day and night, cursing a blue streak at it every few rows.'

Walt felt his troubled heart growing stronger day by day. Marla was her mother's daughter, as resilient as the day was long, and she was getting better with each passing month. It had taken her a while to smile again, and a little longer than that to rediscover her sense of humor. The fact that it was back, even if just a little, was the alpha and the omega for him. There was nothing in life that would matter to him more.

'Well, lucky for you, you and Jacob will be jetting off on your honeymoon right about then, so you won't have to suffer the indignity of your father fighting it out with an old piece of junk. Should have replaced it years ago. But it's old and stubborn like I am, so I suppose we deserve each other.'

Marla shaded her eyes from the sun as she searched the distant line of trees beyond the field. 'Still no sign of him?'

'Nope. Haven't seen him since you came home.'

'There was enough commotion around here to chase him away for a while, but I thought he'd be back by now. Do you think he was finally captured?'

'I thought about that, so I checked with the wildlife preserve and the Department of Natural Resources. Nobody's caught a lion in the past three months, that's for sure.' Walt chuckled.

Marla absently plucked a seeded stem of canary grass. 'This might sound crazy, but sometimes I think that lion was here for a reason.'

'What do you mean?'

She hesitated. 'If you think about it, he was actually the one who found me. The Minneapolis detectives told us themselves that if it hadn't been for the lion hair at the crime scene in the city, they might have never come down here the day of the tornado.'

'I remember something to that effect.'

'So maybe the lion only stayed here as long as you needed him and now he's moved on. Maybe somebody else needs him now.'

Walt had never been much for the spiritual side of things, but Marla always had that tendency, just like her mother, and especially when it came to animals. There was a fanciful aspect to her nature and she'd always viewed the world a little bit differently than he had. And there was nothing wrong with seeing a little magic or a larger purpose to the universe if that was the way your beliefs and your heart aligned. In fact, it seemed like a fine way to live.

He gave her arm a tender squeeze. 'That's a nice way of looking at it, Marla.'

She nodded. 'He'll come back to say goodbye. I know he will.'

Walt had two more rows of corn to go before the harvest was finally in for the season. When he was finished, he would put the ornery old combine to bed for the year, shower and shave and dress in the only suit he'd ever owned, and then walk his daughter down the aisle.

His peripheral vision suddenly caught a flash; just a brief movement in the woods that went still as soon as he looked in that direction. He shut off the tractor and stepped down into the stubble of the cornfield he'd just picked clean.

'Hey, lion. Is that you?'

There was no movement, no rustling, nothing but the raspy buzz of grasshoppers and the nasal honks of geese flying south for the winter. It had probably just been a startled deer. They were active now, larding themselves up on whatever forage was available in preparation for the lean times to come.

Walt waited for a long time, then finally climbed back on his tractor and that's when he saw a large, tawny shape emerge from the woods. His heart started to pound as he watched the lion amble to a strip of dried grass along the field and circle a few times before settling down on his haunches. He was relaxed, but his eyes never left Walt's.

'Hey, old fella,' Walt whispered. 'I'm happy to see you.'

The lion yawned, his mouth stretching wide.

'Where have you been?'

He blinked languidly, not giving up a single secret.

'Marla told me you would come to say goodbye. She's getting married today, you know.'

The beast chuffed.

Walt sat on his tractor for the better part of an hour, perfectly content to watch the lion while the lion watched him. The sun lifted higher in the blue sky, warming the air and casting a burnished autumn glow on a world that seemed just about perfect in this place and time.

Eventually, his old friend rose from his nest of dried grass, shook his great head, then turned and walked back toward the woods, his coat shining gold in the sun. The last thing Walt saw before he disappeared was the auburn tassel of his tail twitching. Marla would have interpreted it as a final farewell before he moved along to help somebody else, but Walt preferred to think the lion was just saying he'd see him again in the spring. Or maybe he was just swatting away flies.

Walt started up his tractor again and continued his steady pace, chewing up the final two rows of corn. When he got to the edge of the field where the lion had been lounging, he noticed something white, gleaming dully in the sun. It was a bone, and a large one at that – too large for a deer. A cow or a horse, most likely. He'd buried his share of lost animals over the years and so had every other farmer in the county.

It briefly crossed his mind that the bone was something the crime scene folks had overlooked when they'd excavated the graveyard. But wherever it had come from, it belonged to the lion now.

Nothing stays buried, he thought as he headed toward the barn.